BURNT NORTON

NORTON

Caroline Sandon

HEAD
ZEUS

First published in hardback in the UK in 2013 by Head of Zeus Ltd.
This paperback edition published in the UK in 2014
by Head of Zeus Ltd.

9 7 5 3 1 2 4 6 8

A CIP catalogue record for this book is available from
the British Library.

Paperback ISBN: 9781781850930
eBook ISBN: 9781781852880

Printed and bound by CPI Group (UK) Ltd., Croydon CR0 4YY.

Head of Zeus Ltd
Clerkenwell House
45-47 Clerkenwell Green
London EC1R 0HT

www.headofzeus.com

BURNT
NORTON

CAROLINE SANDON lives with her family at Burnt Norton in Gloucestershire, the home and gardens that inspired T.S. Eliot to write the first of his *Four Quartets*. Her husband's family has owned and lived in this house for two hundred and sixty years.

In memory of Charlie Coram James
and David Sloane
May they have wings to fly

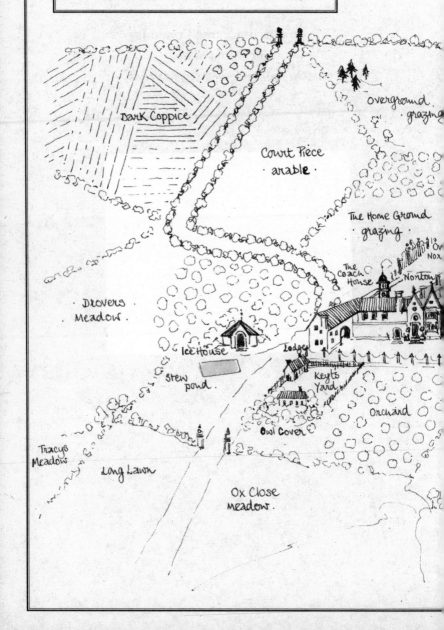

SKETCH OF NORTON HOUSE AND GROUNDS
~ADAPTED FROM ORIGINAL MAP 1745~

Dark Coppice

overground grazing

Court Piece arable

The Home Ground grazing

The Coach House

Norton

Drovers Meadow

Ice House

Lodge

Keyts Yard

Orchard

Stew pond

Owl Cover

Tracys Meadow

Long Lawn

Ox Close meadow

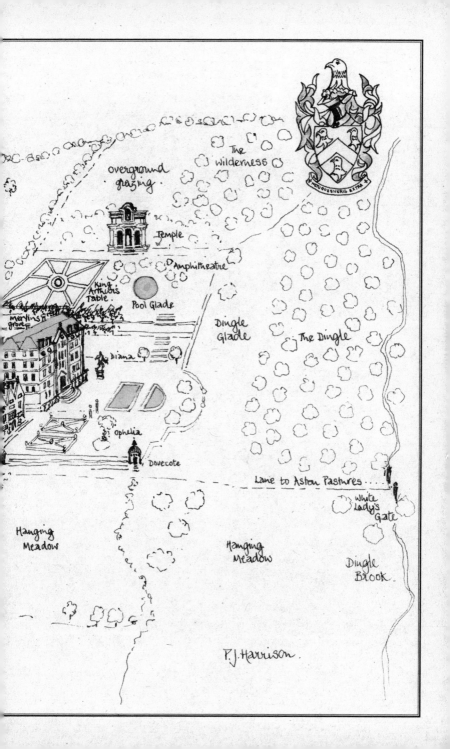

The Wilderness

overground grazing

Temple

Amphitheatre

King Arthur's Table

Pool Glade

Merlin's grove

Diana

Dingle Glade

The Dingle

Ophelia

Dovecote

Lane to Aston Pastures....

White Lady's Gate

Hanging Meadow

Hanging Meadow

Dingle Brook

P. J. Harrison.

But to what purpose
Disturbing the dust on a bowl of rose-leaves
I do not know.
Other echoes
Inhabit the garden. Shall we follow?
Quick, said the bird, find them, find them,
Round the corner. Through the first gate,
Into our first world, shall we follow?

T. S. Eliot

PROLOGUE

In later life Edward could never recall why he had returned to the rose garden, or what had made him look up at that window once more. He did remember that it had only been a glance, yet in that instant, everything changed. He saw the girl leaning towards him, regarding him through a clear pane, her fair hair falling in tendrils about her face. He would remember those sea-mist eyes, reaching out to him, yet distant and unattainable. He stood beneath the window and raised his hand, but a cloud's reflection grazed the glass. When it cleared, the girl had vanished. Once more the window was dark and dingy; only the small face with the down-turned mouth that he had drawn in the dirt remained.

The morning had been hot, September's last stand against the autumn. Across the valley, sheep grazed in the rough pasture and a gossamer haze hung above the ripened wheat. 'Look, Eddie,' his mother said as she stopped the car and pointed across the fields, 'Burnt Norton.'

As Edward followed her gaze towards the wooded hillside, his eyes rested on a Cotswold manor house. Four gables faced north towards the Malvern Hills, and in the changing light, shadows shifted across the thick stone walls. When she restarted the engine, they continued slowly along the drive and over the cattle grid. Below them, amongst the laurels, a stew pond glittered, and lower still, pushing its way through the tangled grass, Edward could make out the ruins of an ice house. A courtyard lay beyond a red-brick archway, and as they drove underneath, Edward could see his future stepfather crossing the cobbles towards them. Conroy smiled warmly as Edward's mother stopped the car and opened the window. Edward could hear the tenderness in his mother's voice when she greeted Conroy, and he recognized the enormity of this new step in their lives. As he climbed out of the car, his mother got out too, shutting the dogs inside.

'This house, Eddie, was once simply known as Norton,' Conroy said, putting his hand on the boy's thin shoulder. 'But after the fire of 1741, it has always been known as Burnt Norton. I hope you'll grow to like it.'

The fifteen-year-old smiled at his future stepfather and shrugged. 'I hope so too,' he said.

The four gables of the north façade rising before him were too severe to be beautiful, but they had another quality, something intangible in the endless stone walls, the countless mullioned windows and the solitary bell suspended beneath the eaves. The coat of arms set above the main doorway held an indefinable fascination. Something deep within Edward made him feel as if he had been there before.

'Curious, isn't it?' Conroy watched the boy's sensitive face. 'Norton can have a strange effect.'

Edward, unable to look away, spoke at last. 'You go on; I'll catch up with you in the garden later.'

'Good idea, we'll leave you to explore.' Conroy and his

mother linked arms and walked towards a small gate at right angles to the house. Edward waited until they had disappeared into the garden beyond, leaving him alone in the courtyard. *Burnt Norton.* The name echoed in his head.

A broken door led to a small internal cloister. He entered and climbed the worn steps to the back door. He turned the handle, it wouldn't move. He pushed his whole weight against the weathered oak, until at last it gave way and he tumbled into the dimly lit hallway. On the wall above him a row of bells from another century remained. He read the names: Drawing Room, Dining Room, Boudoir, Library. He stopped in front of a mirror, and as his face distorted in the mottled glass he remembered Conroy's words: 'In a month or so, you can choose your own bedroom, but you must wait until the builders have replaced the broken boards.'

Ignoring this, Edward crossed the flagstones, unhooked the *Danger* sign from the bottom of the wide staircase and stepped over the first missing tread. He paused for a while on the half-landing and looked over the rose garden below. The two beds were each split into four quarters, separated by a central gravel path. Each bed was enclosed by a low box hedge, but the roses themselves were dying, their petals drifting silently to the ground. Behind them, in the shade of a sycamore tree, a statue of a young horse stretched its neck.

The air was hushed, heavy with sadness. Edward ran his finger across a pane of glass, drawing a small, cheerless face in the thick dust that had gathered there. Then he stood and climbed the last five treads to the first floor.

An old mattress lay propped on its side. He prodded it, watching the dust burst into tiny particles. Beneath a broken skylight, books and magazines littered the floor. He picked up a copy of *Punch*, opened the yellowed cover and was reading the caption to an old-fashioned cartoon when a chair in the corner caught his eye. It had large wooden wheels. He ran his hands along the back, and as the chair moved, the wheels creaked in protest. Edward wondered at its history, for everything had a history in Edward's imagination.

A small doorway disguised as a bookcase further intrigued him. He pulled it open to reveal a winding stairway to the attics, where two rooms led off a small landing. In the first, sixties wallpaper peeled from the pink plaster and forgotten idols posed on faded posters. He entered the second bedroom. The small leaded windows fractured the sunlight into a thousand patterns on the wooden floor. An iron bedstead with rusting springs rested against one of the heavily beamed walls and in the corner a painted cupboard lay open. Flies buzzed on the ceiling, and the room had the air of having been untouched for centuries. This was the room he would choose. Edward lingered there, oblivious of time passing, until the dogs' muffled barks reminded him that they had been left in the car. He ran out of the house, retracing his footsteps into the empty courtyard.

When he opened the car door the dogs jumped out, free at last. He followed them into the rose garden, where they raced ahead of him – galloping beyond the rose beds, past the sycamore tree and the statue of the horse he'd seen from above – leaving Edward alone once more. Admiring the gentle west wing with its three identical gables, he recognized with pride the leaded panes of his new bedroom far above him, and below it, the large and dirty bay window where he had paused only a short time before. He turned away, walking up the bank onto a large flat lawn. At one end, the lawn was enclosed by a crumbling balustrade; at the other, two gateposts were buried in the undergrowth.

He thought he heard his mother's voice. He ran towards it, calling her name, but there was no reply. Only a statue of Diana the huntress, her arm shattered, her face pitted by centuries of weather, stared back at him from below.

Slightly unsettled, Edward returned to the rose garden. He stopped in front of the window, where he looked up again and saw the girl.

The dogs' barking broke the spell, and Edward darted away from the house, under the brick archway, down a gravelled path, and into a wide-open space that merged with the woods beyond. Great oaks bordered two empty pools. He stopped there and leant against the entrance pillar. Shutting his eyes, he breathed deeply, and for an instant the pools filled with water, and children chased each other in and out of the shadows. Edward sat on a stone bench, the echoes of their laughter ringing in his ears. As the sun warmed his face, he reflected that Conroy was right: this house had a strange effect.

His mother's voice recalled him to the present. He opened his eyes and looked around: the pools were empty once more. Following the sounds of their voices, he found his mother and Conroy half hidden by the wild grasses. Edward threw himself onto the bank beside them.

'I thought you said the house was empty, Conroy?'

'The last tenants left thirty years ago, so, yes, it certainly is.'

'But there was someone in the window.'

Conroy smiled as if everything was suddenly clear. 'When I next see you, I will show you something very special. It is a first edition of *Four Quartets* by T. S. Eliot, given to me by my grandmother on my twenty-first birthday. The opening part of the work is "Burnt Norton". I believe Eliot happened upon our garden sometime in the thirties when my family was away, and he sat down to write one of the greatest poems in history. Perhaps one day you will find an explanation, but for now, you can read this astonishing work and appreciate the mystery.'

Looking at the scarred and empty pools, the trees towering above them, Edward wondered if Eliot had closed his eyes and leant against the same stone wall, and if he, too, had seen the children.

CHAPTER ONE

1731

No memorial is guaranteed permanence. Thirteen hundred years ago, a Roman was buried on Kingcombe Hill. The grave overlooking the Vale of Evesham was thought an enduring place for the soul to seek the afterlife, and it remained undisturbed until one frosty November morning when a plough bit into the elaborate stone coffin, the lid was dislodged, and the Roman's peace was destroyed. The fragile bones disintegrated on the morning breeze, the plough moved on, reducing all traces of vanity to useful rows.

But something was left behind: a ring made of gold strands twisted like a serpent's coil. Dorothy knew this ring well; her father wore it until the day before he died. She suspected that this ring had changed her family's fortunes.

The room was dark when Dorothy opened her eyes. She lay quite still, letting the last strands of a dream slip from her. As her dolls stared at her from the shelf, she remembered Miss Byrne's words from the night before.

'It's only London,' she'd said as she tucked the crisp white sheets around Dorothy. 'And it's only for a month. With Ophelia as lead horse, you can have no worries at all.'

But Dorothy didn't want to leave Norton and the security of her routine. She pushed back the covers, letting her feet swing over the edge of the bed. The house seemed quiet, but somewhere in the attics, the first servants would be stirring.

Across the room, dresses like silver shrouds hung in the nursery cupboard. Moving them aside she found an old woollen cloak of her sister's and pulled it around her shoulders. She fastened the hooks, put on her slippers and crept down the back stairs. On the half-landing she paused and opened the window. There was a new sharpness: the scent of autumn. Dorothy shivered. Something troubled her. She shut the window quickly, startling Annie, who looked at Dorothy from the courtyard below, her face luminous in the lamp light. The maid tripped, cursing angrily and stumbled on through the archway towards the ice house. Lorenzo opened the lodge door, pulled on his leather boots, and going in the opposite direction he disappeared into the darkness.

Dorothy decided to follow him. A fox barked in the distance, and above the line of the yew trees, blue-black clouds sailed across the emerging sky. The lawn was wet, and by the time she reached the coach house, the hem of her cloak was heavy with dew. Ophelia turned her head, whickering softly; Dorothy entered the stall and buried her face in the horse's silken coat.

'Does Lady Keyt know you are up?' Lorenzo stood in the doorway.

Dorothy looked at him, her face colouring. 'Please don't tell her,' she said.

'Then come with me; you can help. There's still a lot to do.' She followed him to the harness room. The fire flickered in the grate, and the satisfying smells of soap and leather drifted towards her. She sat on a chair by the hearth, and when the flames rose up, they caught the hollows in Lorenzo's face.

While Lorenzo polished the buckles and greased the leather, Dorothy worked on Ophelia's bridle. They were disturbed by a clatter in the yard outside.

'Mornin', Lorenzo, morning, Miss Dorothy,' Jim Smith, the wheelwright said, his wrinkled face creasing into a lopsided smile. 'This here's taken me nigh on a month to make. Precision, that's what it takes. Precision and skill.' The old man rolled the wheel towards the carriage. 'I'll be along to the back door with me ticket just as soon as I've tightened these bolts.'

'Make sure you secure them well,' Lorenzo said. 'I can't wait, I have four horses to prepare.'

Dorothy returned surreptitiously to her bed at precisely the moment her father, Sir William Keyt, Member of Parliament for Warwick and the owner of two considerable estates, stretched luxuriously in his own. He sat up and looked at his wife sleeping beside him. He traced the curve of her jawline with his finger and lifted a strand of hair from her forehead. She opened her eyes for a moment and smiled.

'The opera,' he said softly, with the pride of someone offering a great gift. 'I shall take you to the opera.'

He settled back in bed, knowing that after twenty-one years of marriage and four children – not counting the poor departed baby – his dear wife deserved every indulgent day of the month they would spend in London. He had no great desire to stay with his mother-in-law, the indomitable Lady Tracy, but he owed it to his family, and though he had visited

9

the Vatican in Rome, the duomo in Florence and St Mark's Basilica in Venice, he regarded his education as incomplete: he had never been to the opera. On this day, the eighteenth of September, he resolved to address this oversight.

He put his arm around his wife's waist and pulled her towards him. 'We will have the best time,' he murmured, before sleep claimed him once more.

An hour later, he woke to the sound of the butler knocking.

'Come in, Whitstone.'

The butler opened the door and hovered discreetly in the entrance.

'Your bath is ready, Sir William.'

'Thank you. Please tell Hawkins I'll be with him shortly, and get him to lay out my burgundy travelling coat and the buckskin breeches, and before we leave could you get my diamond fob from the safe. And clean this, will you?' He pulled a small ring from his finger. 'The ruby eye is barely discernible.'

'It will be done, sir.'

Sir William would never have called himself vain, but if he was truthful, which he sometimes was, he was keenly aware of his appearance. He had a certain fondness for clothes and indeed for jewellery.

After he was bathed and dressed to his satisfaction, he went downstairs to his study. He sat at his desk, stretched his long legs and opened the drawer. Someone had been there; whoever it was had moved his diary. It did not take long to determine the culprit. For a moment he was angry, and then he smiled. If only Thomas had some of Dorothy's spirit, he thought.

***

Miss Byrne found Thomas on the landing. 'Put your book down, young man, and go and have breakfast. It's hard enough to get your little brother's nose into a book, and it's hard enough to keep your nose out of one.'

Thomas laughed. 'Is John awake?'

'It's been the devil's own job to keep him away from your poor mother. He has been up since six, talking about a new telescope. It's all he thinks about. Your father is filling his head with fanciful ideas; that's the job of your old governess, so it is.'

Thomas felt a moment of jealousy. His father loved John the best.

'Now don't you be looking sad. Your father will buy you a present in London, I'm sure of it.'

Thomas smiled at Miss Byrne, though he doubted her words. He could never please his father.

CHAPTER TWO

The Keyt children were waiting in the carriage, with their mother and Miss Byrne, when Sir William came down the front steps, flanked by his dogs.

'Letitia, Sophie, go inside – you're not coming.' He stroked the spaniels.

He approached Ophelia, patting her side, then ran his hand expertly down her legs, checking for any swelling that would signal an impending lameness. When he was satisfied, he climbed into the carriage. 'Good morning, my dear, good morning, everyone.'

'Good morning,' they replied. He parted the tails on his burgundy coat, and after rearranging a ruffle on his shirt sleeve, he opened his journal, the *London Gazette*, took his glasses from his pocket and declared that they were ready. 'John, you may tell Lorenzo to release the brake.'

The small boy clambered from his seat, banged on the partition with a chubby fist, and the coach moved off at a brisk trot. As the wheels clattered under the archway Dorothy turned to see the oak front door close behind them.

'My darling, you were not in your bed this morning when Annie lit the fires.' Lady Keyt turned to her daughter, but Dorothy dropped her eyes.

'No, Mama, I was with Lizzie. I had a bad headache.' She knew her sister would not betray her.

'Well, have a care, or you will have to stay in your room to recover.' Dorothy stared at the window, silent; her mother knew everything about her, even the things she didn't want her to know.

They had just passed Moreton-in-Marsh when Thomas rose to his feet. 'Mama, Father, please listen to me.' Dorothy's heart lurched, for it was the same voice he used when something was wrong. It was the voice that drove her father mad. She raised her head.

'We need to turn the carriage,' he said, his blue eyes intense in his pale face. 'We need to go home while there is still time.'

'Thomas, enough of your nonsense,' her mother said quietly, her hands flying to her throat.

'There's going to be an accident. One of us will die.'

'Thomas, my angel, do not frighten us.' Her mother's voice was firmer now. 'You mustn't let your thoughts run away with you.'

'A still tongue makes a wise head!' her father snapped. 'Sit down and keep your ridiculous ideas to yourself!'

Thomas looked at Dorothy. 'Please, Dotty,' he mouthed, and though the words of support trembled on her lips, she turned away.

He sank onto the upholstered bench, pulled his knees to his chest and stared.

Lizzie tried her best to placate him. 'Dear Thomas,' she said, 'you are an odd one! How could it be a dying day? You only have to look around you, the sun is shining, and it's truly glorious.'

But Dorothy couldn't look outside, for she saw danger in every tree and blade of grass. She buried her face into Hastings, her cloth rabbit, and prayed to all the saints in heaven to keep them from harm.

'Dorothy, my darling, no harm will come to us, I assure you. It is only one of your brother's little turns.' Her mother leant towards her, touching her arm. Dorothy didn't know why, but for the first time in her twelve years she did not believe her.

Two hours passed. Lizzie read stories to John, and Dorothy listened half-heartedly. Thomas remained silent. Just before the coach reached Chipping Norton, Lorenzo slowed the horses. Sir William stepped down.

'Come on, boys,' he said. 'There are too many of us in the coach as it is. We need to walk; it's too much for the horses to pull us up this hill.'

'I'm coming too,' Dorothy said, jumping down. Soon everyone except Lady Keyt was trudging up the dusty track. Dorothy picked up her skirts and ran to the front. She held onto Ophelia's harness, while John rode on her father's shoulders. Thomas lagged behind, every now and then kicking up the dust with his new shoes. Lizzie joined him.

'Come on, Thomas,' she said. 'Father will be cross if you make yourself dirty. I'll give you a penny if you recite one of your poems.' Distracted at last, Thomas put his arm through his sister's and his clear voice carried up the hill towards the rest of the family. Dorothy, glad to be at the front, glanced up at Lorenzo; she always felt safe with the coachman.

When he noticed her looking at him, he gestured to the road ahead and laughed. 'Look at these potholes. In Florence we have proper roads; here, we have dust in the summer and mud in the winter!' Dorothy laughed too, the last of her anxiety disappearing.

As they pulled away from the village of Enstone, church bells rang. On the third chime, the carriage began to sway. 'What's happening?' Dorothy cried. 'What's happening, Miss Byrne?'

The governess's comforting hand was wrenched from her as the carriage pitched sideways. With her face pressed against the window, Dorothy watched helplessly as a wheel rolled unsteadily towards the ditch. Grabbing the leather strap, she pulled down the window. Ophelia was frightened and picking up speed. Dorothy cried out her name. There was a second of uncertainty, an instant of hope, but as the bit tore at Ophelia's mouth, cutting her delicate flesh, the horse threw up her head, and panic coursed through the team. They raced forwards. Lorenzo struggled to control them, his body straining, but the horses only went faster, the carriage vibrating as it dragged along the ground.

When Dorothy later relived the scene, she would remember the noise: the screams of terror and the pounding of hooves as they tried to escape the monster behind them; the splintering of wood and the grinding of metal. A bend in the road flung her backwards into the carriage. Her head hit the ceiling, and she was tossed upon the floor. The curtains fell across the windows and they were separated from the ordinary world, to enter a dark and terrible abyss. It was as if time stopped and then gathered momentum once more.

She cried as her father fell heavily onto her, pinning her to the floor. She tried to push him from her chest. 'Get off me, Papa; I can't breathe. Please get off me.' She struggled beneath his weight until the carriage tipped over and her father fell clear. Dorothy lost consciousness. When she finally opened her eyes, everything was quiet. The curtains had fallen back once more, and light flooded the carriage. She put her hand to her head; a sticky substance oozed through her tangled hair. 'Mama! I'm bleeding! Help me!'

'It's all right, darling. I'm coming, I'm here.' Lady Keyt struggled towards her daughter. Her dress was torn, and hairpins scattered around her. 'William, poor William.' Her father was sprawled in the doorway. 'Oh Dotty, his buttons have burst. It's his favourite coat.'

Dorothy heard her little brother whimpering, but it was the sight of her beautiful sister that horrified her. Elizabeth moaned softly, her head bent backwards. A shard of glass from the broken window was embedded in her cheek. Blood trickled slowly from the wound, a ribbon of red on her white skin. Her eyes stared ahead. She looked like a discarded and broken doll, with her skirts fanned about her body and her legs bent at a strange angle. Dorothy knelt beside her. 'Lizzie, your hand is cold,' she said, bringing the pale fingers to her lips.

'I'm frightened,' she replied, her grey-green eyes fixed on her sister's face. 'I can't feel my legs, and I want to be sick.' Miss Byrne arrived at their side. Apart from a small cut on her lip, she appeared unhurt. She took Dorothy's hand.

'Come with me, my pet, I'll take you outside. The coach is unstable, it could move at any moment.'

'I must be with Lizzie. She's hurt.'

'I know, my love, but your mother will look after your sister, and I need to know that you are safe.'

She pulled the bewildered child into the sunshine.

'There now, you stay right there. I'm going to the village for help and I'll be back before the blink of an eye.' As Dorothy sat on the ground, her father regained consciousness. She was vaguely aware that he was searching for John. He started with the travelling boxes that had fallen from the overhead locker. He scrabbled on the floor of the carriage, hurling the boxes through the broken windows, spilling the contents onto the rough grass. Dorothy watched as his movements became more frantic, and then she noticed her little brother. He seemed to be sleeping; her father picked him up and held him tenderly in his arms.

'He can sleep next to me, Papa. I will look after him,' she said, but he ignored her. He stumbled across the grass and fell to his knees, crying out her brother's name.

Dorothy lay on the grass, tired, separated once more from reality. She could see birds flying above her in the clear blue sky, and she could hear their tranquil song. It seemed strange that in the midst of chaos, ordinary life carried on.

'Are you hurting, young missy?' a villager asked. She shook her head, for though she felt bruised and battered, the pain seemed to belong to someone else. In this detached state she watched the villagers lift her sister from the wreckage, Miss Byrne hovering close by. She saw her father holding John in his arms, and she heard his sobs as he laid him gently down. Finally her mother emerged from the carriage. 'William, where is John? I can't find John!'

'He's on the grass, Mama,' Dorothy said. 'He's very sleepy.'

***

With the return of reality came despair. Dorothy watched, her head throbbing, as the villagers cut the horses from their shafts, steam rising from their heaving flanks, their noble heads hanging down, tongues lolling, mouths red with blood and froth. How could one forget the disfiguring lacerations, the lathered sweat, and the terror in their eyes?

'Apollo, *sia calmo, calmo*,' Lorenzo soothed, trying to calm them. His new livery was spattered with mud, the gold braid torn from his shoulders.

Dorothy got to her feet, every muscle in her body tense as she counted the standing horses. There were only three; Ophelia was not there. Her eyes skimmed the landscape. Beyond the carnage, beyond the people milling around, there was nothing, only the canvas of green fields and blue sky. Then she saw her. Ophelia was lying in the ditch, her limbs thrashing against the muddy sides, her eyes rolling in agony. When she tried to get up, her legs collapsed beneath her. Dorothy watched in horror as Ophelia went down once more, her body twisting as she fell against the bank.

'Ophelia!' she cried, running towards her. 'Ophelia!' She was too quick for the adults, and as the mare's screams of distress became more fevered, Dorothy sidestepped the outstretched arms and threw herself into the ditch on top of her mare. Winding her torso around the horse's neck she wept into the sodden, matted mane. She could smell fear's stench on her. For a moment Dorothy's presence soothed Ophelia, but as the pain gripped her once more, the mare's nostrils dilated and she squealed, her head jerking upwards. The hard bone caught the side of Dorothy's face, and as blood spurted from her nose she felt strong hands dragging her from behind.

'Let go of me!' she cried, kicking and yelling, but Lorenzo would not let go. 'Let go of me,' she pleaded while he dragged her away, her small fists beating his chest.

'Miss Dorothy, don't look. You must not look,' he said, trying to shield her eyes, but it was too late. Dorothy had seen the pistol, and she had seen her father's tears. She watched paralysed and helpless as he steadied his hand and put the cold steel between Ophelia's eyes. The shot rent the air. She smelt the gunpowder, acrid and bitter. For a moment she believed he would turn the pistol upon himself but instead he stumbled down the road.

'I hate you!' she screamed at his retreating back. 'I hate you! I hate you!' until she could scream no more.

It was ten o'clock when Sir William came home. Whitstone met him at the door. 'Let me take your coat, sir. I will fetch you a clean one. Shall I bring your supper?'

'I don't want food; get me a bloody drink, man.' He held up his shaking hands with terror in his eyes. 'Do you see these hands? They bring misery, Whitstone. Misery and death.'

Specialists came and went, speaking in hushed whispers. William waited.

'I'm sorry. Your daughter will never walk again. Keep her warm, keep her well. We can do no more.' There were no tears now, only confusion.

'Sleep in your own room, my dear,' his wife said. 'It is better that way. I shall sleep with Elizabeth.'

The following morning he wrote an entry in his diary. *You*

have taken my child. My God, why have you forsaken me?
He could think of nothing else to say.

Elizabeth remained conscious throughout. The dull ache in her back remained, and her head throbbed. Below her waist she felt nothing.

Miss Byrne fussed around her. 'Now keep still, Lizzie darling. The specialist wants to be looking you over.'

'Yes, Miss Byrne,' she said, but she couldn't move anyway. At night when she was finally left alone, she tried to imagine the future, but no thoughts came.

Her mother held her hand, did all the things that a mother should, but she couldn't fix her broken body. 'Dear God, let me be with John,' Elizabeth whispered in the darkness.

CHAPTER THREE

The days following the accident proceeded as in a dream. Dorothy recalled snatches of conversation, a face swimming above her, a spoon held to her lips.

'She is suffering from shock. I would advise you to wait to tell her, my lady.'

'Yes, doctor, we will do as you say.'

It was her mother's face, but it wasn't her mother. This woman had swollen eyes and unkempt hair.

'Lizzie! I want Lizzie.'

'It's all right. Swallow this and we will bring her to you.' A different voice – Miss Byrne.

'No! Take it away!' she cried.

As she slept, Dorothy was haunted by indistinct recollections of sun-filled afternoons: John playing in the garden, running through the long grass; John chasing the butterflies by the pools; John lying beside her. No matter how peaceful, they always ended in disaster.

In her waking hours she reflected on the days before the accident. One incident in particular plagued her. Dorothy had known her actions were wrong; now she believed the accident could be her fault.

Boredom had driven her to break the rules. Her father had been in Warwick on constituency business, and Dorothy, Elizabeth and Thomas were with the seamstress. After three torturous hours of pinning and measuring, Dorothy was on her way into the garden when she noticed the door to her father's study was not quite closed. She could not resist.

Shutting the door quietly behind her, she headed towards her father's telescope. It had fascinated her for years, for its ability to bring the universe closer. Dorothy sat on the stool behind the telescope, moving the instrument on its pivoting base. She peered into the lens, pointing it upwards. Nothing. The stars remained hidden behind the grey autumn sky. It was a bitter disappointment. She was on the verge of leaving when she noticed the drawer of her father's desk lying open. Her father kept his diary in the drawer.

The passage outside was quiet. Kneeling underneath the big old-fashioned desk, her legs crossed, her heart thudding in her chest, she pulled the diary into her lap, and began to read.

There, on the first page, was her grandmother's writing:

To my Darling William,
A gift on your coming of age.
May you have a full life, and may you fill these pages
with your many successes.
Your loving Mother.

On this first day of July in the year of our Lord seventeen
hundred and ten, I have attained my majority. It is a

relatively insignificant detail in world history, but to me
an auspicious day. A month has passed since I married
my young wife. I am indeed a fortunate man, for she is
handsome and dependable, and an exceptional catch,
being part of the Tracy dynasty, whose lineage can be
traced to Charlemagne. Tonight we will dine with her
parents at Toddington.

Dorothy put the diary down. *Dependable.* What did that
mean? She would have to find out. Picking it up again she
read entry after entry.

The baby died today, only two hours old, God rest his
soul. A boy. Ann is beside herself with grief and if I am
honest so am I. One small mercy: Ann at least survived.

After reading this poignant admission, she was momentarily
shamed, but her curiosity proved stronger.

My mother gave us a dog, one of the Clopton spaniels.
It is black as coal with soulful eyes. Dogs are easy to
love, uncomplicated, and they don't answer back. I
believe it gives her some comfort.
*   Ann miscarried again. Though I believe the setback*
to be temporary, Ann has convinced herself she will
remain childless. She is inconsolable.

A joyful entry the following year told of the birth of her
elder sister.

It is five days since Elizabeth made her speedy entrance into the world. Though the infant is proving to be of sound lung and cheerful disposition, Ann continues to be cautious.

She flipped to an entry three years later, recording the birth of her precious Thomas.

We are rejoicing – at last, another boy! My son and heir, Thomas Charles Edward Keyt, born on this day, twenty-third of November, seventeen hundred and eighteen. He is a bonny chap with blond curls, most unusual. I had no hair. Once again my dearest wife has undergone the ordeal of childbirth, and though I too suffered, for her cries of pain cut me to the quick, I believe I am most glad, my part in this affair was pleasurable.

For a moment she grappled with this piece of information, wondering what he meant, but it was forgotten in her longing to learn more.

I bought a colt today, also black. His conformation is superb. I believe we will produce a great line. My uncle, Gilbert Coventry, offered me ten guineas, but I wouldn't sell were it double.

Finally she came to the entry she had been waiting for.

Another child born yesterday, she is a pretty scrap; we will call her Dorothy after my dear aunt. Miss Byrne brought Thomas to see her; the boy ignored me, a strange child. He held a bunch of violets in his hand as if it were a great prize, dropped them into her crib, scattering them over the blanket. I told him off, and the Irish woman gave me one of her looks. How she annoys me. It is as if she disapproves of me, though what I have done, I have no idea. If she weren't a good governess and the children did not like her so well, I would dismiss her, send her back to the peat bogs.

I hope Dorothy will learn to ride, for Lizzie has shown little inclination. It has been a good week when all is said and done.

The entry contained little excitement at her arrival, indeed, it was critical of the people she loved. Dissatisfied, she read on.

A son was born this week. He smiled at me, clutched my finger; I believe I shall love him most dearly. Ann is exhausted. I am convinced this should be her last pregnancy. If anything happened to my wife I would be utterly lost. Though my mother-in-law would insist on naming him Paul, after the first Tracy baronet, I will hear nothing of it. We shall call the boy John, a good name in my family.

At that moment her mother's voice intruded on her solitude. She returned the diary to the drawer and hastily left the room.

'Ah, Dorothy, I've been looking for you. Where have you been?'

'I was reading in the big chair, Mama. I was engrossed in my book.' Her mother looked at her, her grey eyes solemn.

'Where is your book now, darling? Don't leave it lying around, for it will get lost.'

'Yes, Mama. I'll fetch it at once.'

Later that night she asked Miss Byrne what dependable meant.

'It means that the people in your life are loyal and steady,' she said. 'It means you can go to sleep knowing that we are always here to look after you.'

It was a good explanation but somehow not the one that she had required.

Sleep did not come easily that night, and when it was quiet, she crept back to her father's study. Opening the diary once more she skimmed the pages; estate procedure and her father's constituency were of little interest. When she finally found an entry devoted to her ability on a horse, she glowed with pride.

Dorothy sits as if she were born in the saddle. I put her on Ophelia today and the child showed no fear; it warms my heart. She rode astride like a man. It is a shame that fashion dictates how women will ride. Utter foolishness.

And he spoke of his love for Ophelia.

The most obliging temperament I have yet to see. She is a truly beautiful mare. We put her between the shafts today. I have no doubt she will be a fine carriage horse.

Later entries troubled her once more.

That damned Irish woman, perhaps she is to blame. Thomas gets more peculiar by the moment. He will have to go away to school.

She read another page, hoping the sickness in her stomach would disappear.

We are going to London in a month's time for Lizzie's launch. The child is sixteen years old. Half the country is in love with her. Why on earth does she need to be launched into society? I don't want to lose her to some spineless fool. She has become most dear to my heart.

Stayed at the Charter House again. Much easier if I have two days together in my constituency. I was served by the landlord Johnson's daughter. Pretty girl, she reminds me of Dorothy, with her sharp tongue and quick wit. Unusual for someone of her class.

Dorothy put the diary back in the drawer. Everything was wrong. Her father hated Miss Byrne, Thomas was going away to school, and her father found her comparable to a landlord's daughter.

She made the first mistake at breakfast the following morning.

'Do you know, young man' – her father addressed John, who leant towards him eagerly – 'that a new and better telescope has been invented? I am told you can see much farther than ever before.'

'We can get one when we're in London,' Dorothy said.

Everyone turned to look at her. 'But we are not going to London,' Lizzie said. 'Are we, Papa?'

For a moment her father looked puzzled. 'As a matter of fact we are, but your sister has ruined my surprise. How did you know, Dorothy?'

'I overheard you discussing it with Mama. I'm sorry,' she said, her cheeks burning.

He shook his head. 'Well, I don't remember you being there, Dorothy. And now that the element of surprise has been lost, I had better explain.'

Dorothy wanted to cry. Her humiliation was compounded when her father smiled and told her Ophelia would be coming with them as lead horse.

'How did you know?' Elizabeth whispered conspiratorially, but for the first time Dorothy ignored her and refused to answer.

That evening, Miss Byrne took Dorothy aside. 'In Ireland, it is said that to pry is a sin and to lie is a sin. Nothing good will come of this, my girl.'

That day she had committed two sins; perhaps now the family was paying for them.

CHAPTER FOUR

At Dorothy's insistence, Miss Byrne brought a mirror to the bed. Dorothy's face was swollen and her nose broken, the ache a constant reminder of all that she had lost.

When at last she was on her own, she struggled to the window. Drawing back the curtains she gasped, for it was as if a wand had been waved, and the last of the summer vanished. Gales battered the countryside and trees littered the ground like fallen giants.

That night, when the candles were snuffed, and the wind howled its continuous lament, she pulled the bedcovers over her head, but the terrors continued.

'John's frightened! Help him, Mama!' she screamed, as the rain beat upon the casements.

'He's dead, my darling. John has gone to heaven.' Her mother's concerned face hovered above her.

'Why? John loved us. He would never wish to leave us.'

'I know, my darling, but God wanted him back,' her mother said, gently pushing the damp hair from Dorothy's forehead. 'He was too precious for this world, and God chose your little brother to sit at his side.'

But it wasn't true, for as the household slept, Dorothy crept downstairs. Surrounded by candles, the coffin rested on the table in the hall. She would always remember the sickly-sweet aroma of lilies, strewn and wilting upon the floor. Hesitating, she lifted her lantern and tiptoed towards the coffin. She closed her eyes and, squeezing them tightly, lifted the lid. When she opened her eyes, her brother was there, amongst the waxen flowers, his arms crossed upon his chest, his face as grey and immobile as her dolls'. When she put out her hand to touch him, he was cold like marble. Recoiling, she let the lid fall and ran from the room. She hid in the corner of her sister's bedroom, her arms folded around her knees as she rocked to and fro.

'They have all lied to me,' she whispered.

The following day they buried John. To the villagers who lined the street they made a small sad procession: Lady Keyt, inconsolable in black lace; Miss Byrne, walking with a poker back and an unfathomable expression; Dorothy, who dragged Hastings along the ground, letting his coat trail in the mud; and Thomas, who held his sister's hand within his own. Sir William refused their help and carried the coffin alone.

As the wind tugged at his coat and scattered the funeral flowers, Dorothy wondered why her father rebuffed them. They all suffered. Did he think that he had the exclusive right to unhappiness?

After a simple service her father lifted the coffin once more. They followed him along the nave and over the graves of their forefathers, but when they reached the chancel steps he turned.

'Stay here,' he commanded. 'I wish to be on my own.' When he finally emerged from the newly built vault Dorothy ran to his side.

'Not now, Dorothy. Not now.' If he saw her tears, he ignored them. He strode down the aisle, slamming the church door behind him.

The months aged Lady Keyt. Small lines formed around her mouth, and the clothes which once skimmed her body now hung in loose folds. When Dorothy tried to talk to her she would answer vaguely, 'Not now, Dotty, later.'

Every day, Lady Keyt went to the nursery and selected John's clothes.

'You will launder them as usual,' she instructed the maid, 'and each morning you will lay the fire.' The intention behind her words saddened Ruth, but she did as she was told.

'What are doing, Ann? Why torture yourself?' William said as he entered the room. 'He is gone. John is never coming back.'

She nodded at her husband. 'Don't worry, my dear. They need to be aired, that is all.'

'But you never did this before. Why are you doing it now? He's dead, for God's sake.' He pushed the rocking horse, letting it swing to and fro. 'Come out of here, Ann. It's time you took care of the rest of your family!'

When he had gone, banging the door behind him, she sighed and lay on the child's bed. The ceiling spun around her. It must be the medicine, she thought. How soft the bed was, how cosy for John. Her mind wandered.

'I have seen three of those birds this week, Mama. What is it?' John's hand tugged at her dress.

'It's a kite, my darling,' she had replied, shading her eyes to look up at the large bird that circled above them. 'Do you see the forked tail? Once upon a time they were admired, now they are killed as vermin.'

'We don't kill them here, do we?'

'Of course not. How could we, when our own name is Keyt? Listen to them, to their strange mewing call. Since the time of King Alfred the Great, we have been linked to this majestic bird by name and by legend.'

'Tell me the story, Mama. Please tell me.'

'Yes, my love. Lean against my shoulder and I'll begin.'

When Ann opened her eyes it was dark; she hadn't seen Lizzie and she hadn't thought about her younger daughter at all.

It seemed to Dorothy that no one wanted her. Her mother's universe had narrowed to the confines of Lizzie's bedroom; and if she felt guilty at her own survival, with one son dead, and one daughter a cripple, she seemed to have forgotten that she had two other children who needed her. In this new world Dorothy grew up quickly.

Elizabeth never complained or berated anyone for her misfortune; she accepted her lot with a generosity of spirit that humbled even the most cynical. Sometimes when Dorothy heard Lizzie's gentle voice, she would forget her sister's disabilities, until the chair's creaking on the floorboards reminded her. For Elizabeth's sake, Dorothy tried to be cheerful in her company, but afterwards she would run to her room, pull the pillow over her head and cry. This was the monotony of their new lives, the tedium of days filled with sickness and grief.

CHAPTER FIVE

In the years before the accident, Keyt had been a distinguished name. Sir William had every reason to be proud. His tenants respected him, the wider community valued him, and his family considered him a devoted and loving father. Though Sir William eschewed the idea of favourites, in moments of reflection it was usually his little John and Dorothy who occupied his mind. In those days a bond existed between him and his youngest daughter that seemed indestructible. It was not just their mutual love of horses; Dorothy had a bright, indefinable spark that amused and entertained him, and yet managed to trouble him. He sensed another side to her nature, and though her sense of adventure mirrored his own, he hoped it wouldn't destroy her.

One morning, when the mist still lingered over the meadows, he summoned his daughter to his study. 'It's a perfect day for a ride. Why don't you ask Lorenzo to saddle your pony, and we shall ride over the Hanging Meadow? If you hurry, you can be back in time for your lessons – your mother need never know.'

Before he could change his mind she ran from the room, along the corridor, out of the back door until she reached the coach house.

On this particular morning she ran so fast, she tripped on the stone steps. She looked up to find Lorenzo standing above her.

'Are you hurt, Miss Dorothy?'

He put out his hand and Dorothy took it.

'Thank you, Lorenzo.' She brushed the dirt from her dress. 'Papa wishes to ride with me. Can you saddle Peter?'

'Of course, Miss Dorothy, but will you help me get the lazy *cavallino* out of bed? He will not move for me.'

'I'll show you how to do it,' she said happily, her sore knee forgotten.

Father and daughter set off together. Sir William, who sat easily on the temperamental Apollo, and Dorothy who cantered behind, her legs kicking the fat grey pony at every stride. When they reached the brow of the hill Sir William turned Apollo's head.

'Look, Dotty – my favourite view of the estate. We can see Aston below us, and over there, just off our land, is Meon Hill.' She followed the direction of his hand. On this day there was no distinction between the earth and the sky. As they stood quietly, the horses with their heads down, eating contentedly, she was glad that her father had shared this with her, and had called her by her pet name. As they rode home together through the dappled wood, he told her about the pony he had owned as a child.

'She was thirty-two years old when she finally died. A very good age.'

'I hope Peter will live for ever, Papa.'

'Nothing lives for ever,' he had said, looking at his daughter's

34

earnest face. 'Indeed, one day you will have a bigger horse, and John will have Peter, but you must never forget him, for your first pony will always be special.'

'But he'll have John to love him.'

'You are right, and fortunately your little brother is proving to have a good seat, just like his sister.'

The following week, Miss Byrne came to her bedroom. It was early in the morning.

'Your father asked me to wake you. Be quick now.'

'What is it?'

'Nothing, child, you are wanted at the stables. Put on your green dress, the one with the collar. And put this shawl around your shoulders. It's cold.'

She met her father at the coach house door. 'Come with me.' He put his finger to his lips. 'Quietly now.' She followed him to the foaling box. It was dark, and as her eyes adjusted, the straw moved. A tiny foal struggled to its feet.

'Well, what do you think?' For a moment she couldn't speak, but when the little foal tottered towards them, completely unafraid, she found her tongue.

'She's beautiful Papa,' she murmured, 'quite beautiful.'

'She was born two hours ago. Lorenzo and I stayed with the mare throughout the night. She is the first by the stallion Othello.'

'The one you bought when I was born?'

Sir William nodded, putting his hand on her shoulder.

'May I give her a name, Papa?' she whispered.

'If you can think of a suitable name, then yes.'

'Ophelia,' she replied. 'Please may we call her Ophelia?'

Her father laughed, delighted. 'A child who is familiar with

Shakespeare deserves to name a foal. And when you can ride this Ophelia, when you can truly manage her, she shall be yours.' Dorothy swelled with pride.

Six months later, with her father standing beside her in the appointed place at the head of the rose garden, a statue was unveiled.

'Ophelia,' he said, pulling off the canvas shroud. 'The start of a new bloodline, may she thrive for her new owner, Dorothy Ann Keyt. May her progeny become champions of the future.'

Dorothy ran to the statue, unable to contain her excitement.

'Thank you, Papa!' she said, throwing her arms around the statue's bronze neck. 'Thank you so much.' Her family applauded, but there was one voice missing. Dorothy's face fell to realize that Thomas had not come out to join in the fun. But then he had always been different. And after the accident, things only got worse.

'What's wrong with you?' Sir William chided, walking into the winter sitting room to find Thomas and his sister reading on the floor by the fire. Both looked up from their books.

'The estate is your future, the family's future. Go and get your coat and come outside. I wish you would apply the same passion to your property as you do to your poetry.'

'It's all right, Thomas,' Elizabeth said when he had gone. 'Papa doesn't mean to be unkind; it's just that you like different things.'

Thomas tried to like those things beloved by his father – horses, shooting and hunting, the gentlemanly occupations that made a man – but it was hopeless.

One morning he knocked on the door to his father's study. 'I have something to show you Papa,' he said nervously. 'There is a piece in the *Gazette* that I think will interest you. Would you like to see it?'

He didn't notice the glass of ruby wine or the papers spread upon his father's desk until the newspaper dropped from his shaking hands, spreading the glass's contents into a dark, destructive pool.

'Get out of here, Thomas! Look what you've done! Take your bloody visions and get out.'

'I didn't mean to, Papa! Can't you see it was an accident?' His father refused to look at him. Exasperated, Thomas continued, 'You never have time for me. You didn't before, and you certainly don't now. You shut yourself away, feeling sorry for yourself. If you had listened to me, none of this would have happened. I know you wish I had died instead of John, but let me make it easier for you – so do I.' He ran from the room to find his younger sister.

'Thomas, it's all right,' Dorothy said putting her arms around him. 'It wasn't your fault.'

'At times I wonder if it was my fault. Perhaps the accident happened because I believed it would. Sometimes I think my head will burst with all these strange thoughts. If it wasn't for you and Lizzie I'd go truly mad.' He pulled a piece of paper from his pocket. 'I've written a poem for John. Shall I read it to you?' He brushed his hair from his eyes, and with a faltering voice he read the sad rhyme.'Do you like it?' he said at last, handing Dorothy the crumpled paper.

She nodded, unable to speak.

'Keep it. I would like you to have it.' Dorothy folded it into the pocket of her pinafore, and much later, she took it out and read it again.

CHAPTER SIX

Miss Byrne came from County Cork. Perhaps it was the harsh winds of her native coastline that had fashioned her looks, but the stern façade belied a warm and generous heart.

'I'm from the bogs of Ireland and that's where I'll be returned if you are a bad girl,' she would say, her brown eyes playing behind her wire spectacles.

'No, Miss Byrne, no!' Dorothy would reply in mock horror, and Miss Byrne would scoop her into her arms and they would laugh. Dorothy would feel the prickles of Miss Byrne's rough woollen dress against her face, and she would smell the lavender on the lace handkerchief pinned to her chest.

If she cried at night, the governess would enter her room and take her gently by the hand. 'You had better be coming along to my little room. Up with the stars, so it is, and I'll read to you if you can find my story book.' Dorothy would follow her up the attic stairs, her misery forgotten. With small, skilled hands she would pull the large, leather-bound journal from its hiding place beneath the floorboards; she would leaf through the pages, hoping Miss Byrne had added a story in her neat handwriting. By the time Dorothy was old enough to read them herself, the book was half filled.

'Why do you keep it beneath the floor?' she once asked.

'Because this is private, young lady, and we would not be wanting the prying eyes of anyone else to see it, would we? Now, where shall we begin?'

Before the accident, when children from the neighbouring estates came to see them, Dorothy and Thomas were allowed to roam the gardens and woodland on their own. Children loved coming to Norton, because of the unusual freedom they were allowed. Miss Byrne said that it would stimulate their minds and develop their independence. The estate woodman built a tree house in the branches high above the Dark Coppice. A stream ran below the tree, and a ladder hung from the steps. Climbing the ladder without getting wet was a delicate manoeuvre.

When young men came to see Elizabeth, Dorothy and Thomas would spy through the banisters in the galleried hall. When their sister looked up they would run away giggling, but they were never quick enough, for they were always caught by Miss Byrne.

'What would you be doing, now? Give your sister a bit of peace; she does not want you lot ogling her all the time. Away with you.'

Those carefree days were so far away, Dorothy wondered whether they had happened at all.

Elizabeth was the only person to even mention the past.

'Do you remember when Papa organized a race in the Long Meadow with the local children?' Elizabeth's voice was wistful. 'Come sit here, Dotty; I have the best view of the garden from this window.'

Dorothy sat beside her. There was an unfinished watercolour on the easel in front of her, and an unopened book in her lap. 'I can't seem to read today; I can't seem to do anything,' Elizabeth said at last.

Dorothy was drawn to the small scar on her sister's cheek – she was unable to check her dreadful memories. 'Of course I remember the race. I coveted your prize so much that you gave it to me, as I knew you would.'

Elizabeth closed her eyes for a moment, remembering her small triumph, and the beautiful cherry-wood box. The estate carpenter had made it, Donald with the shortest legs and the widest smile. 'Miss Elizabeth,' Donald told her, 'I know that sister of yours has taken it, so she has. I'll make you another one, and it will be a better one, miss, much better.'

When Donald completed the speciallyb adapted chair with large wooden wheels, there were tears in his eyes. 'I never thought to make you this,' he said, 'but I've made it with my heart.' She now ran her hands along a polished arm, remembering his kindness.

She was distracted when she looked outside. The two rose beds each were split into four quarters, separated by a central gravel path. It's curious, she thought, I'm sure the layout of the rose garden has changed.

She looked away and took her sister's hand. 'I know you are angry with Papa, but don't be. He hasn't abandoned you, he is just suffering. He will come back to you, just give him time.'

Dorothy looked at her sister. 'Am I that easy to understand?'

'To someone who loves you very much, it is not that difficult.'

'I will try to forgive him, but he is not the same.'

'None of us are, my darling. None of us.' She ran her hands through her hair, letting them rest at the back of her neck.

When Elizabeth looked out of the window again, the gravel path had disappeared. The four single rose beds were set in a tidy line.

CHAPTER SEVEN

Dorothy relied on Miss Byrne for a sense of normality. When she refused to eat, Miss Byrne coaxed her, and when she screamed Ophelia's name, she wrapped her in her bony arms. 'Hush there, child. She's up with the unicorns, can you not see her?'

But Dorothy could not.

Her early morning visits to the stables had stopped. Peter, the little grey pony, was neglected. Sometimes Dorothy watched him from her window as he paced along the fence line, his coat long and his mane untrimmed. Occasionally he would stop at the gate, his small head tilted as if listening for a familiar voice, but then he would lower his head and his pacing would continue, as he waited patiently for John's return.

Each day was a merry-go-round of misery. They would sit at the family dinner, waiting for Sir William. He was always late. To pass the time, Dorothy would watch the clock, and as the hands slowly turned, she would remember fragments of happier times, a moment in a dinner full of laughter, or a particular instant in the entertainment afterwards. In those days there had been plays after supper performed by the children. Elizabeth dressed as Titania would play the Fairy

Queen with more beauty than skill, and Thomas as Oberon, would play his part with a solemnity that made the adults smile, while she, Dorothy would dance, with Miss Byrne accompanying. Sometimes John would dance with her. Now, only a year later, the harpsichord was silent, the laughter gone. As Dorothy sat at the long oak table, amongst the panelling and the tapestries, she longed for the forgotten evenings, and for the current one to end.

One night, in an unusual display of frustration, her elegant mother banged her fist on the table. Everyone turned to look at her.

'Is everything all right, my lady?' Thomas Whitstone sprang to her side.

'No,' she said. 'It is not all right, but I would be grateful if you would serve us. We can wait for Sir William no longer.'

'Yes, my lady.' How Dorothy resented the sympathy in Whitstone's eyes.

An hour later her father arrived, agitated and confrontational. He ate quickly.

'Is it too much to expect my family to wait for me?' He drained a glass of wine and reached for the decanter, the sleeve of his velvet coat trailing across his plate.

'Excuse me, sir.' The footman deftly removed his plate, but not before Sir William had shouted at him.

'Leave it, can't you see I haven't finished?'

But he had finished, and when Dorothy looked at her father she was disgusted. His face was bloated and his eyes bloodshot. His once immaculate clothes were soiled and his jewellery had gone. Only the small snake ring with the ruby eye now bit into his puffy flesh.

Later she could hear his shouts and her mother's sobs. When the front door slammed behind him she rushed to the window. He banged on Lorenzo's door.

'Get me Apollo,' he ordered.

'It's late, sir, he is sleeping.'

'I don't care if he's bloody sleeping! Get me a horse, any one will do.' Not long afterwards they were gone, horse and rider galloping into the blackness, their silhouette outlined against the night sky. Dorothy burst into tears and Lady Keyt drew her daughter onto her lap as she did when she was little.

'I hate him, Mama. He's always angry.'

'You mustn't, darling. You should never hate anyone, let alone your father.'

'He used to be kind; now he only drinks and shouts.'

'Underneath he is still kind. Do you not remember, he was loving and generous? Look at the time he spent with you. Look how he spoilt you.' She spent the rest of the evening talking of the past with Dorothy. Sir William was Lady Keyt's first dancing partner and her first love. Dorothy envisioned her mother as a young girl, guiding her father through the storm when, at only thirteen he lost both his father and beloved grandfather. She imagined their wedding at Toddington church, her father waiting for the beautiful bride who would comfort and support him throughout the years.

When her mother spoke again, her voice faltered. 'I will always love your father, just as I will always love all of you. But for now, Lizzie is my priority. She needs me most. Do you understand that, little one?' She held Dorothy tightly.

'Perhaps God has punished me for too much happiness,' she said at last, kissing the top of Dorothy's head. 'So much tragedy: John, Lizzie, Ophelia. But don't make it your own life story, and don't judge your father too harshly. Don't hate him for all our sakes. You can still realize your dreams.'

Dorothy tried to believe her, but she didn't see her father again for five days.

The months passed slowly, and Sir William's absences grew longer. Elizabeth became quiet, immersing herself in painting. Her horizons might have shrunk, but she observed her world with clarity and simplicity. The bust of an ancestor, an embroidered cushion – each took on a new life. The ancestor had thought, breathed and lived; likewise, someone had worked that cushion, pricked her finger, and strained her eyes.

She thought of her own life. 'Do you know what makes me very sad?' she told her sister. 'I always imagined having children, and now I shall have none. I shall simply be a burden to you all.'

'You will never be a burden,' protested Dorothy. 'I will always look after you, so please don't talk like that.'

'I'm sorry, that was thoughtless. I just can't bear the thought of becoming an encumbrance.' Though Dorothy loved her sister, she couldn't help her frustration. How was Elizabeth always so serene when she, Dorothy, was always angry? Elizabeth never judged, she never criticized and she rarely complained. Amongst her family she became the confidante, always ready to listen to their miseries. But Dorothy could not see inside Elizabeth's heart. In private she wept, mourning the loss of her freedom. She grieved for her family, but she also grieved for herself.

CHAPTER EIGHT

Dorothy found Norton stifling. Thomas, who had been her constant companion, increasingly retreated to the library to read or write poetry. The tree house, once a symbol of their freedom and solidarity, remained empty. At times she was tempted to read more of her father's diary, but her lingering guilt discouraged her. Instead she escaped into the fantasy world of novels, romances that she could barely understand. She longed to be one of the heroines, enjoying a never-ending quest for love and adventure.

Had she stayed in her room on that stuffy summer's day she would not have known the truth about Miss Byrne's departure. She was lying on her bed, trying to focus on her reading, with little success. Everything annoyed her: the heat, the flies, her restricting clothes. She dropped her book to the floor and looked in the mirror; her faced was flushed and small beads of perspiration stood out on her upper lip. She grimaced at a patch of sweat spreading beneath her armpits and pulled open the drawer to her tallboy. She found a clean blouse and was about to change when she noticed the diary her father had given her, hidden beneath her petticoats. It was a smaller version of his own. Inside was a card.

To my darling Dotty, within this small book you can record your successes and your failures; your passion for horses and your passion for dancing. May it be your confidante and your friend.

She was touched by the words and remembered the intimacy they had once shared. She picked it up and went outside, heading towards the pool garden. She reached the alcove in the wall and sat down on the stone bench. It was cooler there, the perfect place to write. Her pencil lay sharpened in the pocket of her dress. She took it out.

She had just started upon the first line when she heard her father's angry voice in the garden; she peered round the wall to see Miss Byrne before him, her head lifted in defiance.

'That's it, Miss Byrne, you will pack your bags and get out. You are of no further use here. You can go to hell or back to your father. It is of no concern to me.'

Dorothy watched them, unobserved, her body rigid in disbelief.

'Sir William, your blindness will have its own punishment. Your neglect and self-pity is pathetic.'

'Enough, I said!' he shouted. 'Get out! Get out, you meddlesome old woman.'

'And what shall I tell the children?'

'Tell them what you bloody well like. Anything, I really don't care.'

Dorothy slumped as if she had been hit. She didn't know or care what Miss Byrne had done, she only knew that she loathed her father. He had always viewed Miss Byrne with suspicion, but to deny his daughter her only comfort was unbearable.

'Damn you, bloody woman,' he yelled at Miss Byrne's retreating back.

Miss Byrne turned and looked at him. 'I will pray for you,' she said. 'I can see you are suffering, but believe me, you will suffer more.'

Miss Byrne came to Dorothy's room later that night; she sat down on her bed, and for the last time she tucked in the sheets and plumped up the pillows. There were tears in her eyes. 'I have to leave you,' she said in her soft Irish voice. 'But I will always be with you.' She tapped Dorothy's forehead. 'If you need me, shut your eyes and I will pop up right here.'

Dorothy sat up and clung to her skinny frame. 'Please take me with you. Please don't leave me.'

Miss Byrne looked into her eyes. 'It's not of my will, little one, so please don't be crying. You must be brave and you must look after your sister, and take care of that brother of yours. They both need your strength, I have all the faith in you, all the faith in the world.'

She sat with her arms around the bereft child and stroked her hair, but to Dorothy it was over. 'What will I do?' she wailed. 'Who will read to me now?'

Miss Byrne gently prised her fingers from her clothes. 'You will read to your sister instead, and you will continue to dance and play the harpsichord, for you have a real talent. You will do it for your brother, your sister and for yourself, and when you have tired of Lotti and Bach, remember the Celtic ballads that I have taught you. And I will leave you my story book. Be sure to look after it. When you open it, you will know that I am with you.' She knelt down in front of her. 'Now always remember, my child, how exceptional you are, and that there is a big world out there, with a future that one day will be yours.'

Dorothy followed Miss Byrne to Thomas's room. They sat upon his bed as the light faded from the sky. 'Look now,' she said. 'You are white as the sheets that you are lying on.' She put her arms around him. 'Remember, young man, you did not cause the accident. You have the gift, but you do not have the power to change events, only to see them. You could not have prevented the inevitable. It was written in the stars.' She kissed him on his forehead and walked to the door. At the last moment she turned.

'Don't judge your father too harshly, children. When you are older you will understand the difference between weakness and evil.'

For days Dorothy shut herself away, refusing to eat or talk. She didn't know how to survive without Miss Byrne.

Finally Thomas came into her room. 'Dotty, please come down. I am worried about Lizzie; she has taken to her bed.'

Dorothy was ashamed. In her need to be alone, she had forgotten her sister. She washed her face and went to her. 'Lizzie, will you forgive me?' she asked. 'In my selfishness I put my own misery first. I don't deserve your love.'

'Darling, of course you do. We all miss her. I don't understand any of it, but we can only get through this together.'

Later that evening, when Elizabeth was asleep, Dorothy returned to the room at the top of the house. Opening the door, she stepped inside. The last of the day's sun filtered through the leaded windows, making patterns on the wooden floor. The crucifix remained, and though the wardrobe was empty of her clothes, the faint smell of lavender lingered. She sat down on the floor beside the bed and pushed the small cotton rug to the side. Lifting the floorboard, she removed the book, Miss Byrne's gift to her, and cradled it to her chest. Before long she entered a world of fairies and unicorns. When the writing blurred on the page and the drawings danced in the shadows, she returned the book to its hiding place and went downstairs to bed.

CHAPTER NINE

Molly Johnson sat on the platform at the top of the granary steps. From this position she could see the world – which, to her mind, consisted of her back garden. It was her favourite place. With the hens pecking beneath her, she swung her stubby legs, absorbing every detail with a capacity far beyond her seven years.

From here the black timbers and tall chimneys of the Charter House, a coaching inn in the county town of Warwick, looked large and important. The courtyard on the other side of a low wall stabled at least thirty-six horses. The grooms worked there, and her friend Seth, the stable boy, ran from stall to stall doing the chores. When she saw him now she waved; unfortunately for Seth, whose enthusiasm proved greater than his coordination, he dropped the buckets he was carrying and they clattered to the ground. The horses snorted indignantly, Seth's clothes were soaked, and Molly couldn't help laughing. It was an infectious laugh, and her reddish curls bounced around her pretty face, her tawny eyes shone with vitality.

She was disturbed by her mother. 'Molly Agnes Johnson, you get down here this minute before I tan your backside! If the fall doesn't kill you, I will.'

'Coming, Ma,' she said. 'Sorry, I was feeding the hens.'

'You were feeding nothing, and no more fibs. God will strike you down, so he will.' Mrs Johnson tried to look fierce but failed miserably. Somehow her eldest daughter always managed to make the world a brighter place.

Molly grew into a taller version of the same agreeable child. The future promised adventure, and she found plenty to fuel her dreams. Everything was as it should be, except for one small injustice. 'No, you won't go to school. There is no need for books when you're clearing tables in a Warwick hostelry; you need different skills, woman's skills.'

'But Will goes to school, Da. It isn't fair.'

'Life isn't fair, Molly. Now be off with you, and up the hill with your brother.'

She walked Will to school, climbing the steep cobbled streets towards the castle, and left him at the classroom door. 'One day,' she swore to herself, listening to the hum of children's voices. 'One day, I'll read and write with the best of them.'

Life was eventful at the Charter House. There were horses to be fed and watered, stables to be cleaned. It never stopped. When the stage arrived at noon, her mother would pull her from the window. 'It's nigh on midday. You've had your lunch, now get on with your work. Dreaming won't clean the rooms, and we can't give a lady dirty sheets. Go and help the housemaids with the beds, otherwise it's the chamber pots for you.'

Molly would run away laughing, but when the next coach arrived, and the passengers spilt down the steps, she was back at the window. The women's dresses caught her eye, so tight she wondered how they breathed. She wanted to make beautiful dresses like that and sell them in a shop with a sign outside: *Molly Johnson, Seamstress*, in blue with gold letters.

When she wasn't serving she washed, and when she wasn't washing she mended. There was plenty to mend: her mother's stays, stiffened with glue; her sister's stockings; the sheets and pillowcases – enough to keep her sewing for ever.

'I'll be fifty when I have finished, Ma.'

'You're a good girl, Molly. God will favour you, so he will.'

And God did favour her, for there were few beatings in the Johnson house. Shouting was another matter; Mrs Johnson yelled at her husband, and he yelled at everyone.

When Mrs Johnson wasn't stretching her lungs, she grew flowers, which Molly tended with love. There were flowers for scent, and flowers for colour, but the herbs grown in terracotta pots most captured her imagination.

'For affairs of the heart there's naught better than a pinch of rue,' her mother taught her, 'and for loosening the stool it's camomile and liquorice.' Their plants could cure any ailment.

As the landlord's daughter, Molly amused the customers and became skilled at avoiding unwanted advances. 'She has a tongue like a greyhound, but the face of an angel,' her father admired.

The first sign of trouble was Dan Leggat from the butcher's shop. 'Hello, Molly.' He put his thick fingers over her hand as she tried to lift his mug. 'Come and sit with me.' He patted the bench beside him.

'No, thank you. I'm busy.' She disliked Dan Leggat. He was a blustering oaf with a mean streak. He pulled wings off insects and laughed at the fun of it, and he bullied poor Madge

Hartly because of her crooked legs and simple mind. Molly had seen him lick the blood from his hands after butchering a calf. No, she didn't like Dan Leggat at all.

'Don't come over all prim and proper, it's time you wed. I'm a good match for you, better than most. If you treat me right and show us a little favour now and then, I might even take you down the aisle.'

'Leave me alone. I'm this side of fifteen, and I'm not for marrying anyone.'

When his arm darted forward and he caught her breast, Molly whipped round. 'You get your hands off me this minute,' she hissed, 'or I'll slap your ugly face.'

'Are you bothering my daughter, Dan?' Her father appeared by her side. 'By the look of her she wants none of it. Now get out of my house.'

Dan slunk off, his face red with anger. 'You'll pay for this,' he said.

Molly flung her arms around her father's neck. 'Thank you, Da.'

'He's not good enough for you, Molly, not good enough at all.'

Each June, the whole town went to the castle for the midsummer celebrations. Lady Brooke and his lordship provided pies and pasties, and young and old danced in the meadow by the river. Molly always dressed with care. For three successive years she had altered her pale blue muslin dress, until at last there were no more seams to ease. Using the lace collar from her mother's wedding gown, she inserted a panel at the front. A linen sheet with fancy edging became a petticoat, and with patience and tiny stitches, daisies adorned the bodice and hem. With a garland of flowers on her russet curls and the prettiest dress in the meadow, Molly Johnson was never short of a partner.

She even caught Lady Brooke's eye.

'You're the Johnson girl,' she said, looking into Molly's untroubled face. 'What a complexion. My skin was like yours once, but now . . .' She sighed and turned away, but Molly had seen the marks. No paste or lead could hide the blemishes.

'Never put anything on your face, my dear,' she said, taking Molly's hand. 'Leave it natural; it would be a crime to ruin such lovely skin.'

'Yes, my lady,' she answered, both flattered and confused.

'Be careful, Miss Johnson,' Lady Brooke continued, her grip tightening, until Molly winced. 'Your looks will bring you everything, but everything comes at a price.' She dropped her hand, and Molly ran through the grass to her next partner. When she turned, Lady Brooke was still watching her, with a strange look on her ruined face.

Mrs Johnson came to her bedroom in the attic that night.

'It's late, my girl. Shut your eyes and dream of all the lads courting you today. You could do far worse than the Potter boy. He's a handsome lad with a good future.'

'He doesn't interest me. I want someone special, someone different, and it's not about money. Look at Lady Brooke. She has all the money in the world and it can't mend her face.'

'You're right there, love. The pox is the pox – it doesn't know rich from poor.'

'When I marry, it has to be for love. Nothing else will do.'

Her mother stroked her hair. How could they hold on to this bright and beautiful girl?

Molly saw him immediately; she noticed the cut of his coat, the highly polished boots. He was a gentleman.

'Can I get you some ale, sir?' She stopped at the alcove by the fire, straightened her dress. Flames rose up, casting shadows around the stranger. She noticed his even white teeth, his unpowdered hair and his fine brown eyes.

'Thank you, young lady. A pint of your best.'

'It's only the best here, sir.'

She learnt he was the Member of Parliament for Warwick.

'He has our vote,' her father said. 'Sir William Keyt, now he's a gent if ever there was one.'

Sir William stopped by the Charter House more often after that. Seth told Molly he owned several estates and a large carriage. He said people like him kept their gold under the mattress.

CHAPTER TEN

As the weeks went by, Sir William Keyt became a regular fixture at the Charter House.

'Ah, here you are, Molly. I've been waiting for you; I've missed your company.'

Of course Molly was flattered. He said she had a bright mind and a quick tongue. When she learnt of the tragedy in his family she felt sorry for him, for Molly's heart was warm and generous.

'It goes to show,' her mother said. 'In the eyes of our Maker we are all the same.' But there weren't many men of Molly's acquaintance who wore silk stockings, and velvet coats with fine embroidery. There weren't many men who wore rubies and lace and a golden snake on their little finger.

As she got older, he asked for her more and more. She accepted his interest with the innocence of youth, as she appreciated his courteous words and enjoyed looking at his fine clothes.

'Come and talk to me on this day of all others. It is the anniversary of my hell, Molly. You're a good listener.'

'Doesn't your wife listen to you?' she asked.

'No, not really, but certainly not today; today she will be on her knees asking God's mercy. When has God ever been merciful?'

Molly refilled his mug.

'Everything changed with the accident. Lizzie gets all my wife's time now. It's difficult to begrudge my poor crippled daughter. Have I told you that it was John who died, my beautiful John? As God is my witness, I wish that I had been taken instead of that precious child.'

Molly had never known despair; her life, though humble, was rich in a different way.

'I'm sorry,' she said. 'Really sorry. If our Will was taken, I would hang myself from the nearest tree.'

'That would be a great loss to the world.' Sir William smiled, and for a brief instant he was able to forget his suffering and relax in the light of the young woman before him. When he took her hand, she didn't pull away.

'My other two children seem to hate me.'

'Of course they don't hate you; they're just angry. My mother says that I see things in black and white, and that all young people are like that. I bet you were no different when you were young.'

'I'm not that old, Molly. Forty-three is not old.'

'Forgive me, sir, I must be off. There's a pile of chores waiting, and I've not done the half of them.'

On Molly's fifteenth birthday, Sir William brought her a present. Molly looked at the fine woollen cloth, stroking the soft blue folds. 'You can make a waistcoat for your brother Will. You said he's always cold.'

'Thank you, Sir William,' she said. 'I'll make him something really fine.'

When she ran from the public rooms to show her mother, Mrs Johnson raised her eyebrows. 'Watch it, Molly. He's clever, that one.'

Molly laughed. 'Come on, Ma, it's hardly a romantic present. I don't have many friends, so let me be.' In Molly's eyes this was true. There was Seth, but he didn't have time for chatter; her sisters were too young; and the local girls, on reaching puberty, were kept away. Molly found this baffling. 'It's not as if we're a bawdy house, sir,' she explained to Sir William, and he had laughed and patted her hand.

Even with her sharp tongue and quick wits, Molly was at first naive. She was oblivious to her effect on Sir William. She did not realise that his stifled emotions were returning, and that the wall he had built to protect him after the death of his son was crumbling. But when she mulled over her mother's warning, she wondered at her stupidity. She was a simple girl, an innkeeper's daughter. How could she have believed that her wit and intelligence kept Sir William amused?

'Come and sit with me, Molly. You seem to avoid me.'

'I will, sir, but just a minute.'

'I have brought you something. A bracelet. The amber will complement the colour of your eyes.'

For all his fancy clothes, Sir William Keyt was no better than Dan Leggat from the butcher's shop.

By the time Molly was sixteen she had taken to avoiding the gentlemen in the front of the inn; she ran errands for her mother, helped in the kitchens and took food from the steaming ovens. But it did not go unnoticed. One day her father called her. 'You'll get out in front, girl. What do you think you are doing?'

'But I don't want to. I'm doing a good job helping Ma.'

'You'll do as you're told, or I'll lather your backside. Get out there this minute.'

Her father's harsh tone hurt Molly. When he summoned her to the parlour, he avoided her eyes. 'Sit down and listen clear. You've been acting strange of late. Now you can show me what a sensible girl you are. Sir William Keyt, our valued guest, has honoured you with a position as his wife's lady's maid. It's a step up the ladder, and who knows what it may lead to?'

Molly looked at her father. Shock hit her in the belly. 'You can't mean it. I'm happy here with you and the girls and Will. Please don't make me go.'

'Why ever not? Any girl who knew what was good for them would die for this opportunity.'

'It's no opportunity, and it's no step up the ladder. He wants me in his bed.'

Molly's father raised his hand. She thought he would strike her. 'Enough of your lip! It's your mother's fault, too much spoiling. I always said it, and now it's come to roost. You'll stay in your room until I tell you to come out.'

Molly ran upstairs to the bed she shared with Will, who was thin and sickly and always cold. She held her brother in her arms.

'Is it my fault?' she moaned, staring at the ceiling. 'Did I encourage him? I don't have a choice; there's never been a choice. I'll run away, I'll starve in the gutter and freeze to death. Then he'll be sorry.'

Will held her hand and cried. 'I love you, don't leave.' She cried too, but it didn't change anything.

Her mother begged her father. 'Jack, she's a child. What in heaven's name are you thinking? Have you not seen the way he looks at her?'

But her father remained unmoved.

Three weeks later Molly packed her bag and said goodbye to Will, whose knees dug into her back at night. She took him to school for the last time, and hugged him at the door. 'Be good, and we will see each other very soon. In the meantime, send me letters, fine letters in your best hand. Someone will read them to me.'

'Bye, Molly,' he said, 'I'll miss you.'

'Hush now.' She gently disentangled his arms from around her waist. 'And don't you forget to say your prayers.'

Later that morning a storm came, and as the thunder crashed around the house, she worked herself into an anxious frenzy. Her mother tried to gather her in her arms, but Molly pushed her away. 'Why didn't you stop this? Don't look so bloody stricken. You could have stopped him! He went and sold me like one of his bloody pigs! You know what's going to happen to me, and yet you let him send me away?'

'I tried, my love,' her mother pleaded.

'You should have tried harder! You said you would take a beating for any of us, but that was a lie.'

When Mrs Johnson pulled back her sleeve, the truth was revealed in the bruise that swelled beneath her skin. 'I'm sorry,' she said sadly. 'You know your father when his mind is made up, and I have this to show for it. I couldn't push it, my love.'

'It's all right, Ma, don't cry. I'm sorry.'

'I love you, Molly,' she said at last. 'I want only the best for you. I've tried to persuade myself that something good'll come of it.'

'What good? What possible good?'

'You will be in charge of her ladyship's clothes. You will mend and embroider, and you will dress her hair. You are a smart girl and you will be doing what you really love. Perhaps this is a path to a better future and we've got it wrong. It is quite possible that Sir William is honest in his offer.'

'You and I both know what he wants.' Molly buried her head in her mother's chest. She inhaled her comforting smell, and cried.

'If there's any trouble, you come home. I will deal with your father and be damned with the consequences.'

'Don't let anything happen to Will.'

'Of course I won't. I love him too. I love you all so much, God help me, so I do.'

Molly broke away and opened the door to find her sisters listening at the keyhole. 'Stop gawping, girls, and come and see me off.'

They walked outside. It was Friday, baking day, and the sweet smells made her homesick before she had even left. As the coach clattered away down the street, her little sisters faded into the distance. She waved her handkerchief and she shut her eyes. 'Please, God, keep Will safe.'

CHAPTER ELEVEN

On a dull spring morning, Mr Godwin taught Latin in the schoolroom. Although his teaching did not inspire in Dorothy the same enthusiasm as lessons with her former governess, it did at least provide some distraction. She was returning a book to the schoolroom shelf when she heard wheels clattering on the cobblestones outside. She rushed to the window, hoping for a visitor, but with a sinking heart she saw her father. She wondered what sort of mood he would be in. She returned to her desk, piled her books together and walked over to her brother.

'It's only Father,' she said. 'Will you help me with my translation later?' They chatted as they went downstairs. When they arrived in the drawing room, their father was already there, standing in front of the chimney breast, his hand resting on the large stone mantel. To the children's surprise he had a smile on his face.

'Well, have you nothing to say to your father?' he asked.

'Hello, Father,' they said in unison.

'Good morning, William,' said Lady Keyt as she came into the room. 'I hope you have had a pleasant journey?'

'Yes, thank you.' He kissed her quickly, and Dorothy noticed his new coat and breeches, cream with mother-of-pearl buttons.

'There is something I wish to say.' He pulled out his handkerchief, blew his nose, and delivered his news. 'Ann, I am delighted to inform you that I have employed a new lady's maid on your behalf. Miss Johnson is an accomplished girl, and she will be of great service. Above all, she will release you from the burden of responsibility towards our dearest daughter.'

There was a stunned silence.

'Excuse me, William, but am I hearing you correctly? I don't wish for any extra assistance with Elizabeth; her nurse gives me all the help that I need.' Dorothy noticed her mother's hands turn white as she gripped the back of the chair. 'I am capable of finding my own lady's maid. If I wanted your help in household matters, I would ask you. Mrs Selley leaves two months from now, which gives ample time to find someone that suits me.'

'But my dear, you will like Molly. She is competent and reliable. She is also the daughter of a loyal constituency member. Her father has agreed.'

'I can see you are on first-name terms with this girl. It's most irregular – indeed, it undermines my own position within this household. Looking at you, however, it's obvious that you have made up your mind. I am sorry that we have come to this. So be it, but do not expect my sanction in what I consider to be a blatant disregard for my feelings.' Lady Keyt smoothed her dress, lifted her shoulders and, with a straight back, left the room.

'For heaven's sake, Thomas, why are you fidgeting? Stand still,' Sir William snapped, turning on his son.

'I am standing still, sir. It is you who is agitated, not I. If you will excuse me, I'll go and look after my mother.'

'Well, Dotty, follow your brother. I realize I can do nothing right in this infernal household!'

Dorothy fumed. Molly Johnson was the landlord's daughter that her father had likened to Dorothy.

'Don't ever call me Dotty. Your right to that name went a long time ago. If you bring this girl to Norton, I shall never speak to you again. Never.'

She glared at her father, picked up her skirts and ran after her brother.

The following morning they ate in silence. When Lady Keyt had finished her breakfast, she folded her large linen napkin and rose to go.

'Dorothy, I would be grateful if you would spend a little time with Lizzie. I have a slight headache.'

'Of course, Mama.'

Dorothy looked in on Lizzie on her way upstairs but she was still asleep. She would go to her later. Climbing the stairs to the attic, she passed Annie at the linen cupboard. Sheets lay across her arm, and a jug of water balanced on a china tray.

'Morning, miss,' she said. 'Just going to do the room for the new girl.'

'Would you do my room first, Annie? I would like five minutes alone.'

Dorothy paused on the threshold of Miss Byrne's room for the last time. New sheets would cover the bed and somebody else's clothes would fill the cupboard. She knelt down, prised open the floorboards and removed the book, cradling it in her arms.

***

Dorothy found Lizzie in her usual place on the half-landing. She was reading, her brow furrowed in concentration. 'Dotty,' she raised her head. 'We must give Miss Johnson a chance. She may be just what we need.'

Dorothy was about to reply when Elizabeth leant forward and stared into the rose garden, the book falling from her lap.

'Dotty, can you see the boy in the garden? He is looking this way. His clothes are most unusual.' Dorothy looked outside; the garden was empty and still, save for the leaves eddying around Ophelia's statue.

'I can't see anyone,' she said gently.

'Oh, Dotty, I can see that you don't believe me. Perhaps it is my medication. Now even my mind is going. For just one moment I want to be normal.' She grimaced, the small scar twisting in her cheek. 'Can you imagine what it's like?'

Dorothy couldn't imagine, it was beyond her capabilities, and for a moment she felt unutterably sad. 'I'm so sorry,' she replied at last. She knelt in front of Elizabeth and took her hands in her own. 'I didn't see a boy, but if you did, then he must have been there. You are not losing your mind; you are saner than the rest of us put together. I cannot give you back your dreams, but I can give you this.' She put Miss Byrne's book into her lap. 'Miss Byrne wrote these stories for us, and they have given me strength. Perhaps they can do the same for you.' When Elizabeth didn't answer she turned the pages. 'Do you see, Lizzie? The rest of the book is empty. Will you fill the pages with our story? Will you write about everything, the past, the present, and the future, so that someone, some day, might read it and know about us?' Elizabeth nodded, her eyes filling with tears.

CHAPTER TWELVE

The coachman dropped her bag on the flagstone floor. 'The housekeeper will come for you.'

Molly looked at her face in the hall mirror. It was not the face she knew, the confident and pretty landlord's daughter.

'Morning, miss.' A footman passed. He winked and smiled, a silver tray balanced in his hand. 'Mrs Wright will be along shortly. No need to be afraid, she won't bite.'

'I'm not frightened, sir,' she replied, but her words sounded false. She longed for her bedroom, her Will, her mother, anywhere but here.

'Could have fooled me,' he said cheerfully, pushing the swing door closed with his foot.

Mrs Wright arrived, her grey hair scraped into a bun. She had small eyes in a mean face.

'Miss Johnson, come this way. Don't get any ideas in this house. Do as you are told or you'll be out of here before you know it. You will answer to me and her ladyship.'

Molly followed her under a stone archway and into a large inner hall. Portraits of long-dead Keyt ancestors stared from the walls; Molly hurried past to avoid their silent gaze.

A footman opened a pair of double doors, and Mrs Wright

swept through to the drawing room. Molly cautiously entered after her.

'Excuse me, Lady Keyt, Miss Johnson has arrived.' Three heads turned towards her, the same three heads she had glimpsed through the window. Lady Keyt remained with her face in profile.

'Good morning, Miss Johnson.' She got up slowly, graciously, and walked towards her, her green silk dress rustling as she moved.

'Good morning, ma'am.'

'Curtsy, miss,' the housekeeper barked. Molly bobbed ineffectually.

'Mrs Wright, you may go, thank you.'

It was evident that Mrs Wright had no wish to leave. Her tongue clicked against her teeth as she left the room.

'This is my daughter, Miss Elizabeth.' Lady Keyt nodded at the girl in a high backed chair. 'This is Master Thomas, and this is my younger daughter, Dorothy.'

Molly smiled tentatively. Elizabeth was pretty, with her thick fair hair plaited around her head, but the poor legs hidden beneath a blanket saddened her.

'I believe you are to be my lady's maid,' Elizabeth said in her gentle voice.

'Yes, miss.'

'I shall enjoy that, I know.'

Before she had time to reply, the younger girl walked towards her. 'I can't imagine why Papa employed you; you're hardly old enough to be a lady's maid. And you won't be my companion because I don't need one.' She rushed to her sister's side.

69

Molly stared at her shoes, covered with mud. She couldn't believe that she had neglected to clean them.

'Dorothy, be polite to poor Miss Johnson. We must make her welcome in our home.' Molly looked up shyly. Despite her broken legs, Miss Elizabeth had the kindest manner.

'Miss Johnson,' Dorothy spoke grudgingly, 'that was churlish. I apologize.'

It was obvious to Molly that Miss Dorothy's apology did not come from her heart.

'Dotty, is that an admission of guilt? I cannot believe my ears.' At the sound of Thomas's voice, warm and teasing, Molly found herself blushing.

'Good morning, sir,' she mumbled, aware of Dorothy's scrutinizing eyes.

She was grateful for the arrival of Sir William, who came in with two spaniels at his heels.

'Greetings, Miss Johnson. Welcome to our home. Letitia, Sophie, leave Miss Johnson alone. I do apologize for my unruly dogs.'

'I love dogs,' she replied, suddenly aware of her country vowels. 'I always wanted one, but Ma said there were enough four-legged beasts at the Charter House, and a dog would be one too many.'

'Well, you will have no shortage of dogs here.' He smiled. 'Mathews, I am expecting Mr Clarke; tell him I will be with him shortly.'

'Yes, Sir William,' the footman replied.

Sir William turned back towards her. 'I hope you will forgive me, but I have business with my agent to attend to. I expect, however, that my wife will wish to go through the details of your employment. I hope you will be happy here, Miss Johnson.'

Molly nodded, reassured. His manner was polite. Perhaps her fears had no grounds.

'Children, I will see you later,' he said. 'Ann, I will leave you in Miss Johnson's capable hands.'

'Thank you.' Ann sat down and took up her embroidery. 'Thomas,' she said, putting on her glasses, 'please will you show Miss Johnson the house? We would not want her to get lost.'

'Yes, Mother,' he replied.

'Miss Johnson, after you have unpacked and refreshed yourself, I would be grateful if you would come to my room. I would like to go through the details of your duties.'

Molly followed Thomas from the room, keeping her eyes on the floor ahead of her.

'Don't worry about Dorothy,' Thomas said, when they were out of earshot. 'She's had a difficult time recently; she'll come round.'

Molly doubted that, but remained silent. In the first bedroom they came to, bright curtains hung at the windows, and a Turkish rug covered the floor. There were comfortable upholstered chairs beside the fire, and paintings of flowers and birds filled the yellow walls.

'Elizabeth chose everything in here. She wanted the room to be light and cheerful. The paintings are her own. She's talented, isn't she?'

Looking at the delicately painted flowers, Molly thought of her pots at the Charter House. She nodded in admiration. 'She has a gift. At home we have flowers everywhere. I've learnt a lot about them over the years.'

'Then you can share your knowledge with me.'

Molly looked up, her confidence growing. She glimpsed his faultless profile, the finely moulded jaw. 'Did you know,' she began, pulling her eyes away, 'most of the medicines in these bottles are made from plants? There are remedies for every kind of ailment.'

'I didn't,' he replied, 'but I can well believe it. My mother says that the medicines inside this cabinet keep Elizabeth alive. She had the whole world at her feet before the accident. Now she is reliant on these small bottles. What a waste, don't you agree?' Thomas turned towards her. 'Perhaps you can give her a little happiness.'

'I will try, sir,' she said, knowing she would do anything to gain his affection. When their eyes met, he smiled a resigned, sad smile, and she fell in love in that instant.

That evening, Molly's duties began. When she entered the delightful bedroom, it was possible to believe that her father was right, and that this would be a great opportunity for a simple landlord's daughter.

'Do you like pretty things, Miss Johnson? I believe from the look in your eyes that you have a taste for beauty.' Lady Keyt was sitting at the dressing table. Her dark hair hung to her waist, and the firelight softened her fine oval face.

'I do, milady,' Molly replied. She turned to look at the ornate bed hung with embroidered silk and tassels, the heavy silk curtains at the windows, and the flounced valances. Paintings in gilt frames covered the panelled walls, and there was silver everywhere: the dressing-table mirror, the brushes and combs, the candlesticks on the mantelpiece. 'I love nice things, I believe all girls do, but best of all I like fabrics. I think that is because of my sewing. Ma says I know a good thing when I see it, and I reckon the silk on your bed must have cost a fortune.'

Lady Keyt laughed, and Molly relaxed, knowing they would get along.

'I am unaware of the cost, but I am glad you like sewing for you will be in charge of my clothes, and when they need mending it will be your responsibility to do so. Can you manage that?'

'I surely can. I have mended most of my life, and my stitches are nigh-on impossible to see.'

'That is the perfect requirement for a lady's maid. Now, Molly – do you mind if I call you that, for we are to see a great deal of each other?'

'I would much rather be called that.'

'Well then, it's decided.' Lady Keyt's reflection smiled back at her. 'Ruth and Annie will empty the slops, lay the fires in my bedchamber and change the bed linen, but you will care for my wardrobe and act as my personal dresser. When you are not with me you will sit with Elizabeth. I hope you won't find the position tedious after the bustle of a coaching inn.'

'No, my lady. I'm sure I won't.' Molly's enthusiasm grew by the minute. Lady Ann Keyt was courteous and kind. As she helped her new employer into a gown of the finest silk and lace, her future seemed bearable after all.

When Lady Keyt was ready, her soft arms scented with rose water, her hair piled upon her head, she directed Molly to the servants' quarters.

'It's through the swing door in the ground-floor passage. They have supper at seven, dear, so you had better hurry along.'

When Molly pushed open the door, everyone stopped eating and turned towards her. 'Come here, miss,' Tompkins, the footman who had winked at her earlier, said, patting the empty chair beside him. 'It's all right, love, Mrs Wright isn't here – she eats with the butler, in her parlour, and there's still plenty of time. We get an hour at lunch and at dinner.'

Molly's keen eye counted eighteen indoor servants and noted every detail of the cheerful room: the heavy china, the pewter flagons on the long oak table, the burnished copper saucepans hanging from hooks on the ceiling. She listened as the conversation flowed.

'She's come up the hard way, has Mrs Wright,' Ruth the housemaid said. 'She has the job of hiring and firing and there's the problem: she doesn't think much of you being hired by the master himself. Watch yourself with Mrs Wright.'

Molly smiled, disguising her unease.

'She's been here for nigh-on twenty-five years, and she's climbed up from lower than Annie here and me.' Ruth prodded the girl beside her. 'She had two years on the fenders, hearths and slops and she don't take kindly to you being given right off what took her twenty years to get!'

Ruth shook her head and giggled, leaving Annie to finish her story. 'Now she's in charge of us all indoors. She pays the servants and the tradesmen and if anyone tries to skim her, she don't half get mad. She does all the accounts and if we disturb her, do we know it! She does the marketing, buys all the meat and veg. She acts like my namesake Queen Anne herself, not that I ever met her, her majesty being dead that many years.'

Everyone laughed, but Annie continued, 'She makes me right mad at times. It's always the same. "Annie, have you been thieving?" she says, after she's checked the linens. If something goes missing, it's always me. What does she think I'm going to do with a fine lace napkin, wipe my bum with it?'

'Don't forget the stillroom perfumes,' Tompkins interrupted. 'Molly, me love, if you smell of lavender water, you'll be dead before the day is out – smelling good, mind you.' As the banter and the laughter continued, Molly grew more at ease.

That night she slept in the room at the top of the house. It was not so different from her room at the Charter House, and she fell into a deep sleep. When she awoke the next morning, she rose on one elbow and looked around her. The early sunlight made patterns on the wooden floor, and on top of the washstand a small china mug was filled with spring flowers. It was an attractive room, and with a little imagination she could make it her own. She listened to the silent house, and painfully she thought of Will, the two of them in her own bedroom, whispering before the rest of the household erupted with the day's activity.

She got out of bed and looked through the window. Crocuses burst through the ground, another reminder of home. Once again Molly longed for her mother and for Will, and she hungered to be outside.

She washed her face and hands in the blue and white china basin, smoothed her hair and glanced in the mirror. Her hazel eyes stared back at her. Molly had never liked the colour; she wished they were blue.

She straightened the collar of her sprigged cotton dress. It was faded and a little too short, but it was her second-best dress, and until she could make another, it would have to do.

She went down the back stairs and into the garden. It smelt of cut spring grass, reminding her of the garden at Warwick Castle.

A brick archway led to a pathway between two raised borders. She followed the path, picked a narcissus and held it to her nose. 'The Romans brought them here,' her mother had told her, 'nigh-on thirteen hundred years ago.'

Through two pillars she entered a large untended garden. Wild flowers grew in the long grasses, and amongst the trees, two pools glittered in the early morning light. In the smaller pool there was a statue. She recognized it as Pan. She sat down on a bench and leant forward. Pan's reflection moved across the water towards her. She was lost in thought when she heard footsteps. Thomas was at the entrance to the garden. He looked her way and for a long moment they didn't speak.

'May I join you, Miss Johnson? I am also an early riser.'

'I have to start work soon,' she said, finding her voice, 'but, yes, for a little while. I would like that.'

He sat on the bench beside her, and when he moved, his leg brushed against hers.

'Do you know about this flower?' he asked, looking at the wilting stem in her lap.

'I do. I am not well schooled, but my mother has a story for nearly every flower in England.'

'That means,' he said, 'you will be able to tell me a story every day of the year.' He looked at Molly intently and she felt her cheeks burn.

She struggled to remember the myth. 'This is a narcissus, and it's named for a character in Greek mythology. Surely you have heard the story?'

'I don't think so,' Thomas said. 'Go on.'

'Narcissus was a hunter. He had flowing golden hair and great beauty, but he had no heart. On seeing him the nymph Echo fell madly in love.' Molly paused, but Thomas nodded at her encouragingly. 'Narcissus spurned Echo, and the poor nymph wasted away and died. This angered the gods and they decided to punish Narcissus. One day when he was tired of hunting, he drank from a clear pool of water. On seeing the beautiful face shimmering in the water below, he immediately fell in love, little realizing the reflection was his own. Like Echo, he too faded away, echoing the manner of her death. Aphrodite took pity on him and made him into this golden flower.' As she looked up, their eyes met and he smiled, and though he would smile at her many times, this was the one she never forgot. 'My mother is very wise, Master Thomas. She may not have had a proper education, but she knows more about life than anyone I know.'

'Molly,' he said. Her name sounded so pretty on his lips. 'That is the most enchanting name. May I call you by your first name? Miss Johnson is too formal, now that I know that you love stories and flowers.'

'Indeed, sir, you may.'

'Do you like our house?' he asked, willing her reply to be positive.

'Master Thomas, I like it enough, but the house in the dip with the chickens outside reminds me of home. That one I like a lot.'

Sir William Keyt strode towards them. 'Thomas,' he thundered. 'What are you doing? Your mother has been waiting for you. Have you forgotten? And Miss Johnson, are you going to neglect your duties before they have begun? Do I have to send you back to your father today?'

'I am sorry, sir,' she said, humiliated. She was about to apologize again, when she realized the injustice of his anger. 'I came out to see your garden,' she started uncertainly. 'It was well before breakfast and the start of my duties.' She squared her hips and faced him. 'I did not ask to be in your employment, Sir William. My father forced me. Apparently an agreement was made. It was not my decision, and I will gladly go home.'

'If you feel that we have coerced you, far be it from me to stop you, but have a care, Miss Johnson: your father might not be so pleased.'

He turned on his heel.

'Forgive me,' Thomas said when his father had gone. 'It was my fault. I should have defended you but I didn't know what to say. My father always has that effect on me, but you stood up to him. You are quite extraordinary.'

As Molly headed back towards the house and the day's duties, she repeated Thomas's words like an incantation.

Thomas remained on the stone bench. He picked up the flower and turned it in his hand, remembering the heat from her body as her leg had moved against his own. 'Help me,' he sighed, but nothing could ease the confusion in his heart. He slipped the flower into the pocket of his coat. Who knew what course his life would take, but at that moment he was sure that Molly Johnson would play a part in it.

CHAPTER THIRTEEN

The following morning Dorothy rose early, determined to find her brother. She went to his room but found no sign of him. She was about to leave when Ruth arrived, armed with brushes and the ash pail.

'Morning, miss, just come to do the grate.' She knelt down to clear the remains of the previous night's fire, and Dorothy changed her mind and sat in the armchair to wait for Thomas. For the first time she noticed that all of the relics of their childhood had disappeared – the drawings pinned to the wall, the maps showing their imaginary travels, even the colourful pictures done with Miss Byrne. At fifteen, her brother was nearly a man.

Beside her on the table lay several sheets of paper, the finished translations from the day before. Glancing through them, she noticed underneath a number of poems in varying stages of composition. She was about to put them down when one line caught her eye: 'Oh such beauty is held within thy face.'

She sucked in her breath, tears stinging her eyes, and pushed it hurriedly back into the pile. It had to be about Miss Johnson. She just knew it had been written for her.

Ruth rose and stretched her back. 'I've finished the hearth.

If you're after Master Thomas, he's in the garden. He'll be looking for that new lady's maid, I'll warrant.'

'I did not ask for your opinion!' Dorothy got up and charged from the room.

In the rose garden Molly was picking flowers. As she straightened, wiping her face with her sleeve, she noticed Thomas watching her.

'How long have you been here?' she asked.

'Long enough,' he replied with a smile.

'These are for your mother,' she explained, hastily adding the stems to her basket.

He laughed, aware of her embarrassment. 'You are allowed to pick flowers. You'll not be punished. Mother thinks you are wonderful. In fact, it seems you have captivated the entire household.'

Neither noticed the face in the study window. On hearing their voices, Sir William had peered outside; seeing his son standing with Molly Johnson filled him with fear and helplessness. Though they stood feet apart, their looks and gestures revealed mutual attraction. Sir William slumped into the chair, and with his head cradled in his arms he wept.

Sometime later Dorothy heard shouting in the hall.

'I will not go! You can't make me!'

'You'll do as you are bloody well told! I won't have you moping around here any longer. It's time you went to school. You should have gone at thirteen like every normal boy. I said so to your mother at the time, but she wouldn't have it. Now, you are definitely going.'

'Perhaps you have your own motives for getting rid of me.'

'How dare you, Thomas! You have no respect, and no manners. Perhaps Eton can make something of you, for it seems you have learnt nothing here. You will leave on the tenth of the month, so you had better start packing!'

She heard the door slam and waited for her brother at the top of the stairs.

'He's sending me to Eton,' he said. 'I'll be a target for every bully in the school.'

'Why do you say that? Of course you won't be.'

'Look at me, Dotty. I hate shooting, I hate sport, and Father says I act like a girl.'

She put her arms around her precious brother. She remembered the entry in her father's diary and realized that this was no idle threat. 'It will be all right. He can't have meant it. If you don't want to go, he won't make you. Even Father can't be that vile.'

Thomas held her at arm's length and looked into her eyes. 'Believe me, Dorothy. If he thinks I'm a threat, he will send me away for ever.'

Dorothy didn't understand the implication of his words, but she knew that her father would be responsible for yet another loved one leaving her.

It was not long before the gossip had reached the servants' quarters.

'He's been sent away to school, poor boy.' Annie's face was long and disapproving.

'Perhaps it's better for him. Too many girls in the house,' Ruth said.

Molly folded the petticoats away in the cupboard for the third time. She rearranged the vests and the camisoles, the stockings and the bodices. Keeping busy was the only way to get through the morning.

As Thomas's departure drew near, Molly's anxiety increased. She had been hanging a dress in Lady Keyt's wardrobe when he walked through the bedroom door.

'I have come to say goodbye.'

'It's true, you are going, then?'

'Father's packed me off to school.' He picked up a hairbrush distractedly and put it down in the wrong place. He walked towards her, then turned back to the dressing table.

'Stand still, sir, or you'll wear out the carpet.'

He smiled. 'Molly Johnson, you are quite unique. I have never met anyone like you before.'

'You can't have met many people, then. I believe I'm quite ordinary.'

He laughed and took her hand. 'I'll write if you would like me to.'

She nodded, too flustered by his touch to tell him she couldn't read.

'Goodbye, Molly. I must go.'

'Goodbye, Master Thomas, and good luck.'

'Molly, may I kiss you?' She looked at him in assent, and he lowered his head to hers. It was a fleeting, feather-light kiss, but it bound her to him.

'This is a poem especially for you.' He tucked a folded piece of paper into her fingers and pressed them to his lips. No one had written her a poem before. No one had made her heart pound in her chest. When the time came for him to leave, it took all her will not to run down from her attic bedroom and throw her arms around him. Instead she watched helplessly as the footmen carried the trunks to the awaiting coach.

'Cheer up, Miss Dorothy,' Lorenzo said kindly. 'He'll be back before you know it.'

'He won't,' she wailed. 'I know he'll be gone for ever.'

When the family assembled for the last time, she ran to Thomas and hugged him, burying her face in his shoulder.

'These are for you.' She pressed a small bunch of violets into his hand. 'I picked them this morning. They will remind you of home.'

He pulled his prayer book from his inside pocket, and placed the tiny flowers inside.

'I shall keep these for ever, Dotty. Not only will they remind me of home, but they will be a constant reminder of my little sister.'

'Don't be frightened,' she replied. 'I shall pray for you every single day.'

'Thank you. Please do keep me in your prayers, for you shall always be in mine.' He gently unhooked her hands. 'Mother,' he said. 'I shall miss you so much.'

'And you, my beloved son.'

'Goodbye, Lizzie, I shall think of you.' When Elizabeth lifted his hand and held it to her cheek, her eyes welled with tears. Thomas kissed her forehead. 'Write to me. Send me drawings of home.'

Their father stood apart from the family, his arms steady at his sides. 'Make good use of your time, Thomas.'

Thomas did not reply.

As the coach pulled away, he turned towards the house and waved, but this last gesture made Dorothy gasp with disappointment: it was directed to an attic window, far above her.

CHAPTER FOURTEEN

For the next few weeks, Molly buried herself in her work. She soon settled and mastered her new duties. Here she mended silks and satins instead of cottons and coarse wool. The company of her boisterous family was exchanged for that of aristocrats, who viewed the world from a different perspective. Her mistress expected obedience, but she was also kind and generous.

'You're doing well, Molly. Your mending is faultless, your care of my wardrobe impeccable, and Miss Elizabeth has become attached to you. I'm sure you'll be with us for a long time.'

Molly felt proud. Life at Norton was getting better.

One morning, when Molly's work was all but done, Lady Keyt went to the wardrobe. She pushed aside the dresses to pull out a gown. 'This no longer fits me,' she said. 'Would you like to have it? It has a rip in the seam, but that should be easy enough to repair.'

Molly was lost for words.

'Don't you like it?'

'Thank you, my lady. I never expected I would own dress like this.' She held the mint-green silk in her arms, cradling it like a child. She touched the lace on the bodice, the delicate pin tucks on the sleeves, the silk sash. 'Thank you, my lady. It is the most beautiful gown in the world.'

Later, standing in front of the cracked mirror in the small bedroom at the top of the house, turning this way and that, her cheeks flushed, it was easy to dream. When she put on the dress, its bodice cut very low, it was easy to imagine hands caressing her body, and lips on her neck.

In Dorothy's eyes, Molly Johnson had one purpose in life: to ingratiate herself within the Keyt household. Dorothy eavesdropped, learning everything she could about the landlord's daughter. Elizabeth liked her, and as Lady Keyt's distrust evaporated, she heaped privileges upon her new maid. The servants, particularly the men, openly admired her.

Mrs Wright was an exception, hardly bothering to conceal her dislike. 'Airs above her station, that one! She'll learn the hard way, she will.'

Her father's feelings were more difficult to discern, for though he had employed Miss Johnson, he seemed indifferent to the sound of her name.

Early one morning, Ruth knocked on Dorothy's door. 'Are you dressed, miss? Your father is asking for you in the hall.'

Dorothy went downstairs and found her father in his riding clothes. 'Dorothy, will you come with me to the coach house? I have something to show you.'

Lorenzo appeared leading a bright bay mare.

'This is Ophelia's half-sister. I thought you might want her. She's rather like Ophelia, don't you think?' Her father sounded uncomfortable, but when Dorothy saw the mare nothing else mattered. She put out her hand and the filly pushed her nose towards her.

'Thank you, Father, thank you,' she said, her arms already clasped around the horse's neck.

'Ride again. It'll do you good,' he said. 'Now, I have to be at my constituency this afternoon. I must be off.'

Dorothy watched him canter away. She wanted to trust him, to give him affection, but she remained wary. Her father was too unpredictable.

She named the mare Fidelia, and from that day, a happy new ritual began. At eleven o'clock each morning, her unruly hair tied beneath her veil, she would wait impatiently at the mounting block. When Lorenzo arrived with the horses, his handsome face smiling, her heart lifted. As they cantered through the pasture, she would laugh in exhilaration, for Fidelia proved a worthy successor to Ophelia. As they ambled through the woods, letting the horses cool, she felt contented. She learnt of Lorenzo's background: of his mother, an idealistic Italian girl, who was romanced by an English valet on Sir William's grand tour of Italy. He told her stories of his mother's journey to England with the Keyt entourage, her subsequent misery and return to her own country, taking her young son with her. She heard of the sixteen-year-old boy's courageous decision to return to England, his love of horses, and his apprenticeship as the Keyt coachman. She learnt of his unfailing loyalty to her father and his sense of accountability.

'I should have checked the bolts,' he said. 'Your father has never blamed me for the accident, but if only I had checked the bolts . . .'

He told her of his half-brothers and sister and his cousins, all living and working on the farm near Florence, and his dreams of one day returning there. 'In September, when the grapes are picked,' Lorenzo said, his voice soft with memories, 'we celebrate the *vendemmia*, the harvest. In October, the olives are gathered and the world is good.' Dorothy imagined him at ease amongst his own people. Occasionally her imagination went further.

The seasons moved on, and Dorothy's life gained equilibrium. She rode with Lorenzo (the hour she most looked forward to), took dancing lessons once a week, and continued with her schooling. She made a conscious endeavour to control her emotions. With considerable personal effort, a tactical understanding formed between herself and Miss Johnson: they avoided each other.

One morning, running to the landing with a feather she had found, Dorothy noticed Lizzie hiding her sketch book beneath her blanket. 'Lizzie, I found this in the woods and thought you would like it. Why have you put your pad away? I want to see.'

'You can't,' her sister said, a little abruptly, 'but thank you, it's a gorgeous feather. I shall use it for my painting tomorrow.'

Although Elizabeth smiled, her tone concerned Dorothy. She found her mother in her sitting room writing letters. 'There's something wrong with Lizzie,' Dorothy said anxiously.

'Of course there is, Dotty,' her mother said, putting down her pen. 'She can't do any of the things you can. We all think Lizzie is all right because we believe she accepts her fate, but her heart is more troubled than you think.'

Dorothy left the room, chiding herself for her blindness. She vowed to be a better sister, and for a good while, she was.

CHAPTER FIFTEEN

Thomas had been away for four months when the post boy arrived at Norton, carrying a packet of letters. 'I've brought these myself, miss. The postmistress is busy, and it's on my way home.'

Dorothy thanked the boy and gave him a generous tip, taking the packet into the house. Two letters were for her father, but at the bottom of the pile were three letters tied together with string. She recognized the script instantly. After delivering her father's post she ran upstairs to her room and untied them. On top there was a letter from Thomas to her mother, then one to herself. The last was a letter to Molly. With shaking hands Dorothy looked at the envelope. After a moment's hesitation she broke the seal.

Dearest Molly,
    I hope I may call you that.
    Firstly, may I say that you have occupied my mind. I thought of you on the long journey to Windsor, that last look – your dear face smiling in the window – and I continue to think of you at the most odd moments. I will hear your laughter whilst translating Latin texts, or in the college chapel in the middle of the Nunc Dimittis.

I believe there must be a name for my foolish fantasies.

My first few weeks here were lonely and frightening, but at least the worst is over. They have a ritual here called 'Tossing the Blanket'. Its sole purpose is to terrify and torture the new boys. I survived it, but only just, and indeed, I have survived my housemaster, Mr Kirkpatrick, who is as cruel as any man can be. There are ten boys in my dormitory, and each evening at eight o'clock we are locked into this bleak comfortless place, and left in the merciless hands of our tormentors – boys not much older than ourselves.

The misery may sound relentless, but that would be wrong. I have made my first friend: his name is Gilbert Paxton-Hooper. He passed me a note in our first lesson together. 'We will be friends, ignore the bullies.' You can imagine what that meant to me. He is bright and artistic, with exuberant dark curls.

My personal tutor is as kind as Kirkpatrick is cruel, so it isn't all bad. One day I shall inscribe my name in the ancient desks as others have done before me, and I shall come home.

I hope you will wait for me, Molly, and that these simple words haven't been too tedious.

Always,

Thomas

Dorothy balled the letter within her fist. She clutched her sides, all of her resentment and frustration welling over. She sank to the floor, panting in fury. Never in her life had she known such jealousy. Molly Johnson had stolen her brother.

When she felt she could stand she walked to the fire. She smoothed the creases in the letter and held it over the grate. The edges curled, slowly smouldering, until at last the flames consumed it. It gave her satisfaction to watch the words turn to ash and fall.

Calling for the dogs she ran outside. They trotted after her through the gate and into the wilderness beyond. A blustery wind pulled at the trees around her, and as the branches creaked and groaned above her, she drove herself up the hill, the dogs barking in excitement. The exertion calmed her, and her anger dissipated. By the time she reached home and returned to her bedroom, only despair remained. She sank into the armchair and with great difficulty read her letter.

Darling Dorothy,

I know it has been a while since I said goodbye. Forgive me. Your letters have kept me going when school has been intolerable. You have a talent for bringing Norton to life.

Lizzie tells me you have a new horse, a gift from our father? I am glad, for you must have resolved your differences. Do you think he will ever tolerate his unconventional son?

Has Molly Johnson settled in well? I hope you like her a little better, for I have sincere hopes she could become your friend. Though she is in service, she is also a companion to our dearest sister. Try not to be hostile, and remember, while she is in our home, it is our duty to make her welcome.

Dorothy put the letter down. It was as if Thomas were beside her, reading her mind. Picking up the letter again, she skimmed the details of his initial miseries, which she had already read.

I am moving in exalted circles. A new friend, Horace Walpole, is the son of our current first lord of the treasury. I smile when I imagine our grandmother's delight at my social elevation. He is more eccentric than your brother. He writes sonnets, and his rhymes are more fantastic. Can you imagine the irony? Father hoped I would be made into a 'man' and I am encouraged to write poetry! I have actually received commissions of a romantic nature, though as the author I am required to remain anonymous. Whilst my pockets remain heavy with change I have no cause for complaint.

We have something else in common: Walpole despises physical exercise and any sport which involves killing one of God's creatures. At last, I am not alone! Anyway, sister, I have run out of time. Know that on my first night, your violets were my only source of consolation. They remain in my prayer book, and the scent, though diminishing, reminds me of you.

Keep well, and keep the sordid details of this letter to yourself. Mama would be horrified. Please write to me with your news, and I apologize if I have lectured you in any way, it's only with the best intentions.

Send my regards to Lorenzo.
Yours always,
Your devoted brother,
Thomas

She tucked the letter into the pocket of her pinafore. He had lied. The violets were not his only source of consolation – Molly had seen to that.

She went downstairs, and seeing Lizzie alone in her usual window, she sat down beside her and took the letter from her pocket. 'From Thomas?' her sister asked eagerly.

'Yes, shall I read it to you?'

'Please, Dotty. I long for Thomas's letters.'

When she had finished, Elizabeth took her hand. 'You mustn't be envious, little one. He's a boy. Maybe one day things will change and girls will go to school, but for now we have to accept our lives as they are.' Once again her sister surprised her. It seemed that both of Dorothy's siblings recognized her inner torment.

'Elizabeth, am I a bad person?'

'Of course you aren't,' she laughed. 'But jealousy can eat into your soul. I love you with all my heart, but life is what you make of it. Don't let the things you don't like about yourself destroy you.'

Dorothy smiled wryly. Fortunately her sister hadn't witnessed the scene in her bedroom, and she didn't suspect any other reasons for her jealousy.

CHAPTER SIXTEEN

Molly's honeymoon with Norton lasted for less than three years, but it was long enough to make friends and establish herself within the household. Then, two separate events hastened her undoing: Sir William gave up his constituency in Warwick, and Thomas returned home a year earlier than expected, having passed his final exams.

Sir William's manner changed slowly – a smile, a lingering glance – but with each day Molly's isolation grew. If Sir William were to make an advance, would her new friends believe her? Would Annie and Ruth accept her story? She doubted it, for like a cloud, trust breaks in a storm. Never mind Dorothy, with her knowing looks – clever Dorothy, who watched and waited – or Mrs Wright, who would take out her innards with a spoon.

The worrisome scenarios she had formed in her head remained there and were never given voice. She sat with Elizabeth, her head bent to her sewing, her mind a thousand miles away.

'Are you all right, Molly? You look troubled.'

Looking into her sweet face, she longed to confide. 'I'm fine,' she said. 'It's only a headache.'

As Christmas approached, a fever of anticipation coursed through the household. Only Sir William shared none of the good humour. His eyes followed Molly relentlessly. She began locking her door at night. Fear shadowed her.

On the night of the servants' party, the tenth of December, she had finished her work and was closing the door to her mistress's bedroom. 'And Molly? No need to hurry in the morning. Enjoy yourself.'

'Thank you, milady. Goodnight.'

She leant against the wall, resting her tired shoulders. She smoothed the folds of her beautiful mint gown, the silk rustling beneath her fingers. It was mended now, the seams invisible, the bodice altered, and where the hooks were fastened she had sewn her own initials. She straightened, looked this way and that. The landing was clear; no one loitered in the shadows. But as she hurried to the stairs, a hand grabbed her in the darkness.

She ducked and tried to get away, but he held onto her skirt. She could hear the silk rip as it tore between his fingers. She screamed, but he caught her, covering her mouth. 'Be quiet, I only wish to talk to you. Why do you avoid me?'

'I don't, sir. Please let me go.'

'But you do. Are you saving yourself for someone else? My son, perhaps?'

'No, sir, please let me go. There's no one, sir.'

He leant towards her, his words slurred. She smelt the whisky upon his breath. 'All lies from your pretty lips. Do you know the punishment for lying? Dismissal. Shame on your family.'

She was trapped: the humiliation of disgrace or of compliance. A black cloud exploded in her head. She punched at his chest, clawed at his face. 'Leave me alone! Your wife will hear. For pity's sake, let me go!'

He pinned her arms. Tears poured down her cheeks as he dragged her through his bedroom door. 'You're not getting away from me this time.'

He slapped her face. She staggered, holding her ringing ears. He grabbed her hair, pulling her head backwards. His mouth crushed hers. His hands tore at her clothes. Her breasts slipped free of the last restraining fragments of silk, and for a moment he stopped and cupped them in his hands. 'Molly, you are driving me mad,' he whispered. Thrusting his knee into her groin, he threw her onto the bed, skirts pulled upwards, hands between her legs, pushing, forcing, invading.

He fumbled at his breeches. She closed her eyes and turned her face away as he mounted her. The pain ripped through her body, and she could smell his alcohol-pungent sweat, could feel the rough bristles on his cheeks as he struggled to hold her down, could hear his panting as he forced his way further between her thighs. She prayed for unconsciousness, but it didn't come, only a sickening shuddering as he pushed himself violently into her. Then it was over, and he fell heavily forward, his weight crushing her chest.

She pushed him from her and climbed from the bed. Taking the towel from the washstand she rubbed at the blood on her legs, and covering her body with the remains of her dress, she stumbled from the room.

Sir William woke to a pounding head and a heavy heart. He had broken every code of honour. He had betrayed his family. He had violated a young girl who was under his protection, and whose exuberance brought nothing but pleasure to those around her. Had he found the courage to kill himself at that moment, he would have done so, but now he accepted cowardice as yet another of his vices.

An empty bottle lay on the floor beside him – whisky, hazel, the colour of her eyes. With a sick feeling in his stomach, he threw it against the fireplace, where it shattered. He rose to his knees and crawled across the broken glass, hoping the shards would carve his corrupted flesh.

CHAPTER SEVENTEEN

When she was twelve, Molly Johnson had sat in church with her mother while they listened to the Very Reverend Charles Pearson, Dean of Warwick, deliver his sermon. 'And God said: If a man find a damsel that is a virgin, which is not betrothed, and lay hold on her, and lie with her, and they be found, then the man that lay with her shall give unto the damsel's father fifty shekels of silver.' When she had questioned the validity of the sermon, her mother had been unable to reassure her.

Now she remembered this. If these were God's words, then God was a man no better than all the rest. She stared at the ceiling, but no sleep came. She raised herself up, took off her ruined dress, and walked to the mirror. Dead eyes stared back. She touched her bruised thighs, her swollen mouth, and as she hid the dress at the back of the cupboard, a small laugh escaped her lips. *You thought you could have it all, but you have certainly paid the price.*

She took Thomas's poem from beneath her pillow, tore it in half and threw it away. She lay down again, closed her eyes and slept restlessly, a lonely figure curled on an iron bed. In her dream Thomas was waiting for her. His arms were open, and she ran towards him, but when she reached him, Sir William stood before her instead. 'You'll never be free,' he said.

In the morning she retrieved the torn paper and replaced the two halves beneath her pillow. She washed her body, scrubbing her thighs with a brush until her skin chafed. Still she felt soiled, for the stain lay deep.

'Are you all right, Molly? You look sick,' Ruth asked, full of concern.

'Yes, a little tired, that's all.'

'Lord,' Ruth said to Annie, 'she's been having it with someone; I'd stake my life on it. Do you think it's our Mr Whitstone? He's lusted after her for weeks, so he has.'

By the morning's end, all the downstairs staff were talking.

Mrs Wright stood before Molly triumphantly; the bloodied sheet a trophy in her arms.

'Found this on the master's bed. When the mistress finds out, you'll see what happens, my girl. It's the workhouse for you! What do you think of pretty Molly now, Mr Whitstone?'

Dorothy was on an errand for her mother when she heard the whispering.

She pushed open the swing door and was halfway down the passage when she heard hushed and excited voices coming from the scullery. Dorothy couldn't make out the words, and when she entered the room, the talking stopped.

'Please, may I have some rose water?' she asked Mrs Wright.

'Yes, Miss Dorothy. I'll get you some immediately.'

When Dorothy retreated down the passage she wondered what had caused such fuss. Mrs Wright's sharp eyes had looked flustered, and her prompt response was unusual.

She forgot about it upon seeing a letter on the hall table. It was from Thomas, his final letter from school. On this occasion, hers was the only letter. She took it to her bedroom and shut the door.

Darling Dotty,

I am not sure whether you will receive this letter or your brother first. Either way I am writing to you with a mixture of anticipation and regret.

I shall see you at last, but if I am honest, my days in this damp, low-lying town beneath Windsor Castle have been some of the happiest in my life.

How time has flown. I imagine you must have grown enormously. I hope not as much as your brother, for I am now over six feet.

I have grown to love Eton. I play fives in the buttresses of the college chapel. It is a sociable form of exercise which needs cunning rather than skill. (Would our dear father count it as sport? I rather think not.) I am a member of the college chapel choir – how you would love the singing.

Two incidents occurred last term. I won't bore you with the details, but it is now generally believed that I have supernatural powers. It has secured me quite a reputation. In retrospect both occasions were rather more luck than anything else but it seems sometimes even this most unwanted gift can have certain advantages.

There have been many changes, mostly good. The dreadful ritual 'Tossing the Blanket' has been banned from my house and lock-up abolished, and though we work hard, we are given more time for our own amusement.

On Sunday afternoons in fine weather, we row on the River Thames. We tell stories, anecdotes of things we have done, and countries we would like to visit. I believe my dreams have been rekindled and I shall travel after all. In the winter months we take tea in our lodgings and regale each other with news and political gossip. Even Kirkpatrick has softened and shares the occasional joke. Gilbert Paxton-Hooper continues to be my friend and I have spent time with his family. You would love them – chaotic, learned and totally unlike us.

Yesterday, according to tradition, I inscribed my name into the lid of my desk. When I had finished, Paxton-Hooper added a postscript, 'Thomas Charles Edward Keyt has the gift of second-sight.' And so I am there, buried in the wood for future generations to find. Tomorrow I will say goodbye to my friends and teachers. Lorenzo will come to collect me, and, little sister, I will see you again. We shall spend Christmas together, and you will help me to decide how to spend the rest of my life.

In anticipation,
Your affectionate brother
Thomas

Dorothy folded the pages. Unlocking the bureau, she placed it beside his previous correspondence. Afterwards she took out another letter, one addressed to Molly Johnson. Many times she had considered destroying it too, but something had restrained her.

When Thomas arrived two days later, they were all waiting in the drawing room: Lizzie, her mother, even her grandmother had come for the occasion – everyone except Sir William. When the carriage stopped in the courtyard, Dorothy was the first to the door, opening it before Whitstone or the footmen had time to get there. Lorenzo stepped down from the box and held the horses while the grooms ran towards him. At the same moment, the dogs dived down the steps and hurled themselves at Thomas. Dorothy followed, throwing her arms tightly around her brother's neck.

'Are you trying to kill me before you have said hello?' he asked, laughing.

'Well now, quite the handsome gentleman, aren't we? I'm sure you must have cut a dash amongst the female population of Windsor.'

'And you are as pretty as ever, if a little taller, and still with the same impossible tongue!'

Dorothy laughed and glanced at Lorenzo.

'Good afternoon, Miss Dorothy,' he said, his gaze fixed upon her.

'Good afternoon, Lorenzo,' she replied.

Seeing Lizzie in the doorway, Thomas ran up the steps towards her.

'Lizzie!' he said, taking her hands. 'How I have missed you.'

'I have counted the days until your return,' she said.

Finally he walked towards his mother. If the sight of her careworn face startled him, he did not show it. 'Hello, Mama.'

'Hello, my son. And what a fine young man you are.' She put her hands either side of his face. 'How proud I am.'

'Where's Father?' Thomas said at last.

'He's in his study; he wanted us to let him know when you arrived,' she lied. 'I suggest you go to him.'

'I'll go now, before I change,' he said, his disappointment obvious. 'I hope we shall be dining together tonight?'

'Of course, my darling, at thirty minutes past the hour, as usual.'

Dorothy walked with him to their father's study. 'You go in, Thomas. I'll wait for you here.'

'Thank you, Dotty, but please come in with me.' He knocked and carefully opened the door.

'Oh, it's you,' their father said gruffly.

'Yes, sir.'

'How was school? Have you learnt anything?'

'I have learnt a great deal, sir.'

'Well then, perhaps you should now finish your education at Oxford. You're seventeen years old. It's time you went.'

Her father's words rekindled Dorothy's resentment; her poor brother had only just arrived.

'I would like to stay home for a while, if I may? I have spent so much time away from my sisters.' A hint of sarcasm sharpened his tone.

'Very well, but Oxford soon. Now forgive me, I have work to do.'

As they walked out along the passage, Thomas smiled wryly at his sister. 'That was a jubilant welcome, was it not?'

Dorothy squeezed his arm. 'I'm sorry.'

Molly hurried past, her head turned away from them. Dorothy dropped her hand from her brother's arm.

'Molly, is that you?' Thomas asked, bewildered.

Molly turned around. 'Hello, sir.'

'It's me, Master Thomas.'

'Yes, I know, sir.'

'Is that all you have to say?'

'I don't know what you mean. Should there be anything else? Forgive me, I have to go.'

Whitstone pushed through the servants' door. 'We appear to be going somewhere in a hurry, Miss Johnson. Anywhere in particular? Oh, Master Thomas. I'm sorry, I didn't see you. I hope you have had a pleasant journey.' It took the butler a moment to regain his composure.

'Yes, thank you, Whitstone,' Thomas replied. 'I would like to bathe and change for dinner. Please, will you have the water brought up for me, and would you get Hawkins to put out my evening clothes?'

'Of course, sir, immediately.'

When he had gone, Thomas caught up with his sister. 'What's going on? Why do I sense an atmosphere?'

'I'm not aware of anything,' Dorothy replied evasively.

While Thomas went to his room, she collected a coat and shawl and took refuge in the garden. She leant against the wall, letting tears of self-pity and frustration stream down her face. It seemed that even now, after well over two years of absence, her brother's thoughts went first to Molly Johnson. She looked up as the back door opened.

Her father came outside dressed only in his shirtsleeves, his eyes like a madman's. He grabbed an axe from the woodpile and disappeared towards the wild garden. Dorothy couldn't help but follow.

Outside the white gate the woodland he had planted only two years before flourished. The fifty saplings had survived their first harsh winters, but they would not survive Sir William's self-loathing. He lifted his axe and drove it into his precious trees. Dorothy watched in horror until he finally exhausted himself and sank to his knees amongst the ruin.

Dorothy tiptoed back through the gate until she was certain her father couldn't hear her, and then she started to run. She didn't stop until she reached the sanctuary of her bedroom.

Molly had longed and prayed for Thomas's return, but now she hid in the shadows. When he came near her that evening, she tried to slink away, but he caught her arm.

'Molly, you evade me. Come, and let us talk.'

'No, sir, I have to go,' she answered, aware of his new masculinity: the rich voice, the shadow on his chin.

'You did not answer my letters. Don't you care for me? Have I no hope?'

As she hurried away from him, she wondered what he meant. 'What letters?' she whispered. 'There were no letters.'

That evening, Thomas joined Elizabeth and Dorothy on the half-landing. Elizabeth was wearing a white dress, her fair hair secured with combs. 'You look beautiful, Lizzie.'

'Thank you, Thomas.' She pointed to her shadow moving on the wall behind her. 'Can you see my shadow floating?'

'I certainly can,' he replied, kissing her forehead.

'I think that when I die it will be like that. I shall be free at last.'

'Don't talk of death. You are still so young.'

'Forgive me, Thomas. I don't mean to be morbid. Please . . . tell us about your time at school. We have read your wonderful letters, but let us hear it from your lips.' Thomas sat down, and with his arm around Elizabeth's shoulders he told his sisters anecdotes about his days at Windsor. As they chatted in the candlelight the melancholy mood broke.

Elizabeth turned to her sister. 'Dotty, please will you pass me Miss Byrne's book? It's there, on the window seat. I'd like to show Thomas my drawings. I believe they are passable.'

Thomas stood up and leant over her shoulder. 'Look at John – such a likeness. That's how I remember him.'

'That's exactly how I remember him too,' Dorothy said.

Elizabeth clasped her sister's hand. 'Dotty, when I am gone, will you look after the book?' She closed the cover, speaking quickly and earnestly. 'It has become my life's work. It's the one thing I am proud of.'

'Now, now. We have banished any sad thoughts.'

'But listen. I have a request. If for any reason our family leaves this house, will you return the book to its original home? I'm convinced Miss Byrne would approve. I dream of it hidden beneath the floorboards, waiting to be found in hundreds of years from now.'

'I give you my word,' she replied.

Thomas kissed her on the forehead. 'Come on,' he said, lifting Elizabeth easily into his arms. 'Let's go to dinner.'

***

Dinner that night was a strange affair. The wine, the finest from Sir William's cellar, was drunk liberally, and the footmen, dressed in their new livery of burgundy and gold, hovered respectfully, but it was not the celebration Lady Keyt had intended. Though Thomas's coat of midnight-blue velvet with pearl buttons and lace cuffs drew admiring glances from Lady Keyt and Elizabeth, Dorothy alone wondered bitterly whether his elegant clothes were a mark of respect for his family, or an attempt to attract Miss Johnson's eye. While Thomas watched his father warily, he wondered at Molly's reticence. Sir William, wearing an embroidered coat of his grandfather's, could only stare at his glass.

After white soup, followed by roasted duck, glazed carrots and potatoes, Thomas's favourite trifle was produced with a flourish. As soon as his plate was cleared, Sir William brought the dinner to an abrupt end.

'If you will excuse me,' he said, his speech more than a little slurred, 'I'm for bed. It seems I can't contribute much to the conversation.' He rose to his feet unsteadily, barking rudely at the footman who tried to help him.

Dorothy looked up, as if seeing her father for the first time that evening. She looked at the embroidered coat she had loved so much as a child.

'Papa, why do the dragons on your coat have fire coming from their mouths?' she had asked him many years before.

'Because they have very bad breath.' At the time she had laughed, but now as she watched him, she wondered what had happened to the man she had so loved. Part of her pitied her father, but she knew that she couldn't help him. He insisted on self-destruction.

The rest of the family retired to the drawing room. Thomas lowered Lizzie onto the sofa, tucking a rug about her knees, and Dorothy settled into her favourite armchair. She wished this cosy tableau could be fixed in time. She sensed transience in the air and was afraid. She looked up at the armorial shield hanging above the fireplace, representing the union of the Keyts and the Coventrys. The three kites emblazoned on the blackened wood appeared ominous and threatening.

Shortly before eleven Thomas stood up. 'If you will excuse me, it's been a long day and I'm very tired.'

Dorothy, Lizzie and their mother remained in the drawing room. They played cards until they were distracted by Molly's voice in the passage. 'Take your hands off me, Mr Whitstone! I beg of you, leave me alone!'

'You would have let me touch you once, but I've heard there are bigger birds in the sky, and you want a brace of them.'

They heard footsteps running, followed by Whitstone's bitter words: 'I'm sure Lady Keyt would be interested to know who has been warming her husband's bed!'

Dorothy turned to see her mother's cards drop from her hands, scattering on the floor beneath her. Lady Keyt picked up the bell and rang it fiercely.

Whitstone came in, his head bowed. 'Forgive me, milady. I thought you had retired.'

'No, Mr Whitstone, I have not retired. Would you be good enough to explain the meaning of your words?' Her face was ashen in the candlelight.

'They meant nothing, milady, absolutely nothing.'

'Do not lie to me. If you don't answer me truthfully, you will leave my employment tonight.'

Despite her distress, her mother kept her dignity. 'Whitstone, you have thirty seconds.'

The butler shuffled his feet, cleared his throat and began. Elizabeth's hands clutched the sofa, while Lady Keyt sat rigidly in her chair. Dorothy got up and stood in front of the fireplace, her eyes bright with fury, while he told them about Sir William's infidelity and Miss Johnson's betrayal.

'She didn't deny it,' he said at last, his eyes darting from one member of the family to the other. 'Mrs Wright confronted her with the bloodied sheet. I'm so sorry, milady.' Dorothy noted the sweat on his forehead and hated him. This pathetic man had destroyed her mother's fragile equilibrium.

'Thank you, Whitstone, you may go,' her mother said, quietly. 'I think for your own safety you should leave the house. My husband has been drinking and I can't answer for his actions.' Dorothy noticed a small pulse at the corner of her mother's eyes.

Lady Keyt stood and turned towards her daughters. 'Lizzie, I'm truly sorry. We have all been deceived by Miss Johnson. Dorothy, please ask Mathews to carry Elizabeth to her room. Forgive me. I will see you in the morning.'

Elizabeth had pushed herself into the corner of the sofa, where she sat shivering uncontrollably. Dorothy went to her and held her tightly.

'Oh, God,' Elizabeth sobbed, 'is there no end to this?'

CHAPTER EIGHTEEN

Lady Keyt was not given to anger. Only under extreme provocation did she succumb to rage, as was the case on this particular night. After unpinning her hair in her bedroom and brushing it furiously for several minutes, she slammed down her silver brush and marched across the landing to her husband's room, opening his door without knocking.

'How could you do this to me, William? How could you betray me?' She stopped in front of him, her eyes narrowed.

He looked up at her from his chair and felt afraid. He placed his glass of whisky on the table beside him. 'Calm down, my dear. What are you talking about?'

'No more lies. I've had enough of your lies. The servants know of your infidelity, and so do the children.'

'You are mistaken. I have never been unfaithful to you.' He stood up unsteadily, his nightcap askew on his head.

'I know about Molly Johnson.'

'What are you talking about? That is a ridiculous suggestion.'

'Whitstone told me,' she said flatly. 'I beg of you, don't belittle yourself further.'

William couldn't breathe. He felt as if he was drowning. 'Ann, you must believe me. The man is a servant, a cheap and common liar.'

'Molly Johnson is also a servant, and yet you chose her above your wife. It's too much. I'm leaving.'

William's face crumpled. 'I'm sorry. Please don't leave me, I beg of you.'

'It's too late. I've put up with your black moods and your drinking. We've both suffered the same tragedy, but you have compounded it with your adultery.'

'Forgive me, Ann. Please. I can't live without you.'

'I cannot. I have had more than I can bear. I don't want any more lies and misery. Elizabeth and Dorothy have seen enough. I will take them to The College, if that is acceptable to you.'

'Ann, please don't do this. I swear to you, it will never happen again. Please give me one more chance.'

'You have shared your life with me, and yet you have taken her to your bed without a care for my feelings. Tell me, why should I give you another chance?'

William was quiet. He turned from her, and with his hands gripping the mantelpiece he lowered his head until his forehead rested on the cold marble. When he spoke, it was with the pain and uncertainty of a lost man. 'Since the accident, you have denied me your body and your bed. You have given your love to the children but not to your own husband.'

The truth of his observation cut Ann, and she moved towards him, her anger turning to regret, but she stopped herself and pushed her hands deep into the pockets of her silk dressing gown. She had dealt with too much to feel capable of starting over again.

William looked at his wife. 'I will not allow you to leave,' he said, his voice rising. 'You are my wife. It is your duty to stay. You are the only woman I have ever loved. I beg you to reconsider.'

Ann looked at the broken man before her, the man she had once loved so passionately, and turned sadly.

'I'm sorry, my dear,' she said, her own heart breaking.

CHAPTER NINETEEN

Dorothy remained by the fire long after her sister had gone to bed, staring into the fading embers. She now understood Mrs Wright's excitement, the hushed gossip and furtive looks. She stretched out on the sofa, burying her face in the pillows, but she could not blot out the repulsive images. Her wrath turned solely on Molly. Her father's destruction of his trees told her all she needed to know: her father could not live with his transgression; he was obviously remorseful. But Molly was far from repentant.

Dorothy's mood bounced from hatred to despair and back again, until at last she fell asleep. When she awoke, the fire had died and the room was cold. She stood up, shivering, and dragged herself upstairs. Halfway up, she heard her parents' angry voices. For once Dorothy had no desire to listen.

She shut her bedroom door and went to her bureau. Inside lay Thomas's letter to Molly. She picked it up and, striking the tinderbox, watched the flame ignite and grow. She held it to the letter, then dropped the burning paper into the fire. Staring into the flames she felt her anger tighten like a vice in her chest. She climbed onto her bed and tried to sleep, but it was useless. She rose and went to her washstand. As she stared at her exhausted reflection in the mirror, she considered that neither parent was blameless – her mother's rejection had played its part.

When quiet returned to the house and her father's door closed, Dorothy went to find her mother. Lady Keyt was in her bedroom, sitting at the foot of her bed, when Dorothy knocked to come in. As her mother looked up to greet her, Dorothy saw more lines of pain etched into her face.

'Is this my fault, Dotty? Was any of this my fault?'

'Of course not, Mama,' she lied.

'I can't bear to think of it. I trusted Molly, and I thought I could trust my husband.' Her words rekindled Dorothy's indignation. He had betrayed her mother, banished Miss Byrne, and shot her beloved Ophelia. He had ruined all of their lives.

'Mama, I'm sorry. I'll look after you,' she said, putting her arms around her.

Returning to her bedroom, Dorothy sat at her bureau and finding her notebook she wrote furiously. Molly would know of her anger.

Though you would whore with my father, and prey upon my brother's affections, have no false hope: you will be sent from our house. I saw through you the moment I set eyes on you. You are nothing, Molly Johnson. Nothing.

She crossed it out and started again. By the third draft she was satisfied; she would write it out tomorrow. She climbed into bed and fell into a deep and dreamless sleep.

CHAPTER TWENTY

In the middle of the night a scream awakened Molly. She lit the candle on her night table, sat up in bed and listened. For a moment there was silence, but the scream came again. She pulled a robe around her, and unlocking the door to the passage, she ran down to the large, central landing.

Ruth stood by the broom cupboard, white-faced, in her white gown and frizzed brown hair.

'What's wrong?'

Molly followed her gaze. Thomas Whitstone's door lay open.

'Sir William! He has a sword,' she whispered. 'He's killed Mr Whitstone!'

The servants came, one after the other, rubbing the sleep from their eyes. Dorothy arrived with Lady Keyt.

'Out of my way. Get out of my way.' Sir William barged out of Whitstone's room, his sword raised. Everyone drew back. 'He betrayed me!' he cried. 'He betrayed me to my wife.' He looked wildly around the room until his eyes fixed upon Molly. 'And you, you have bewitched me,' he gestured towards her, the sword waving dangerously.

All eyes turned to Molly: Lady Keyt, frozen in shock; Mrs Wright, her lip quivering, her nightcap squashed on her greying curls; Dorothy, her eyes bulging in her pale face.

You do what you can, when you can, my love. Molly remembered her mother's words as she walked towards the man who had raped her. He swayed before her, his eyes unfocused. Her heart beat wildly as she gazed at the raised sword. 'Give that to me, Sir William. Someone else will get hurt.'

She reached up, but he waved it threateningly. She stepped back but maintained her composure.

Dorothy was forced to admire Molly Johnson's courage, even as it highlighted Dorothy's own weakness. 'Sir William, give it to me. I beg of you.' Molly put out her arm and this time he didn't resist. Slowly she caught his wrist and lowered his hand, gently prising open the clenched fingers, until the sword clattered to the ground.

He seemed to awaken as if from a dream. 'What have I done?' he asked, his muddled brain clearing.

'Come, sir; let's go downstairs. It's all right, sir. You can come with me.'

'But Molly . . . do you hate me?'

'It doesn't matter now.'

He let her take his arm and lead him like a child.

Thomas passed them on the stairs. For a moment Molly looked into his eyes.

'What's going on? Will someone tell me what the hell is going on?'

No one answered.

This time Thomas shouted. 'What has he done?'

'I think your father has murdered poor Whitstone,' his mother replied. Dorothy burst into tears, not because of 'poor

Whitstone', but because of the look that had passed between Thomas and Molly.

'It's all right, Dotty,' her brother said, taking her in his arms. 'Don't cry.' He took her hand and led her to a chair. 'Dotty, you wait there. Mother, you sit down, too. This won't take long.'

Dorothy watched him disappear into Whitstone's room, and within seconds she heard his laughter.

'It's fine,' he called. 'Come and look. There is no one here. Our drunken father has driven his sword into a pile of pillows.'

She crossed the threshold. A candle burnt on the dresser, and feathers like snowflakes settled on the floor. On the bed, the slashed and torn pillows bore witness to her father's rage.

'You see, the bird has flown.'

Dorothy shook her head. 'Mama warned him. She told him to get away.'

'What's going on? Please will someone explain why Father should wish to kill Whitstone?'

'Oh, for pity's sake, can you not see what is in front of your eyes? Molly is Father's mistress and Whitstone had the stupidity to tell Mama.'

Thomas looked at his sister, comprehension dawning in his eyes. 'No, I had no idea. How stupid of me. All these years, I've been a fool.' He turned and stumbled down the stairs.

Dorothy followed. 'Thomas, forgive me! Please come back.' He looked at her in amazement, his eyes filling with tears, and continued on, deaf to her voice.

He left the back door open; she ran after him into the garden. It was raining, a freezing rain that pelted down her neck and into her eyes. Her steps were urgent. She ran down the path, stones piercing her thin slippers. 'Thomas, where are you?'

Reaching the entrance to the pool garden, she heard her brother's voice shouting against the wind. 'My father will be rid of me, and I will be rid of the world.'

She saw him near the pools and feared he would drown himself. 'No, Thomas!' she yelled. 'Please God, no.'

He looked up at her for a moment, then laughed hysterically and ran off into the darkness, his wet nightshirt clinging to his body.

She ran after him but he was gone, out through the upper gate and into the woods beyond. 'He will die if he stays out in this,' she sobbed. 'He will surely die.' She returned through the garden and into the courtyard, hammering on the door of the man whom she trusted above all others.

'Lorenzo, help me, please help me!'

Lorenzo, unaware of the unfolding drama, put his head through the window. On seeing Dorothy below, he ran downstairs.

'You are soaked through! Put this around you.' He laid a coat around her shoulders while Dorothy told him what had happened.

'You must help me,' she pleaded.

'Of course,' he replied, pulling his breeches over his underclothes and nightshirt. 'You go back inside the house and I promise I will find him.'

'No,' she replied, 'this is my fault and I'm coming with you.'

They ran through the white gate at the end of the courtyard and down the track towards the Hanging Meadow. They called his name but there was no reply. They looked in the

Dingle and the woods above the deer fence, but still there was no sign.

'Think, Miss Dorothy: where would your brother go?'

Dorothy, panting from exertion, suddenly remembered. 'He'd go to the tree house,' she said. 'He always went to the tree house.'

They ran together towards the stream and stopped underneath the large beech tree. When they called he didn't answer.

'I will go up,' Lorenzo said, his foot already on the first rung of the ladder.

Lorenzo found Thomas huddled in the corner. His arms clutched his knees and his teeth chattered.

'Leave me in peace,' he said as the dark head appeared through the entrance.

'I will not,' Lorenzo replied, taking a seat beside him. 'It's freezing and we should be by a good fire. I have whisky in the cupboard for just such an occasion. Will you have one with me?'

'I don't want to live. What is there to live for?'

'You should not say this, you who have everything. Come now, you crazy Englishman, and get down that ladder.'

Dorothy stared helplessly at the tree house waiting for a sign of progress, until at last Thomas appeared at the doorway. Without looking at her he climbed down the steps and walked into her waiting arms. Lorenzo had only taken the second step down when the wood, rotten from years of neglect, gave way. He plummeted to the groundt.

He lay amongst the wet leaves and rotting vegetation,

groaning at the sharp pain that shot through his ankle. 'It may be broken,' he said. Dorothy knelt beside him.

'This is all my fault,' she said miserably.

While Thomas ran to the house to get help, Dorothy remained with Lorenzo. 'What can I do?' she asked.

'I need to take my boot off before the swelling gets too bad.'

'I'll do it,' she said, gently removing the boot. Pulling a handkerchief from the pocket of Lorenzo's coast – still about her own shoulders – she bound it round his ankle. He raised himself onto his elbow and watched her. When the handkerchief was secure, she tore the ends with her teeth so that she could tie a knot. And all the time she was aware of Lorenzo watching her and of her own heart beating.

Thomas arrived with Elizabeth's nurse, and two footmen ran down the slope, carrying a door between them. They lifted Lorenzo onto the door and carried him back to the lodge. Dorothy jogged along; she wouldn't leave his side.

It was only a bad sprain, and Lorenzo within a short time was able to return to limited duties. For Dorothy, however, the event was momentous: she had lost her heart to her father's coachman.

CHAPTER TWENTY-ONE

Dorothy awoke the following morning to light streaming through the bedroom curtains and the sound of her father's desperate voice.

'You may have The College,' he continued, 'and any income from the Stratford estate. I only hope that in time you will come to forgive your contemptible husband who is no longer worthy of you.'

Dorothy held her forehead, trying to ease the pressure. Too much was happening, too quickly. Yesterday she despised her father; today she wanted her mother to forgive him. They couldn't leave Norton.

'Thank you,' she heard her mother say. 'How sad that we have come to this, when I have loved you so dearly.'

'Then give me another chance. I beg of you, Ann. You are the only woman I have ever loved.'

'No, it's too late,' she said. 'How could I live with the indignity of our servants' knowledge, our children's knowledge, and the humiliation of last night?'

'She is not my mistress. It was one night of stupidity; can't we put it behind us?'

'It's impossible. I couldn't run this house now.'

'Will you take all of the children?'

'Elizabeth would be off better with me, but we will have to ask her, for she is old enough to make up her own mind. I will take Mrs Wright and Whitstone. I think it's better if they were out of your service, as I'm sure you'll agree. Lorenzo, of course, will wish to remain with you.'

Dorothy heard the door close behind her mother. There was no animosity in their discussion, only sadness. She turned into the pillow and wept.

Her mother supervised the packing. Books, treasured ornaments, pieces of silver and her great-grandmother's candlesticks were placed carefully in wooden crates. She worked with the servants until the light began to fail.

'I suppose Miss Johnson has been sent home?' Dorothy asked, walking into her mother's bedroom. She saw dresses and slips, the contents of her mother's drawers strewn all over the floor.

'To be honest, I have no idea.' Her mother leant against the bedpost. She pushed the hair from her eyes. 'I believe I must speak with her first, but at this moment I am too tired to think about it. Oh Dotty, come here and sit down.' She put her arm around her daughter's shoulders. 'What a dreadful muddle.' She smiled ruefully. 'We were so happy once. When I close my eyes, I can still smell my wedding flowers.'

'I'm sorry, Mama. Everything seems to have gone wrong,' Dorothy said, settling into her mother's arms. 'I would like to be married some day, but not for a while.'

'And so you shall, to someone who will cherish you, and love you.'

'I wonder,' Dorothy said quietly.

They stood in silence until at last Dorothy whispered, 'As Thomas will be away at university I shall be on my own. Please say that Lizzie will come with us?'

'I don't know, my love; it has to be her choice.'

'Shall we ask her together? Perhaps if I'm there, it will make the question easier for you both.'

Her mother looked surprised. 'I would be grateful, for though I believe in my heart that it would be better if she came to Stratford, I don't want to place pressure upon her.'

They went downstairs, holding hands.

'Hello, Lizzie.' She touched her sister's shoulder.

She looked up at her mother and sister with a sad smile on her face. 'Dotty, you must go with Mama, but I will remain here with Father.'

Her intuitive sister had pre-empted them both.

'But we can't leave you here on your own,' Dorothy cried, kneeling on the floor beside her.

'Hush,' her mother said gently. 'Let Elizabeth speak.'

'I will not be on my own,' she said. 'One of us must stay with him. I assure you, I will be more than fine.'

Dorothy pulled away from them both and slumped onto the window seat. 'Why are you so good, Lizzie? You don't have to stay. Come with us, I can't bear to leave you.'

'You can leave me, and you must. You must be with Mama. Is that not so?' She looked up at their mother.

'Yes, I believe Dorothy should come with me.'

'Don't be sad, Mama.' Lizzie took her wrist, tracing the small blue veins with her fingers. 'My life is here now; everything that I know is here. With my disability the change would be impossible. And Papa needs me; he can't be left on his own.' Dorothy realized that her fragile sister was the strongest of them all.

'Darling Lizzie, I can bear it only if you promise to visit; to lose you would be my final punishment.'

'I give you my word, Mama. You will not lose me, not for a while at any rate. The journey to Stratford is short, and when I am not with you I will think about you all the time.' She held her mother's hand. 'Don't cry. I'll be content. Papa and I shall care for each other, and Lorenzo will bring me to you every single week. Please understand that I wish to finish my days at Norton.'

Her mother put her arms around Elizabeth, and as Dorothy looked at the two of them, she was filled with a sense of loss.

'I'll leave my two girls together,' her mother said at last. 'There is still so much to do.'

When she had gone, Elizabeth turned. 'Dorothy, I'm not sure if this is the beginning of the end, or the start of the beginning.'

CHAPTER TWENTY-TWO

Mrs Wright stood inches from Molly's face. Her mouth was a knot of resentment and delight. 'The mistress is leaving, but she will see you before she goes. It's reckoning time! Though you would deceive us with pretty airs, I was never fooled. Put the linen back on the shelves and hurry up about it.'

Molly followed her down the corridor to the winter sitting room.

'Wait in there and leave your thieving hands in your pockets.'

Molly did as she was told.

Lady Keyt walked through the door towards her. Molly was struck by the change in her bearing. Her fluid grace had gone: her shoulders were rigid, and her mouth set in an ugly line. 'Miss Johnson, have you anything to say?' She looked at Molly, her eyes steely. 'Can you tell me why you did this to us, when we have given you so much?'

Molly longed to explain. She had rehearsed it many times, but when the moment came, she could say nothing. Lady Keyt had suffered enough.

'I don't know, my lady,' she replied.

'I'm disappointed in you.' The word hung in the air, more hurtful than any tirade. 'You will have to leave; Luke will take you today. Did you spare a thought for our feelings, or were you so intent upon your own pleasure? Did you think you could gain advantage by sleeping with my husband?'

'I'm sorry, my lady.'

Anger flared in her eyes. 'Sorry for breaking up our home, our family? Sorry is a poor word for the suffering you have inflicted. Please get out of my sight.'

Molly ran up the stairs, past Ruth and Annie on the landing. She pulled down the small bag she had arrived with nearly three years before and filled it with the same clothes she had come with. She opened the cupboard. Several gowns now hung from the rail, all beautiful gifts from her employer. She caressed the soft satin, the fragile lace, the tiny stitching on a carefully mended hem. Pushing them aside she knelt down, her hands searching for the tattered silk, the soiled skirt. Lifting out the dress, she hung it up beside the others, the solitary evidence of the truth. Standing for a moment in the quiet room, the weak winter sun slanting through the windows' diamond panes, she remembered a girl, just sixteen years of age. Her instinct had been sound. Now with only a torn piece of paper, an unread poem folded against her heart, she left the room.

She walked past the servants down the back steps. She kept her head high as she climbed into the cart.

After three hours of jolting over the rutted roads, the horse slowed to a clop. Molly pulled her shawl closely around her and rotated her stiffened back. Outside in the bleak Warwickshire countryside, black crows settled in the stark, leafless trees. Cattle huddled together around the hayricks, and farm workers trudged homewards with weary faces. Once she had dreaded leaving; now she dreaded coming home.

On the climb towards the Charter House she passed the familiar black and white cottages. When a child ran past, red ringlets falling below her fur bonnet, she remembered happier times, a girl who had danced around the maypole, who had eaten roasted apples with her friends. She remembered Lady Brooke with her marked face and disconcerting eyes. Creeping through the side door, she avoided her father. She climbed the stairs to the top of the house, to the room that was once her own. Throwing herself upon her old bed, she slept.

The next morning at Norton, Thomas sat beside his sister, his shoulders slumped. 'I expect everyone in the county will know of this,' he said.

'Does it really matter?' Elizabeth said. 'They are not important.'

'What an idiot I have been. For years I treasured the thought that our affection was mutual. What a blind, stupid fool.'

'I am sure Molly had feelings for you. Every time your name was mentioned she looked uncomfortable. It is quite possible Papa noticed this too.'

'Where is she, Lizzie?'

'She left yesterday. Luke took her in the cart. Mother feels betrayed, but somehow I have my doubts about it all. Last week I was convinced she wanted to tell me something, to confide in me. I think it's possible that Molly was the victim.'

'What do you mean?'

'Oh, I don't know, but maybe by not revealing the truth,

she was protecting our mother. I still feel certain that there is something intrinsically good about her.'

'Do you think that Father took advantage of her?'

'I have no knowledge of men, but I could not mistake the way he looked at her.'

'Oh my God, what a fine man he is!' Thomas guffawed. 'What an example to us all!'

'We can prove nothing, so you must put it behind you. Molly has gone, and it's best for everyone.'

'I wrote to her, but she never replied.'

'How could she, Thomas, when she can neither read nor write?'

'I never knew! The poor girl; there is so much I didn't know about her, and I didn't even ask.'

'One day you will look back and see this as youthful passion.'

'Perhaps. How wise you are, my beautiful sister.'

She sighed. 'Wisdom from inexperienced lips.'

Dorothy overheard their conversation from the corridor outside Elizabeth's room. She frowned, and walked on purposefully across the landing and down the back stairs. Undetected, she slipped through the study door, and for the last time she opened the drawer to find her father's diary. It was not there. Frustrated, she rifled through his papers; he was trying to hide it from her, she knew he was. She found it at last hidden at the back of the bookcase. Triumphantly, she drew it out. She was looking for mention of Molly and then her eye fell upon a single entry scrawled across the page. It was from the day of the accident. You have taken my child. My God, why have you forsaken me? The biblical reference revealed his despair, and for a moment Dorothy wanted to comfort her father. These sentiments were short-lived when she found another entry.

I am obsessed, I can think of nothing else. She brings light into this hateful, sad world. Thomas will not take her from me.

She snapped the book closed, unable to breathe. She could not, would not, read another word. Any pity she had felt changed to rage. She stood up, her legs shaking, and walked to the door. Leaning against the architrave she wondered what inspired this infatuation. Why were both her father and brother obsessed with Molly Johnson? She was pretty without being beautiful. She was quick, but uneducated. In a moment of honesty it dawned upon Dorothy: Molly Johnson inspired happiness in others.

CHAPTER TWENTY-THREE

They were leaving Norton, the only home Dorothy had ever known. Two trunks remained on the floor, the nursery globe packed in its own wooden crate. She shut the larger trunk and sat on it, rocking to and fro.

Sometimes she had imagined a new beginning away from this house, away from her father, but now she cursed those dreams.

She would miss her beloved sister. Perhaps she would miss her father. Her feelings changed by the hour. That morning he had found her in Fidelia's stall.

'Your mother told me you're going with her,' he said. 'Better take the horse; she'll do no good without you.'

'Thank you, Father,' she replied, recognizing dejection in his eye.

He walked towards her as if to take her in his arms, but before he reached her he turned. 'I must go.'

She could have thrown her arms around him, begged for reconciliation. Instead she cried into Fidelia's mane.

And there was another reason for her anguish. Logic told her it was feminine weakness, but her heart said otherwise. This was Lorenzo, a man who was ten years older, and who came from a station far beneath her own. With a rueful smile, she remembered an incident the morning after his fall. She had gone to the kitchens with the intention of collecting some broth; the heat hit her as she opened the door. On the fire, two cauldrons of water bubbled fiercely and through the steam she could make out Annie, red-faced and sweating as she stirred the clothes.

Rose, the cook, looked up from the board where she was kneading a large piece of dough. 'Sorry, miss, it's washing day.'

'Please, may I have some broth? I wish to take it to Lorenzo.' Rose glanced at Ruth; Dorothy noted their surprise.

'Here you are, miss. I think the doctor is with him now. Ruth could take it if you'd prefer?'

'No, no thank you.' She had taken the soup and dashed from the kitchens, slopping it along the way.

She entered the cottage just as the doctor was leaving. 'You did good work with the bandage, Dorothy. Well done.'

She walked up the small stairway and knocked on the bedroom door. 'It's me, Lorenzo. I've brought you something to eat.'

Lorenzo was sitting up in bed, propped against the pillows. She remained standing near the entrance. 'Come in,' he replied, a look of astonishment on his face. For a moment they stared at each other, but finally she approached the bed. She thrust the tray into his hands and would have fled, but he caught her wrist.

'Thank you, Dorothy,' he said, dropping all formality.

'It's nothing,' she replied, but it wasn't. It was everything.

Dorothy shut the other trunk and went to the window. She looked out over the orchard, past the stew pond and the granary, the ice house and the dovecote. Hastings remained on her bed; his single eye looked at her accusingly, reminding her of her early childhood.

'Father, will you buy me a rabbit for Christmas? I want a rabbit.'

'I'll see what I can do, Dotty.'

That Christmas, Hastings had arrived.

'Oh Father, I love him! He is much better than a real one. I will treasure him always.'

Now she glanced at the balding toy and left it on the bed, closing the door behind her.

That cold December morning was one of reminiscence. For as long as she could remember, the Christmas decorations were kept in the coffer in the hall. They came out the week before Christmas and were put away on Twelfth Night.

'Dorothy, you'll be hanging the angels, and John, you put the apples on the windowsill. The paint is dry, go on with you.' She could remember their laughter as Miss Byrne fussed over them. When she was sent back to Ireland, Dorothy did the decorations with Thomas, but after he left for school, it was her solitary task. She picked up one of the ornamental apples and touched the fading golden paint, remembering a particular Christmas.

'In Italy we call this a *presepio*,' Lorenzo said, pulling the straw from a wooden crate. 'Donald has carved the figures but I have painted them. At home we put them in the window for everyone to see. It is for you, Lady Keyt, for you and your family, as a thank-you for your kindness to a lonely Italian boy.'

Every year Dorothy would unpack the holy family, the baby Jesus, the Virgin Mary, the cows and the little wooden donkeys, and every year it was her favourite part of the holiday.

Perhaps she had loved him even then.

She sat down at the harpsichord and lifted the lid. Picking out a few notes from one of the long-forgotten Christmas carols, she started to sing. The carol singers no longer came to Norton, and the little girl in the velvet dress had grown up, but her love of music was as strong as ever.

Her voice was tentative at first, but as her fingers sped across the keys, she lost herself in the melodies, her voice rich and full. When she had finished, she heard clapping.

'That was lovely! How I shall miss it.' Her sister was sitting in the corner.

'You were so quiet, I didn't hear you. Shall we sing something together?'

'Do you remember that Celtic ballad Miss Byrne taught us?' Elizabeth asked. '"The Wind and the Rain"?'

'Yes,' Dorothy replied, picking out the tune. 'I think this is correct.' Together they started to sing, their voices rising and falling together. They didn't see their father standing in the doorway, his eyes wet with unshed tears.

When they finished Dorothy ran to her sister and hugged her. 'There is the harpsichord at The College; it may not be as beautiful as this, but I will play for you every time you come, and we can sing together. I must go now, I can't keep Mother waiting.'

'Thank you, and don't forget I shall write to you every day and think of you every minute. You are grown up and so very pretty. In no time at all you will be courted by all the young men of Stratford-upon-Avon and beyond. You must swear that you will tell me every little detail to keep me amused. Be sure that you look after Mother.'

'I'll try, but I will never be as kind as you.'

'You are a good person, but you are headstrong and opinionated. Endeavour to think before plunging forward.'

'I will strive for perfection, but with me I am afraid it's not always possible.' They laughed and she kissed her.

Thomas passed her on the stairs. 'The coach will be outside shortly.'

Dorothy touched his arm. 'Have you forgiven me?' she asked.

'Of course,' he said, smiling ruefully, 'you only told me the truth, after all.'

Sir William watched from his window as the carriage and wagons, piled high with boxes and trunks, passed under the archway. His wife had done it. She had left him. He sat down and rubbed his head in his hands.

The house seemed a barren, dismal place. Dorothy, for all of her antagonism, enlivened the house with her energy, and Ann warmed it with her kindness. He went to the bookcase to retrieve his diary. Finding it moved yet again, he smiled sadly. Dorothy had always found the temptation impossible to resist.

He craved a drink, but alcohol had ruined him. He resolved to put it behind him for good.

Elizabeth remained at Norton. She had put her trust in her father, and in return, he would dedicate his life to her. In the small silent room he vowed to God that he would never hurt her, that he would always protect her. He would no longer use John's death as an excuse for his behaviour.

For the next hour he wrote in his diary. He examined his

obsession for Molly, and he didn't exonerate his actions.

The drink was a cancer, destroying any rational thought. This devil from without became the devil within.

Just before putting down his pen he wrote a final line. *If I ever have the chance to earn the forgiveness of Molly Johnson, I will earn it a thousandfold.*

Closing the door to his study, he went to find Elizabeth. He would tell her about Molly and accept her judgement. He would also prove that he could change, and any suffering that he had caused was in the past. Then they could look to a brighter future.

CHAPTER TWENTY-FOUR

'Lord, what's this? If it ain't my Molly! But what are these tears?' Her mother sat on her bed and scooped the girl into her arms.

'Oh Ma,' Molly cried, enclosed in her embrace at last.

'It's a bad do, girl, a bad do. I knew trouble would come, but I prayed and I hoped.'

'Forgive me, Ma. I've brought shame on your house.' She buried her face in the ample chest.

'You've done no such thing; it's the rich buggers, Lord forgive my foul tongue. They think they have a right over us simple folk. But you mark my words, my love, what goes around comes around.'

'What about Da? He wanted me to do well, to improve myself. He'll kill me.'

'He might like to, love, but he'll have to kill me first. I'll deal with him. He should have listened to me, the silly old fool. He was taken with it all, flattered. There's a divide, and you can't cross it.'

'I never wanted to.'

It was only a small lie.

'Molly Agnes Johnson, get down here this minute!'

When she heard her father's voice coming up the stairs she sighed. She stood in front of him, emptiness washing over her as she waited for the onslaught. 'Do you know the humiliation you have brought us, the disgrace to our good name? You have dishonoured this house and all who live here. Couldn't keep your legs shut, eh?'

'Father, it wasn't like that! He took advantage of me.'

'If you are saying he raped you, there's no rape without encouragement.'

She looked at her father dispassionately. She had once idolized this huge man. Now she realized her childhood hero had feet of clay.

It wasn't the return of the prodigal son, but amongst the misery there was a degree of pleasure. Will came home from school, taller, stronger. He rushed up the stairs towards her.

'You're back! Oh, Molly, I've missed you. Ma thought I'd had it last year, coughed my lungs out, but it didn't finish me. I had to see you.'

She hugged him, put her arms around him. 'I've missed you too, Will, so much.'

'Tell me, what was it like? Were they nice to you?'

'They were,' she answered. 'Lady Keyt and Miss Elizabeth were generous and warm-hearted, and Thomas—' She stopped, her personal thoughts too painful to express.

'Then why are you home?'

'It's hard to explain, but Sir William was not kind, and he hurt me.'

'I'll kill him, then.'

They laughed.

'You're too big to share the bed with me now; it will have to be one of the girls.'

'I'll sleep on the floor,' he protested. 'You'll not send me to another room.'

Molly tied sacking between the beds, but she might as well not have, for that night with the curtain tied back and their faces together, they talked and laughed and cried a little, and Molly's wounds started to heal.

'I'm going to be a lawyer, an educated man. We can move up, you know – not into their class, but we can make a new one of our own.'

'You will be my lawyer if I can afford you. When you are famous you can look after your big sister.'

'For you, Miss Johnson, I'll waive my fee.'

Molly pulled the poem from beneath her pillow. She gave it to her brother.

'Please could you read this to me?'

'What is it?'

'Just something I found, but I would like to know what it says.'

'You've pieced it together. Did you really find it, or is it something special?'

Molly remembered the night she had torn it in half.

'Get on with it, don't be so nosy.' They laughed again and he read it to her, his voice clear and tutored.

When he finished he handed it back to her.

'What does it mean?' he asked.

'I don't know,' she said, her tears falling. 'I think it means that I was once loved, but it's all too late now.'

'Then, he's an idiot. I will always love you, no matter what.'

As the weeks turned into months, a routine was established at the Charter House. Molly did the household chores, mended as before, minded the girls and helped her mother. Sometimes, as she sat in the window gazing into the yard below, she would think of Norton, of the wide-open spaces, and the flowers, she would remember the silks and the satins and the opportunities missed. The first time she was ordered below she went reluctantly.

'I'm short-staffed,' her father had chided her, 'so don't go thinking anything else.'

What should I think? she wondered wretchedly as she crossed the room. She could feel eyes staring into her back. Customers' knowing eyes.

'So?' Dan Leggat's arm shot out and stopped her in her tracks. 'You're back then. Missed your chance, didn't you?' He was sitting in one of the high-sided pews. He made to grab her, but Molly stepped sideways. His thick tongue lolled from his mouth and dribble slipped from his lips. Dan Leggat was more odious than before. Molly turned and fled, but not before she had seen his obscene gesture.

Upstairs in her room she wept into her pillow. She was condemned whichever way she turned. Her mother tried to comfort her but as far as Molly was concerned her life was over.

CHAPTER TWENTY-FIVE

The coach clattered over the cobbled streets of Old Town and into College Lane. Opposite the church of the Holy Trinity, the under-coachman from Norton carefully negotiated a turn through narrow gates and into a driveway. Dorothy stared from the window. Stratford had been bustling; people enjoying the Christmas festivities. *It was so unfair.* By the time they drew up in the courtyard of a large medieval house she had made up her mind to be utterly miserable. A footman ran from the side entrance to collect the luggage. She watched him dispassionately as he unstrapped the trunks, then following her mother she stepped down and walked towards the front door. Weeds sprang though the gravel, and bare roses, blue with disease, clung limply to the walls.

'This is the Great Hall,' Lady Keyt said, climbing the steps cautiously, 'and this,' she said, pointing to the green slabs beneath her feet in an effort to amuse her daughter, 'is moss.' She stopped at the top step and took Dorothy's hand. 'Don't be sad, Dotty, it's been a horrible time, but we will make this work, I promise.'

She looked at the wing facing the river. The four gables housed the library, the Great Hall, and the winter sitting room. When she had come to The College shortly after her marriage, the estate had flourished. It had been filled with servants who maintained it with devotion, and a constant stream of friends who had come to visit the young and happy couple. Now the friends had gone, the house and gardens looked unkempt, and the dejected child at her side was to be her main source of company. She tried to shake off her feelings of self-pity and chatted to her daughter as if unaware of her silence. 'Look at the fine specimen trees planted by your Clopton ancestors. And the river, do you see how close it is? We have a boat; it used to leak, but I shall have it restored.' With only the occasional frown from Dorothy, she gave up trying to be positive and sighed. 'I'm sorry, I know it's Christmas, but it's miserable for me too. The College was our first home together. Your father and I were happy here; your sister was born here.' She shook her head. 'Now I will have to find something worthy to take up my time.'

The solution to her problem presented itself shortly after Christmas. As prayer was her only consolation she spent much of the religious holiday in church, praying for the soul of her departed son, for her sick daughter and for her foolish husband. After many hours on her knees, an idea came to her with divine clarity. She would open a school. The College had been built for the habitation of priests; they, in turn, had taught and assisted the community. The house could serve a similar purpose once more.

'I shall give some of the illiterate children of our parish the chance to read. Will you help me, Dorothy?' she said as they sat down to lunch in the dining room. Dorothy looked up – she could see the excitement in her mother's face and for the first time in days she smiled.

'Of course I will, Mama.'

Over the next few weeks Dorothy helped her set up a classroom within the house and, with Sir William's consent, forty desks and chairs were made at Norton. When they arrived at Stratford in the estate cart, a feeling of renewal brightened the house. Every morning the children came, and from ten o'clock until two, Lady Keyt with the help of her daughter taught the rudiments of writing and arithmetic.

Dorothy added another class to the curriculum: geography. She brought down her nursery globe, and with Miss Byrne's voice echoing in her ears, she took the children on a voyage of discovery.

With the inconstancy of youth, she forgot her sorrows. Thomas, the future baronet, was in great demand socially, and as his popularity in the local community increased, so did his visits to The College. In the evenings, they went to balls and social gatherings, concerts and dancing classes. Elizabeth came for her weekly visits as she had promised, brought by Lorenzo.

Life, Dorothy thought, was getting better.

CHAPTER TWENTY-SIX

'The coachman is here,' Molly's mother called. 'Good luck, God bless. I won't see you off, my duck, it's too painful. But you remember, hold that pretty head up and make them treat you right, promise me?'

'I promise, Ma. I'll do my best.'

Molly was returning to Norton; her father had summoned her only the week before. She had been cleaning the grate in the best bedroom when she heard his angry voice.

'Molly, get here this minute! In the parlour, now!'

She stood up, stretched her aching back, and wiped her reddened hands. 'What is it, Father?'

He shook a letter in front of her face, a thick envelope marked with the Keyt crest.

'You've been back at the Charter House for months now, yet I still worry every time the post comes. Will I always be punished for my daughter's behaviour?'

His hands ripped at the envelope. Molly waited for the rage, but a grin spread over his face.

'Good Lord in his mercy. He wants you back. Go, Molly. Go this instant, clean yourself up and pack your belongings.'

'I can't go back.'

'Don't look at me like that. You're nothing but trouble.'

'Don't you love me any more? Once upon a time I was your special girl,' she asked sadly.

'You ruined that when you spread your legs, so do as I bid or it's the workhouse for you.' Molly's shoulders sank; she was still one of his bloody pigs, sent off to slaughter.

'Ma, help me! I won't go back.'

'Darling Molly, you have to go. There's naught for you here. No local man worth his salt will take you now. News travels fast.'

'Please, Ma.' She threw her arms around her neck. 'Don't make me go, not this time.'

'Look now, you have a big heart. Think of it this way: that poor young cripple needs you; she wants you back. Your father told me that it's her wish, not only his. I am afraid we do what our betters tell us. Do you want to be emptying slops for the rest of your days?' She picked up her daughter's chin, and looked deep into the tawny eyes. 'I'm sorry, child, but your sweet beauty is also your downfall. Go, my lovely girl, and make a good life for yourself.'

Her sisters tugged at her cotton dress, pulling her back to the present. 'Molly, can we work in the big house when we grow up?'

Will stared at her with a face full of hurt and confusion.

'But why, Molly, when you hate him?'

'I have no option. Da says I'm no use to anybody, and Mother says that something good may come of it, though I can't think what.'

'What about me? I'll miss you so much.'

'I know, love, but I'll learn to write, I really will, and then

I can send you letters. In the meantime, make sure you work hard, for you're going to be a lawyer and a fine gentleman.'

They clung together once more, and though she ached inside she knew that there are some who had choices and some who did not.

Molly tucked her feet beneath her on the velvet cushions and drew back the curtains. The mud had given way to the freshness of early summer. The sky outside was a crisp blue, and the trees were the brightest green. With the world bursting with God's beauty, it was hard to feel miserable for long.

After a stop in Clifford Chambers the carriage drove through the gates of Norton, the horses trotting briskly along the newly finished driveway. The fencing was repaired, the crops were sown, and in the walk-round, fat lambs jumped in the air, all feet off the ground together. Molly's spirits rose.

They pulled into the courtyard and Lorenzo jumped down.

'So I bring your bag to the door.' He almost smiled, and she thanked him, and less than a year after being sent home she walked towards the servants' entrance once more.

'Miss Johnson, you have arrived. Would you please follow me?'

It was a new butler, polite and courteous. He led her to the drawing room, where Sir William waited for her.

'I hope you are well, and the journey not too uncomfortable?' Sir William was smartly dressed, jewelled buckles, newly polished shoes, the little snake burnished. She looked up cautiously, and then turned away. His eyes were bright, his complexion clear.

'Yes, Sir William, it was quite comfortable, thank you.'

When she heard Elizabeth's chair in the passage outside, she looked towards the door.

'Miss Elizabeth,' she said, and Elizabeth smiled. There were the same grey-green eyes, but if she was fragile before, a puff of wind would now blow her away.

'Hello, Molly. We are pleased you have returned.'

Molly smiled warmly, for Elizabeth would never want her pity.

'Only Father and I live here now. Thomas is away at Oxford and comes rarely, so your duties will be as my companion. If you wish, you may still dress my hair, but you will no longer need to act as a lady's maid. I hope this suits you and you will want to stay, for I'm afraid I've been a little lonely.'

'Thank you, miss,' she said relieved. 'Thank you,' she whispered again.

'You will be in your old room, and if there is anything that you need, be sure to let us know.'

Upstairs in her bedroom, she unpacked the small leather case and put her coat on the hook. She opened the cupboard; the dresses were there, untouched, even the remains of her mint-green gown.

'Hello, Molly.' A shy face peeped around the door.

'Hello, Ruth.'

'Look here, I'm sorry we weren't kind when you were sent home, but I've had time to think. It was me that did out your room, and I saw the dress, and I said to Annie that I think the master had more than a little to answer for, so I did.'

Such gratitude overcame Molly that she went right up to Ruth and put her arms around her, finding comfort in her sturdy frame. She knew the truth, and Molly felt free to cry at last.

When she had dried her eyes she asked Ruth to tell her how life had been at Norton.

'After you were gone, blimey, what a fuss. The mistress, off she goes to The College, taking Mrs Wright and Mr Whitstone. Master Thomas went to Oxford straight after Christmas. What a Christmas it was, long faces all round. Anyway, it's better again, thank the Lord. Miss Elizabeth is in charge. She's employed a new butler and housekeeper, and two new girls for the dirty jobs, and I'm risen to first housemaid. So there we are, and you are back and Annie is still here, and we are sorry.'

After her little speech they laughed, and Molly felt confident that she could deal with anything.

'I'll be a real friend now,' Ruth said on her way out. 'And if it happens again, I won't run out on you like the last time.'

'Thank you, but God willing, it will never, ever happen again.'

Despite her worsening health Elizabeth seemed at peace. She had taken control of the household with her mother's grace. But in her dealings with Molly, Elizabeth remained tentative and formal.

'Miss Johnson, are your parents well, and your brother Will?'

'Miss Johnson, I would be extremely grateful if you could darn a small tear in my blue petticoat.'

A bout of grippe forced them past their formality. When Molly found Elizabeth's nurse also coughing and wheezing, she banished her from the sickroom and took over herself. For five days she tended to Elizabeth's every need. She changed the linen, washed her feverish body and prepared her food. She also banished Sir William.

'I'm sorry, sir, but she must remain quiet and on her own.' He complied reluctantly, but she noted new respect in his eyes.

When Elizabeth regained her health, their former friendship resumed. One day Elizabeth put down her needlework. 'Molly, I wish to ask you something.'

Molly looked up from her own sewing. 'Yes, Miss Elizabeth?'

'Did you hate coming back here? Were you coerced, or was it of your own free will?'

Molly was not sure how she should reply, but within certain parameters she could be truthful. 'It wasn't my choice, miss; it was my mother who persuaded me. She said that there was no future for me at home. It's true, I don't want to spend my life emptying the slops. Then of course there were the letters; Will read them to me, and yours was very persuasive, but when Sir William said you needed me, I couldn't say no.'

Elizabeth smiled gently.

'Of course I needed you,' she replied.

After her sickroom ministrations, Sir William treated Molly with more consideration. He remembered the day when his daughter had suggested Molly should return.

'Would you like her to, Lizzie?' he had asked, choosing his words carefully. 'I am not sure she'll want to come.'

'Yes, Papa, I would love her to return.'

'How do we persuade her that I'm a changed man?'

'You write to her, and I shall write a separate letter. In that way I can assure her of our good intentions. I will of course tell her that she must come only if she wants to. We would never want her to return against her will.'

'You have it all worked out, don't you?' he said, smiling at his daughter.

To Molly's surprise, Sir William acted with a degree of uncertainty in her presence. He made no further advances, and gradually she began to relax and even enjoy his company. He had stopped drinking, and Molly could only be touched by the concern he showed for his daughter.

'Lizzie darling, I will fetch a rug for your knees.'

'Lizzie, can I carry you into the garden?'

These small gestures made her regard him in a new light. She would never be able to forgive him, but she managed to push the unspeakable incident to the back of her mind.

One evening, as she piled Elizabeth's thick hair on top of her head in preparation for supper, Elizabeth touched her arm.

'Molly dear, I know you have dresses from Mama, but would you be offended if I added one to your collection? As you can see, I have lost a little weight and the aqua gown with the cream trim is far too big. I think it will suit you.'

Molly could hardly refuse.

Shortly afterwards she was invited to dine.

'Molly, would you be embarrassed to join my father and me for supper? I understand if you would prefer to be with Annie and Ruth, but I find myself missing your delightful company.'

Unable to turn down such a sweet and thoughtfully worded request, Molly was more than happy to join them.

That night, dressed in aquamarine silk with cream lace ruffles that cascaded to her elbow, she joined Elizabeth and Sir William in the dining room. Tapered candles burnt in the silver candelabra and venison was served on crested platters. As she sat amongst the velvet hangings, Mr Heron, deferential and inscrutable, poured wine into her etched glass goblet. She couldn't help but smile: if only her father could see her now.

Thomas returned to Norton infrequently, his studies at Oxford taking up most of his time. When he did come to see Elizabeth, Molly remained out of sight.

Very occasionally he dined with his father, but according to Ruth, 'You could cut the atmosphere with a knife, so you could.'

When Thomas had left, Molly would stand at the same attic window where she had stood once before. For a while she would dream the same dreams, but then she would shake her head and turn away.

CHAPTER TWENTY-SEVEN

Elizabeth looked across the fields. 'Do you see up there on the hill? There is evidence of a Roman settlement. I used to love going there.' She shrugged. 'I'll ask Father to show you where they found the ring.'

Molly was intrigued. While she would not have chosen an expedition with Sir William, when he asked her she couldn't bring herself to say no. It was fixed for the following week and, despite herself, she looked forward to it.

In the meantime, she was learning to read.

Elizabeth drew the familiar characters in her notebook and called Molly over. 'The alphabet is made up of twenty-six letters, and you must learn them all.'

Molly practised and repeated, until slowly the mysterious puzzle came together.

'I've done it, Miss Elizabeth, I've done it!' she cried.

When Sir William came across them, he was amused by their girlish laughter.

'I would be interested to know what has given rise to such merriment.'

Molly told him and he smiled.

'I congratulate you both, for I know the struggle only too well. Believe it or not, Elizabeth's mother taught me to read when my tutors failed.'

Molly was surprised to feel pleasure at his shared confidence.

'You must use the library as you learn,' he said. 'Take any book you please.'

Soon she was able to read Thomas's poem, and before long she knew it by heart.

Her first letter home was of no great length.

Darling Will,
    I am writing this on my own.
    It will not be long for it is difficult.
    Write me your news.
    I am beginning to enjoy my life here.
    Love Molly

This was true enough, for her life had taken an unexpected turn. She was devoted to Elizabeth, and she was beginning to trust Sir William. The only blot on her otherwise content life was the occasional arrival of Dorothy. Her feeling of goodwill was further endorsed when Sir William enlisted her help in a matter of extreme urgency.

It was a particularly hot day at the end of her first summer back at Norton; Elizabeth was dining with her father in the small panelled dining room, Molly was in the rose garden outside. She had put the last flower in her basket when she heard Sir William calling her. Hearing the panic in his voice, she rushed through the garden door and down the corridor to find Elizabeth gasping for breath.

'Move away,' she ordered. 'Please, I need space, she's choking.' Binding her hands beneath Elizabeth's ribcage, one over the other, she gave a short, sharp tug, using all the weight in her body. At once a small piece of carrot shot from Elizabeth's throat. She coughed until she caught her breath.

'Thank you,' Elizabeth said, when at last she could speak. 'I believe you have just saved my life.'

Sir William stared. 'Wherever did you learn that?' he finally asked.

'From my mother.' Molly smiled. 'It's not unknown for a woman to have some practical uses.'

The day of the expedition arrived and a picnic was prepared. With one of the grooms accompanying them, Sir William drove the cart to Dover's Hill. He parked in the shade beneath the trees, and while the groom waited he and Molly set off to climb the hill.

At the summit William pointed to a patch of rough grass. 'This is where we found our Roman. A good spot, don't you agree?' Molly did agree, for below them, stretching as far as the eye could see, were the villages and hills and woods of middle England.

He took the ring off his finger and passed it to Molly. 'I know this was not mine to take, but I honour this man, so it can't be wrong.'

Molly held the small winding snake in her hand, looked into the tiny ruby eye, and passed it back thoughtfully. Its expression struck her as insidious.

'I hope you are right,' she said to herself.

They ate their picnic sitting on a wooden seat, the sun warming their backs.

***

From that day forward whenever Molly was dressed for a walk, Sir William would appear by her side. At first there were excuses, a fence-line to inspect, or a tree to examine, but soon the walks simply became a daily event.

As the dogs raced up the hills ahead of them, he talked to her about the estate and about his family. Occasionally he asked her about her own family. When Will was offered a position in Warwick as an apprentice clerk she told him gladly, and though she was still a little guarded in his company, it seemed to William that she no longer despised him.

She enjoyed stories of his childhood.

'I spent a lot of time at Hidcote with my grandfather,' he told her. 'I always wanted to be like him, but I haven't made a very good job of it, I'm afraid. Each morning we walked a different part of the estate. He told me where to plant corn and when to plant clover to enrich the soil.'

He recounted the story of his family's elevation and knighthood, when his great-grandfather, John Keyt, had raised a troop of horse for the late King Charles in the civil war, and he described the formal Sunday outings with his grandparents to the church in Ebrington. 'Generations of our family are buried there. John is in the vault, and one day I shall join him.'

On a warm autumn day, when the leaves were turning and the apple trees in the lower orchard were laden with fruit, Sir William took Molly and Elizabeth to Sunday service. When it ended, and the congregation had filed slowly and curiously past, they stopped in front of a small stained-glass window in the south transept. As the sun illuminated the Keyt and Coventry coat of arms, he told them of the Keyt connection to one of the richest families of England. He showed them the altar tomb of his grandfather – also called William Keyt – who started the Ebrington Cow Charity, giving every poor man in the village free milk.

'He died when I was still a child,' he said. 'The guiding figure in my life left me, and I never said goodbye. My father died five weeks before him, but it was my grandfather whose loss was the greater.'

He wheeled Elizabeth slowly down the path, but in his mind he was once again a thirteen-year-old boy, walking behind the coffin of his grandfather.

That evening, when Elizabeth had retired to bed, Sir William turned to Molly. 'Miss Johnson, may I ask you something?'

'Of course, sir.'

He inhaled deeply. 'My grandfather taught me many things, but one of them of particular significance. He taught me to follow my conscience. I have failed him, just as I have failed you, and I want to ask your forgiveness. What happened that night will never happen again.'

His admission touched her, but Molly could only be truthful. 'I'll try to forgive you, sir, but it will take time.'

'I'm prepared to wait, for ever if necessary. I merely want to make it up to you.'

CHAPTER TWENTY-EIGHT

1737

Molly's relationship with Sir William changed slowly. He did not rush her: indeed, his greatest desire was to win back her trust. He did this in small ways, by including her in discussions and inviting her to dinner, by consulting and listening to her. On questions of Elizabeth's health he always deferred to her. And slowly Molly's feelings changed. Thomas appeared less frequently in her dreams. She found herself watching Sir William, looking at his mouth and wondering what it would be like to be kissed in tenderness. She found herself imagining his body, for he still had fine legs and a broad chest. In the evenings she would sit with him and Elizabeth in front of the fire, and William would read to them. Molly, a little intoxicated by the wine she had drunk at dinner, would listen contentedly, her body warm and sensual. One evening Sir William looked up from his book and found Molly's eyes upon him. When he smiled she did not look away.

Eleven months after returning, Molly made her decision: she would become the mistress of Sir William Keyt. Emptying a jug of hot water into the blue and white china basin, she opened the stopper on a jar of fragrant oil. Trailing her hand in the scented water, she washed herself slowly, caressing her breasts, running her fingers along the outline of her hips, and touching the most intimate parts of her body, and all the while she thought of William.

She would wear the nightgown painstakingly made from his gift of silk. She slipped it over her head, a voluptuous glide that rippled to the floor. She snuffed the candle and walked to his bedroom.

He was lying in bed when she entered. He rose onto his elbow and stared. She put up her hand. 'Stay there,' she said. 'Do not move.'

She pushed the thin straps from her shoulders, letting the silk fall, until it lay in a pool on the wooden boards. She stood before him, her bare skin white in the moonlight. She motioned for him to come to her, and when he stood before her, looking questioningly into her eyes, she picked up his hand and cupped it to her breast. Slowly he began to touch her, reverently as if she were a goddess. Her body responded as he stroked her breasts. Her nipples hardened at his touch, cool on her skin, his mouth covering her and teasing. Then his kisses were on her neck, his body straining against hers, his arms pulling them together. She felt his strength, but still he caressed her gently while he whispered her name over and over again. When she could bear the waiting no longer she took his hand in her own and pushed it down, between her legs.

This time, she did not resist. Greedily she relished this strange new passion.

If Elizabeth knew what had happened, she remained diplomatic, and it was not discussed; and if Sir William tried to be discreet he was not entirely successful. 'Molly, let me carry your work. It must be heavy.'

'Sir, my mending is really of insignificant weight. I assure you, years of carrying buckets up and down my mother's house have made me strong and workmanlike.'

'Strong maybe, but workmanlike? I think not.'

For Molly, it was a time of fulfilment and peace. She found pleasure in being his mistress and enjoyed feeling needed.

CHAPTER TWENTY-NINE

1737

One August afternoon, while Molly read to Elizabeth on the terrace, William approached with a handsome stranger at his side.

'Lizzie, my darling, and Miss Johnson, may I introduce Mr Cartwright?'

Perhaps it was the hint of colour in Elizabeth's cheeks, or the flattering scatter of freckles on her nose that flustered Mr Cartwright.

'Ah, yes . . . ahm, good afternoon,' he stammered. 'I see you are enjoying the weather?'

'We are indeed,' Elizabeth replied.

Mr Cartwright nodded, staring at the ground.

'We will see you shortly, my dears,' William said, leading poor Cartwright away.

When the two men had safely disappeared into the house, Molly and Elizabeth started to laugh.

'He was so overcome! What nonsense he spoke.'

'Oh,' Elizabeth said, wiping the tears from her eyes, 'how glad I am indeed that it is not raining.'

Despite his embarrassment, Mr Cartwright accepted an invitation for dinner, and with considerable feminine delight, preparations began. After an excessive amount of time and indecision, Elizabeth selected the pale blue organza, set off by the Tracy pearls.

'Beautiful,' Molly said, when Elizabeth's hair was dressed to her satisfaction. 'Absolutely lovely.'

Fortunately Mr Cartwright found his voice that night, and throughout dinner, the party made animated conversation. When they had finished their meal, William picked up his daughter and carried her into the drawing room. It was the only outward sign of her misfortune.

'Well, Lizzie, it seems you were also a little taken,' Molly teased when Mr Cartwright had left.

'Certainly not,' she replied, but her eyes shone.

Three weeks later, William, Elizabeth and Molly were finishing breakfast when William rang the bell. George Heron immediately appeared.

'Heron, please remove the plates. I need the table to be clear.'

'Yes, sir,' he replied, deftly removing the coffee cups and saucers, the plates of muffins and toast. 'If you will allow me, I will get one of the housemaids to sweep away the crumbs.'

Molly was heading towards the door when Sir William called her back.

'Miss Johnson, could you spare a moment and stay behind with Miss Elizabeth? I have something to show you both; I will fetch it from the library.'

He returned carrying a long tube. Pulling out a sheet of paper he spread it on the table in front of him. It was the plan for an impressive four-storey mansion with seven bays. An ornate balustrade ran along the roof line, and pediments and pilasters adorned every inch of the masonry. The inscription read *Over Norton House*.

'Well, what do you think?'

It was a moment before Elizabeth replied. 'It's lovely, but what is it for? We are not moving, are we, Papa? I should hate to move.'

'No, of course not, but I am going to build you the finest house in Gloucestershire. It will be here on the top lawn, and Mr Cartwright will be overseeing the work as our architect. You will see from the plan that I have devised a passageway from one house to the other. It will be at first-floor level. Think of this as an additional wing and nothing more.'

He turned to Molly. 'Do you like it?' he asked.

'It is handsome, but hardly a single wing. Surely, this house is big enough?'

'How practical you are, but what is practicality, my dear, when I wish to do something for the two women in my life?'

It was the first time that William had aired his affection for Molly in front of his daughter, and in front of the servants. Molly noted George Heron's look of surprise.

It flustered her. 'I don't know what to say, sir. Please don't take any notice of my opinion.'

William held up his hands. 'Enough. Consider it a gift to you both.'

'Please forgive me, I feel a little unwell.' She ran from the room.

For Elizabeth's sake, Molly had prudently kept her own bedroom in the attic. Her dresses still hung in the wardrobe, the little vase beside the washstand was always filled with flowers; when she attended the dining room it was as

162

Elizabeth's companion. She had worked hard to regain her friendship and feared Sir William's indiscretion had ruined it.

Walking downstairs the next morning, Molly found Elizabeth on the landing, working intently on a drawing. She closed the pad and looked up, her fingers covered with black charcoal. 'Do you think so little of me, Molly?' she frowned.

Molly was flustered. 'I don't know what you mean.'

'You should know me better, so please don't ever judge me again.'

It was the same with Ruth.

'It's all right, love; we won't hate you just because you've got lucky. As long as you don't act like a spoilt duchess, I'll still love you.'

It was not long before the building work started. Teams of craftsmen hired by the director of works appeared. Stonemasons, bricklayers, carpenters and plasterers filled the site. On the first Monday of every month, Mr Cartwright came to inspect the progress. Molly, at Sir William's insistence, was usually at his side. She was flattered, but though she did her best to limit his extravagance, on these occasions he ignored her, so determined was he to create a house that would outstrip all others. As the end of the first stage approached, it became evident that the building lacked sophistication and refinement.

'Something seems wrong with the proportions, Papa, though of course the design is excellent,' Elizabeth observed.

'I agree with you,' Mr Cartwright said apologetically. 'My efforts appear cumbersome and top-heavy. I have failed you.'

'Of course you haven't,' she replied. 'I'm sure you'll find a solution.'

In the end Elizabeth came up with the solution. She asked her father to contact the architect, and only a week after their previous meeting, she arranged to join them on the building site. George Heron pushed the chair over the uneven gound and stopped at the small group assembled in front of the house.

'Thank you, Mr Heron,' Elizabeth said, re-arranging her skirts. 'Not an easy task I know.' She watched for a moment as he picked his way back through the mud, then turned to Mr Cartwright and smiled apologetically. 'I would be grateful if you would cast your eye over my drawing.' She opened her notebook. The central portion of the house remained the same, but the two new wings added balance and symmetry, and the intricate railings and elaborate iron gates gave the desired elegance.

'It's merely a suggestion,' she said.

George Cartwright took the pad from Elizabeth.

'I believe you would make an accomplished architect,' he said, beaming at her. Elizabeth blushed and turned away, but not before Molly had noticed.

When the group returned for tea in the library, Molly voiced her concerns again. 'The mansion is already magnificent and there are only three of us to live in it. Do we really need the extra space?'

'Just think of ways to furnish it and leave the worrying to me,' Sir William said flippantly.

'You see, Mr Cartwright,' she said, defeated, 'I have little influence. Sir William will not be outdone. After all, what is a Kite without wings?'

During the following months the building work continued, and as the two extra wings rose steadily from the ground, rumours began to filter Molly's way. Then she heard it straight from the foreman: he walked up to her while she was picking rosemary in the herb garden, and spat ungraciously into the ground. 'The carpenters weren't paid last month, and the plasterers the month before.'

'I will talk to Sir William and Miss Elizabeth,' she mumbled lamely, retrieving her basket. She knew her excuse was inadequate, for while William ignored any financial implications, Elizabeth was unaware of them. She had never dealt with bills, and throughout her life money had always been available. Why should that change?

As the house grew, so did the garden. Henry Clark, the steward, began a scheme as elaborate as the house itself. Several hundred trees were planted, and above the yew walk, two large parterres were established, their central feature being a round stone table. When Molly asked about this, Sir William smiled. 'I admit to an obsession: we have Merlin's grove, and now we have Arthur's table.'

It seemed to Molly that a new project was undertaken every week.

'Molly, will you accompany me to the new plantation?' Elizabeth asked. 'Lorenzo will come for us at nine.'

As the cart drew up beside the young woodland, Elizabeth clasped her arm. 'These trees will outlive us all. Think of it: they will be here for hundreds of years, long after you and I have been forgotten.'

While Molly worried about the immediate future, Elizabeth looked beyond. She imagined the children from many future generations running beneath the trees; children from a new and altered world.

In early spring, William asked Molly and Elizabeth to join him in the garden.

'Don't look so stern, Molly. After this we will tighten the reins.' He gathered his daughter into his arms and carried her, urging her to close her eyes. Molly followed. They had left the garden long behind them when William stopped in front of a grove of trees.

'Open your eyes, Lizzie. Look what I have built for you. I have called it "The Temple".'

Before them, light flickered intermittently through the dark canopy of branches. Hidden amongst the foliage was a small version of the new mansion.

'Papa, it's beautiful!' she cried. 'Molly, do you see the bust in the niche above the entrance? I'm sure it looks like me!'

'It is you.' Molly laughed.

'And what do you think, Molly?' William asked.

'It is very beautiful, but—'

Molly pushed all thoughts of escalating costs and financial ruin aside, and surrendered to the spirit of the occasion. 'And yes, of course I like it very much.'

Less than a week had passed when these same doubts were brought severely home. Sir William was in his study; Molly resisted the urge to knock and opened the door.

'Come to bed,' she said softly. 'It's late and you'll make yourself ill.'

'Go away!' he snapped, putting his hand over the ledger in front of him. 'If I don't sort these figures, I really will be ill.' William avoided her eyes, refusing to see the hurt he had caused. When the door closed behind her, he returned to his books. He tried to concentrate. He licked his lips, running his tongue around his dry mouth. The expenditure columns were filled with black numbers, row upon row of jumbled figures. They made no sense. He pushed the ledgers away from him and groaned. Shaking his head, he accepted that his desire to be known as a man of wealth and culture would come to nothing. Unlike so many of his class, who had built upon their family's good name and their fortunes, he would have destroyed a name revered for centuries, and squandered a fortune accumulated with prudence and sense. While there was no doubt that some of his sentiments had come from generosity to his daughter and mistress, a large part of this enormous folly had appealed to his own vanity.

'I shall be remembered only as a fool,' he said, hysteria creeping into his voice, 'a stupid, bloody fool.'

Molly returned to her room and sat down at her dressing table. She stared into the mirror, flinching at the pained face that stared back at her. She knew the Keyt coffers were emptying fast. William's demeanour, the rumours, the unpaid workmen all told the story. As William continued to spend, and as the money dwindled away, so too would his interest in his mistress.

Molly's dread escalated when he insisted on her presence only days later.

'Come now, Molly, and don't be cross.'

'Why should I be? I'm hardly ever cross.'

'You look at me with disapproval, and that is just as bad. I know you'll think this an unnecessary extravagance, but I wish to build a theatre arranged around a circular pool. It will be a permanent open-air setting for concerts and plays. We must, after all, have somewhere to open our celebrations.'

'What celebrations?' she asked.

'The county will wish to see all of this,' he said. 'We can't let them down. It's my last indulgence, the very last, I give you my word.'

While William described his vision, she tried to listen, but she remained suspicious of an auditorium carved from the hillside, a column of limes and a circular pool. She could only see it all crumbling around her.

Fifteen months after the first stone was laid, the building of the mansion was nearing completion and only the final details were left.

'Do you like it?' Elizabeth asked, as Molly pushed her around the hall.

'Of course I do,' Molly replied, choosing her words carefully. 'It's magnificent, it would be impossible not to like it.'

They stopped in front of the chimney breast. 'Mr Cartwright commissioned this in London,' Elizabeth murmured, admiringly. Molly looked closely. Amongst the carvings of fruit and flowers, a violin rested on its side, the fineness of the strings demonstrating the supreme artistry of the wood carver. She was about to turn away when she noticed a skull buried amongst the foliage. She recoiled and Elizabeth laughed.

'Papa thinks the skull a little morbid; I can see that you agree.'

'Morbid? Whatever gave you that idea?' Molly laughed also, but it was a feeble laugh. She took hold of the chair and pushed it towards the door.

'I don't feel like going to The College today – would you mind if my sister came here?' Elizabeth asked, when Molly had manoeuvred her down the steps.

'Of course I don't mind. I will be out of the way, I promise you – I have several errands to run locally.' She squeezed her friend's shoulder. Sharp bones protruded through the flimsy material.

CHAPTER THIRTY

A maid was dressing Dorothy's hair when she heard the coach. She stood up, brushing the girl's hand impatiently aside, and rushed to the window. The Keyt horses were trotting down the short drive towards The College. She could see the coach clearly: Lorenzo was on the box, his face in profile; her eyes fixed on him, but when she realized the coach was empty, her excitement changed to concern. Without waiting, she ran onto the landing and down the polished stairs.

'Where's my sister?' she cried, nearly colliding with Lorenzo as he entered the door.

'Your sister's a little unwell but in good spirits,' he reassured her. 'She wishes to see you. I have a note from your father.' Dorothy took the note, and after quickly reading it, she ran to fetch her coat.

'I will tell my mother and come with you at once,' she said.

Lorenzo helped her up the steps and into the carriage. For months Dorothy had thought about him, and though she had seen him briefly, on the occasions he arrived with her sister, they were never alone. Now with his face only inches from her own, she could see the attraction in his eyes. Throughout the journey she remained silent but all the time she was aware of his presence, she was aware of the smell of soap and sweet molasses and dry winter hay. When she stepped down at the journey's end, he held her hand longer than necessary, and the pressure of his fingers remained with her all day.

It was strange for Dorothy to be back at Norton; and though she didn't see Molly, her presence was everywhere. She walked from room to room; the atmosphere was calm and tranquil. Staff greeted her, but to some she was a stranger. Everything was the same and yet it felt different. She sat down to lunch with her sister, but though she talked and laughed and feigned interest, her mind was elsewhere. Outside, the building of a mansion continued unchecked, while she, Dorothy Ann Keyt, had no part in it.

On her journey back to Stratford, Dorothy seethed at the injustice of it. This woman had stolen her father's and her brother's hearts, she had regained her sister's friendship, and now she was having a house built for her. It was more than Dorothy could bear.

When they arrived back at The College, Lorenzo took her hands as he helped her down.

'I know how difficult this is for you,' he said, 'but Miss Johnson will learn that in this world you cannot have what is not yours by right.'

Dear Lorenzo! He was a good man. She longed to forget about propriety and formality.

She looked into his eyes. 'Please, will you come for me on Monday? My sister won't be well enough to return to Stratford, but I wish to see her. I will ride with you to Norton.'

When Monday arrived Dorothy woke early. After putting on her riding habit she checked herself in the mirror; the dark blue cloth suited her. She pushed a strand of escaping hair behind the veil of her new velvet hat, applied rose water liberally to her face and neck, and went down to breakfast. Her stomach fluttered with nerves.

'Are you all right?' her mother asked, looking at the untouched roll on her plate.

'I am well, thank you, I'm just not hungry.'

'Give my love to Lizzie. I long to see her, but you know how it is.'

'I know, Mama, Lizzie understands.' She kissed her mother quickly and went to the hall. Once again she glanced in the mirror. After adjusting the veil to cover her face, she collected her favourite whip from the umbrella stand and went out through the side door and down the passage to the mews. Fidelia whinnied before she saw her. Dorothy smiled and slid the bolt to her stall.

'She's all done, miss.' A stable lad looked in on her. 'I've tightened your girth. She's too bright, that one, she always knows when you're going to ride her, and she has better hearing than any horse I know.' By the time Lorenzo's horse had clattered over the cobbles, Fidelia was stamping the ground with impatience. Lorenzo jumped down, handed his horse to the stable lad, and helped Dorothy up. For an instant she relaxed against him, but then with a small laugh she dug her heel into the horse's side. Fidelia leapt forward and they were gone, galloping down the drive and out into the lane. Lorenzo soon caught up with her, and together they rode towards Norton. Throughout the ride she admired his hands, the long slim fingers that slipped expertly through the reins. When their legs touched, brushing imperceptibly against each other, she could hardly breathe.

'How is your family?' she managed.

'They are all well. My sister married last year and her first child is on the way. Massimo now has four.'

'You must miss them.'

'Of course, but my life is here, not in Italy.' He looked at her intently, and she blushed.

When they arrived at Norton, Dorothy found her sister lying on the sofa in the drawing room with Letitia curled beside her. She bent down and kissed her.

'Don't look anxious, Dotty; it's all right, I'm better now,' Elizabeth promised. 'Read to me, will you?'

Dorothy sat down in a high-backed chair, picked the book up from the table beside her and opened the cover.

'I love you reading to me,' Elizabeth said, when Dorothy had finished a chapter. 'It reminds me of our childhood, but then, of course, it was the other way round.'

'Well, now it's my turn,' Dorothy said gently. She started on the next chapter but Elizabeth was asleep before she had finished it. Getting up, Dorothy rearranged the rug over her sister's shoulders, and quietly left the room.

Letitia ran after her and together they set off towards the mansion. She could see the house was nearly finished and as Dorothy entered the light and spacious hallway, and looked up the elegant staircase to the landing above, she thought she would be sick at the extravagance of it all. The ornate plasterwork was the obvious work of a master craftsman, and the curtains that even now were being hung at the tall windows were made of the finest silks. Flemish hangings adorned the walls and French chandeliers hung from the ceilings. Nothing had been spared the lavish display.

Upstairs, one of the exquisite panelled bedrooms would be *her* bedroom, where *she* would sleep with Dorothy's father. It was too much. She had to escape.

She called Letitia to her side, and going through the French doors at the back, they descended the recently laid steps towards the pool garden. Today even the garden annoyed her. The elaborate stone balustrade was new, as was the statue of Diana, the huntress. With the spaniel at her heels she returned to the old house, more wounded than before. When Letitia barked and ran to the winter sitting room, Dorothy followed her. Molly Johnson was reading there. She looked up from her book and stood uncertainly, but Dorothy made no move. Her pulse pounded in her head and she feared she would faint.

'Miss Dorothy.' Molly nodded, struggling to maintain her composure against the forceful hatred in the other woman's eyes.

'It's you.' They stared at each other a long moment before Dorothy fled through the door, clutching the collar of her dress as if it were choking her.

She found Lorenzo in the coach house brushing Fidelia.

'It's too much,' she sobbed, running towards him, and when he opened his arms to receive her, she fell into them, clinging to him for support.

He kissed her hair, inhaling the delicate scent of rose water, and when she turned her face towards him, he kissed her lips. For a moment they were locked together until she pulled away, her hair falling around her shoulders.

'Can we go home?' she said in a small voice, and he held her in his arms while her tears came.

They rode together in silence, each aware of the proximity of the other. But in coming face to face with Molly, Dorothy had recognized the parallels between her father's love of a servant and her own. It could never be.

As they neared Stratford, she slowed to a halt. 'Goodbye, Lorenzo.' She leant towards him, lifting the veil from her face, and she brushed his lips with her own.

He looked at her for a moment and pulled her towards him. 'Please, Dorothy. I love you.'

'It can never be,' she said gently. 'Don't you see it's impossible?' She could feel the rough wool of his open coat, his warm chest beneath the coarse shirt. The temptation was strong, but she would not become her father.

'You go back,' she said as she pulled away, her face stained with tears. 'I'll ride the rest of the way on my own.' She cantered off, leaving Lorenzo staring after her, his face a mixture of pain and confusion.

That night in bed, she accepted her love for him as a cross she would have to bear. She longed to give herself to him, but she knew that she could not.

CHAPTER THIRTY-ONE

Dorothy dreamt of Lorenzo. She wrote his name on small scraps of paper which she later burnt, but when she heard the Keyt carriage in the courtyard she hid upstairs.

She was distracted from her misery by a young man who came to visit her brother.

'There is a gentleman at the door,' Thomas Whitstone announced, entering the breakfast room early one morning. 'He is here, I believe, at Master Thomas's invitation. His name is Mr Gilbert Paxton-Hooper. Shall I show him in, Miss Dorothy?'

'I'll come out,' she said, putting down her newspaper. She entered the hall, intrigued to see the friend her brother had spoken of so often.

'Forgive me; I hope I'm not too early,' the young man said, bowing.

'Of course not,' she said, looking into his playful eyes. 'My brother has told me all about you. He'll be down in a minute.'

The arrival of Gilbert was just the distraction the household deserved. He was bright and, in the words of her mother, pleasing to the eye. Dorothy liked him; in fact when Gilbert was around, the house changed. There was something appealing in his pale sensitive face. Dorothy liked his smile and the vulnerable expressions that passed fleetingly and were gone. She liked the brown wavy hair, which flopped over the collar of his velvet coat, and though her heart didn't race with anticipation when she saw him, he made her laugh. It was just what she needed.

The first social occasion they attended, a few weeks later, was for Dorothy a thrilling affair. The Lucys were old family friends, and at Thomas's suggestion, Gilbert was included in the invitation. When the coach drew up at Charlecote Park, Dorothy stepped down eagerly; she had a partner socially and intellectually her equal, and from the glances that came his way, he was far from unattractive.

The ball was opened by their host and hostess, who danced a minuet. As the harpsichord started to play, Dorothy gazed at them wistfully. She knew each movement, each pattern their intricate footwork made on the floor, and as they turned and circled, touched hands and separated, she danced each step in her mind. When it was over, Gilbert turned to Dorothy, his eyes amused.

'I can see you're impatient to show off your skills. Will you honour me with the first dance? I am poorly practised but can follow your lead.'

Dorothy laughed happily and allowed him to escort her onto the dance floor for the longways country dance. Thomas and the Lucys' youngest daughter formed the next couple, and as the ten couples faced each other down the line, Dorothy felt the same excitement she always felt when about to dance. She curtsied to her partner, Gilbert bowed, and the dancing began. It started with a rond, a circle to the left and right. Gilbert moved gracefully, and as they worked their way to the top. His hands were precise and his footwork was elegant, and yes, Dorothy decided as she put her hand behind her back for the allemande turn, he was a delightful partner. When the music stopped, they left the dance floor and moved into the library. Thomas settled down to a hand of basset and Dorothy, who had never liked gambling, watched nervously. Fortunately the card game was interrupted by the announcement of supper, and Gilbert took her arm and led her through to the dining room. Thomas sat down on her other side. Throughout supper she was conscious of the magnificent surroundings: the vast table covered in a white damask cloth, the silver candelabra, the porcelain plates embossed with the Lucy crest. After the fish course of the lightest salmon dressed with cucumber and lemon, Thomas leant towards her.

'Well, do you like him, Dotty?' he whispered.

'Of course I do,' she giggled, 'but what about the pretty Lucy girl?' He winked conspiratorially. It would be so easy to marry Gilbert, she thought, as she helped herself to a sweetmeat from a dish in front of her, everyone liked him.

After they had finished, Gilbert took her hand once more. The laughter had gone from his eyes and he was serious. 'Will you dance with me again, Miss Dorothy?'

'I haven't stopped dancing with you; but of course, if you wish.'

'I do wish, quite definitely, like every other man in this room.' And when he led her onto the floor, she knew they were being admired. When the last country dance was over and the small orchestra packed away their instruments, Dorothy turned to her partner.

'Look,' she said, 'we are the last to go. The fiddlers are leaving, the flautist has gone and even the harp is being packed away. It's time to go home.'

Over the following weeks, Thomas, Gilbert and Dorothy were constant companions. When he met Elizabeth, he was attentive towards her, engaging her in conversation, and pushing her mind beyond the parameters of her restricted daily life. Dorothy watched gratefully.

Dorothy's relationship with Gilbert flourished. When Thomas asked his friend to extend his stay, Dorothy was glad. She appreciated his company; she liked challenging herself intellectually. She decided that life as the future Lady Paxton-Hooper could be extremely comfortable. It seemed even her grandmother approved of the relationship: when Lady Tracy summoned them to a ball at Stanway, Gilbert was on the guest list.

Elizabeth, who hadn't been out socially since the accident, at first refused.

'I can't go to a ball,' she said. 'You know it's impossible.'

'But it's family. We'll pick you up on the way; you won't be left alone, not even for a minute,' Dorothy pleaded.

'I wouldn't come in the coach with you,' Elizabeth said finally, 'but I will come. There is, however, a condition attached. Lorenzo, with whom I am familiar, will carry me into the ball, and likewise he will come inside to collect me when I wish to go home.' Dorothy, who hadn't considered this possibility, felt the colour flooding her cheeks. She would have to see Lorenzo. It was unavoidable. For a moment her equilibrium was shattered. She could feel the panic building in her chest.

'Of course, I'll write a note to our grandmother,' she said.

Dorothy needed a dress and she needed it quickly. There were several seamstresses in Stratford, and after finding one willing to undertake the task within the allotted time, she chose a cream organza, with lilac silk for the trimmings.

'I must look beautiful,' she insisted, as the seamstress pinned her into the muslin toile. 'And cut the bodice lower.' Dorothy refused to consider the reason behind her vanity.

On the night of the ball, as The College coachman drove them to Stanway, Dorothy sat quietly. The dress was a work of art – of that there was no doubt. The silk violets encircling the bodice picked up the colour in her eyes, and the wide hooped skirt trimmed with the same violets swayed gently as she moved. Even her hair was for once immaculate, the dark curls tamed and woven with fresh flowers. For the first time in her life Dorothy felt entirely beautiful, but it gave her little satisfaction. She stepped down, her breathing impeded by her restricting bodice and by her own agitation. She would see Lorenzo. Walking up the stairs, she recognized with dismay that her happiness could so easily be destroyed. Why couldn't she forget Lorenzo and be content with the young man at her side?

They were in the packed ballroom when she saw him, carrying Elizabeth. The crowds parted to let them through. Lorenzo lowered Elizabeth into one of the gilded French chairs that had been placed along the walls. Dorothy made her way towards them. 'Hello, Lizzie,' she said. 'Good evening, Lorenzo.'

'Miss Dorothy.' His reply was curt but Dorothy knew that nothing had changed. She sat beside her sister and her mother, refusing to leave them until supper was announced. In deference to Elizabeth a buffet was laid out in the dining room, and Dorothy went to choose for them both. Every kind of creation was displayed on the table. There was venison from the deer park and swan dressed in aspic. There were trifles and jellies and cheeses. After making her selection she returned to the ballroom. Only after they had finished eating and the footman had cleared away their plates did she agree to dance with Gilbert.

Towards the end of the ball her grandmother took her aside. 'You will dance a solo; the *sarabande pour femme* from Lully's *Le Bourgeois Gentilhomme*. I have the music here.'

It was not a question, it was an order, and Dorothy, whose dancing master came on the recommendation and on the generosity of her grandmother, could only comply. She stepped onto the floor and waited for the harpsichord to begin. Normally she would have relished the opportunity to show off the intricate and complicated steps her dance master had taught her, but tonight when the orchestra started to play her mind was elsewhere. When Lorenzo entered the ballroom to collect Elizabeth, Dorothy saw him out of the corner of her eye. She realized she had been waiting for him. She was now dancing for Lorenzo: *coupé*, *pas de courante*, pirouette. The graceful lift of her arms, the lightness of her feet, the tilt of her head, all for Lorenzo. When the harpsichord finally stopped playing and her dance came to an end, she curtsied and raised her eyes. Lorenzo was looking straight towards her. Their eyes met. Moments later he was gone, carrying Elizabeth to the awaiting coach. Elizabeth waved to her sister.

'Goodnight, Dotty; that was wonderful, thank you.'

Dorothy was bereft; the evening was over, and she knew she could never love Gilbert in the way that she loved Lorenzo.

When Gilbert had returned to his house in Surrey, Dorothy was at first relieved; she couldn't marry him, it would be unfair to them both, but during the long winter months these sentiments changed. His letters, full of amusing and eloquent anecdotes, gave her an insight into his life, and how different hers could be, with him. She would be mistress in her own home. On the death of Gilbert's elderly father, she would become Lady Paxton-Hooper. When in the spring of the following year Gilbert returned to The College and declared his intentions, Dorothy accepted his proposal. It was the wise and sensible option. She hoped that marriage to this charming and suitable man would cure the ache in her heart.

Lorenzo, she knew, would not share in her expectations.

CHAPTER THIRTY-TWO

March 1739

Molly sat in the old winter sitting room, her feet tucked beneath her. For all the grandeur of the new mansion, this remained her favourite place. Her cheeks were pink from the fire, and with a book in her hand and the two dogs on the floor beside her, she should have been content. They had moved into their new apartments. She was now, in every sense of the word, mistress of her own home. She had every reason to be happy, but the hatred she had seen in Dorothy's face haunted her.

And something else was wrong, too. The nights Sir William lingered in his dressing room, hunched over the figures – the nights he didn't come to bed at all.

Elizabeth had made an innocent remark: 'Thomas made a property in Stratford over to Papa, something to do with the bank, I believe. Wasn't that considerate? They seem to be getting on well at last.' Molly had worried at the time, a nagging feeling of disquiet that wouldn't go away, and only a few weeks later, she made her own awful discovery.

'I will have a tray in my study,' William said, declining supper. 'Come and say goodnight before you go to bed.'

When Molly knocked there was no answer; she quietly opened the door. William was asleep at his desk, a document spread before him, a pen in his outstretched hand. As she bent to retrieve an empty glass, the words he had been writing caught her eye:

I, Thomas Charles Edward Keyt, convey the remaining third of the house known as 'The College' in Stratford-upon-Avon, to my father, Sir William Keyt, Baronet, as security against the loan on Norton House.

At first it appeared to be another deed, Thomas signing over yet more property to his father, but on closer inspection, the ink on the signature was not yet dry. Sir William was stealing from his son.

CHAPTER THIRTY-THREE

1739

For a short while, William, Elizabeth and Molly lived quietly in their new home. Molly hoped that a peaceful and simple existence would avert calamity, but sadly it didn't last. In late spring plans began for a grand celebration. Magnificent invitations on thick, embossed cards were sent out, and as the day drew nearer Norton buzzed with activity. Additional gardeners were employed, and while they pruned and weeded and filled up the beds, an army of servants polished the house.

Elizabeth went through the menus. Syllabubs were tried and tested on the household, and jellies were set. The blacksmith made a mould in the shape of the new mansion. Extra maids worked in the kitchens. Linen was pressed, silver polished, and glasses rinsed and rinsed again. No expense was spared. There were questions and decisions: would guinea fowl in port wine be appropriate, or stuffed roasted pigeon in pastry, and jellied venison? In the end, it was agreed on both.

'This will be my greatest achievement,' Elizabeth said as she counted the replies. 'I have done so little in my life, but at least now I shall have done this.' Molly could only smile in agreement. Her friend had never understood money, and it was too late to teach her.

That evening, Molly was thinking about Elizabeth's words when William entered the bedroom. He pulled her towards him. 'Darling, will you stay with me if I'm penniless?' To Molly, he sounded like a drowning man.

'What are you saying?'

'I think I may have lost everything. I'm a fool for not sharing this with you before, and now it's too late. I can't tell Elizabeth. She has so little; I only wished to make up for her loss.'

'I'll never leave you, William,' she replied, feeling suddenly defensive of him. 'Never,' she repeated, surprised at the strength of her emotion.

'Come here,' he said, pulling her gratefully towards him and burying his face in her hair. As the sweet scent of jasmine filled his lungs, his misery disappeared, replaced with other sensations. 'Though I like your dress, I'd much prefer you without it,' he said gruffly, his lips moving to her neck.

On the fifth of August, the festivities began with champagne and canapés to the strains of George Frideric Handel's Water Music. As dusk fell, guests were invited to make their way to the theatre. At precisely eight o'clock, five hundred candles were lit in the circular pool, and when the guests were seated, the fountains were turned on, extinguishing the candles with their spray and plunging the pool into darkness. Fireworks lit the sky with blazes of colour. After a short concert, the guests were invited to supper.

The evening was Elizabeth's triumph. The cooks surpassed themselves, and William's cellar was emptied. The jellied sculptures of the new mansion caused a considerable stir, and Elizabeth, dressed in a gown of the palest lavender silk, was showered with compliments. George Cartwright stayed by her side.

Molly could not share in Elizabeth's pleasure. She had expected Thomas, but not the sophisticated Miss Lucy who arrived on his arm. Molly greeted them brightly. She shouldn't care.

Though William was attentive, the guests, for all their pretty smiles and fine words, gossiped. 'So that's his whore?'

'Well, she opened her legs and emptied his purse.'

When the last guest had departed, William lifted his tired, elated daughter into his arms.

'My darling, I hope the evening was everything you wished for?'

'Papa, it has been the happiest evening of my life, thank you – and thank you, Molly, for being my friend.'

Those small words of appreciation drew Molly and William together, and in the dark years that followed they would have cause to remember them again.

CHAPTER THIRTY-FOUR

1740

Spring had just begun, yet Elizabeth didn't have the energy to enjoy it.

'Molly, I am going to stay in bed today. I'll be better tomorrow.' Her pallor and the dark smudges beneath her eyes told otherwise.

'What's wrong with Lizzie? She looks so fragile,' William asked.

'She's tired. For the last three years she has had so much to plan and organize. Sleep is the greatest healer.'

'This is my fault; I can see I asked too much of her.'

Molly touched his arm reassuringly. 'You did nothing of the sort; she loved being part of it all.'

'I pray you are right,' he said.

While Lizzie tried to regain her strength, Letitia became her constant companion.

'I like to have her on the bed. Father won't mind?'

'Are you asking me, or telling me?' Molly smiled.

When she finally asked if Mr Cartwright had called in to see her, Molly resorted to a small lie. 'He's very busy with work on his new project. Your father had word this morning; he'll be in touch soon.'

But in a small community gossip travels fast, and Molly soon heard news of Mr Cartwright.

'I never liked the look of him,' said Ruth. 'He was sucking up to you all, and making sheep's eyes at poor Miss Elizabeth. And now we hear he's engaged.'

Molly was appalled. 'What do you mean? Who is he engaged to?' she asked.

'I've always got my ear to the ground, and Sarah over at Armscote says that he's got hitched to one of the daughters at the big house. Apparently he'll get five hundred pounds. The bugger, I could kill him.'

'Ruth, I'd be grateful if you'd keep this information to yourself.'

As Molly walked back to Elizabeth's bedroom, she realized she could never tell her. If Elizabeth became aware of the engagement, she didn't say, but she never spoke of Mr Cartwright again.

On a hot afternoon in early August, Molly pushed Elizabeth into the wild garden.

When they came to the foot of the oak tree, Elizabeth shut her eyes. 'I wish to imprint every inch of this garden on my mind,' she said, as they reflected on the beauty before them.

'Listen to me, dearest,' she continued, catching Molly's hand. 'My time is running out. Don't turn away, and don't look so sad.' She pulled up her skirts to reveal her poor wasted legs. 'My body will not survive another winter. No, please don't interrupt. You are my friend, and I've grown increasingly fond of you, and I must say this now. I know my father has not always been a gentleman towards you, but I am convinced that he now loves you truly, and I hope that he has made up for his mistakes.'

Molly looked away, tears springing to her eyes. 'So you knew?' she said at last.

'Not at first, though I had my suspicions. But after Mama and Dotty had left, and Papa and I were on our own together, he told me everything. He was so ashamed, and though I did not make it easy for him, I said that one day, hopefully, you would forgive him.'

'Thank you for telling me. I'm glad you know the truth. I would never deliberately hurt you, or your mother, you know.'

'I do, Molly, and you were shamefully wronged. I hope you will forgive us all.'

'You, my dear, have given me only happiness, and your father . . . well, I forgave him a long time ago.'

As summer receded they retreated indoors. Elizabeth kept Miss Byrne's book beside her at all times and wrote continuously. One autumn afternoon, while the rain lashed at the windows, Elizabeth gasped and dropped her pen to the floor.

Molly sprang to her side. 'Elizabeth, what's wrong? What can I do?' She followed her gaze into the desolate windswept garden.

'I have just seen the boy again; he was outside the window, but he's disappeared.' When Molly looked confused, Elizabeth smiled sadly. 'I'm sorry, dearest, of course you don't know about the boy.' Molly remained silent while Elizabeth explained. 'I am not sure if he is real, or a figment of my imagination,' she said finally, 'but I believe he's calling me. I think my time must be coming and he wishes to set me free.'

Molly put her arms around her friend and held her gently.

In mid-October Elizabeth caught a chill; to keep her spirits up, Sir William commissioned the building of the clock tower.

'William, are you mad?' Molly asked, filled with frustration. 'The money is gone.'

'If I wish to indulge my daughter, I shall do so. You would do well to be silent.'

'Do you think this will help her? All she wants is peace. Don't you see, my love, nothing short of a miracle will save her now?'

'For months you have done nothing but nag me. Get out of my sight. I am no longer your love.'

And so Molly devoted herself to Elizabeth. She remained at her bedside and did everything she could to amuse her.

Meanwhile, William turned to God.

'Take my own life,' he prayed, 'but spare my innocent daughter. I am guilty of every crime, but she has done nothing – nothing at all.'

The building of the clock tower continued.

Elizabeth managed to sit in the window for the unveiling. While William and the servants gathered in the courtyard below, the new bell rang its first peal. The servants clapped and turned towards her, and Elizabeth smiled, raising her arm to wave. Even this small gesture exhausted her, and Molly helped her back to bed.

'Molly,' she whispered, 'Papa has tried so hard to make up for my disabilities. I know he has indulged me, and if I'm honest, I have also been a little carried away. But it's all right, isn't it?'

'Of course,' she said, squeezing her hand. 'Your father is a very rich man.'

But as Elizabeth's health declined, so did Molly's relationship with William. He was convinced that the Lord's judgement was upon them and he turned against her. 'It's over. We are being punished. We must repent. Now dry your eyes, for your tears mean nothing.'

'Please don't shut me out,' Molly begged, throwing her arms around him. 'Please don't do this.'

He pushed her away. 'You should know that Lady Keyt, Dorothy and Thomas will be arriving this afternoon. They will stay in their old bedrooms. I think it unlikely that they will wish to see you. I will move into the east wing, but you may remain here if you wish.'

This new coldness astounded Molly; his rejection of everything they had shared. In the eyes of God, and the world, she would always be the mistress, never the wife.

Still, she stayed at Norton, for she could not leave Elizabeth.

CHAPTER THIRTY-FIVE

As the carriage turned into the Norton drive, Lady Keyt caught hold of her daughter's hand. Her normally stoic grey eyes were filled with panic.

'I left here thinking I would never return, and now my choice has been taken from me. I have to be with Elizabeth.'

'Of course you do,' Dorothy said, knowing how much it had cost her mother to return to Norton, even if it was only for a short while. 'We will stay in the old house. Father will be in his new mansion; so don't worry, it's not as if his sleeping quarters are near our own. We'll go home just as soon as Lizzie is better.'

Lady Keyt said nothing and looked out of the window. As they neared the archway, she saw the upper windows of the new mansion rising well above the roof line of her former home. She drew in her breath, noticing the statues and the clock tower with the blue face and gilded hands. 'So much extravagance,' she whispered, wondering at the influence of her former lady's maid.

When the coach drew to a halt, she summoned her courage and stepped down. 'Please God, let this have a happy outcome,' she prayed.

***

At the arrival of her family, Elizabeth rallied. She started plans for their Christmas celebration, but they were abandoned as her temperature rose and her lungs filled with fluid. Sitting by her sister's bed, holding her hot hand, Dorothy heard the ominous rattle in her chest.

Elizabeth's dark lashes fluttered over her sallow skin, and for a moment she opened her eyes. 'Dotty, you will be all right.'

'What do you mean, Lizzie?' Dorothy leant towards her, straining to hear.

'You know, my darling. When I am gone.'

'But you are not going to die. I have prayed so hard, I know God will spare you. You will be well.'

Dorothy laid her head upon her sister's chest and Elizabeth stroked her hair. 'God is not a magician. My time has come and you must let me go. But you will never be on your own. God will always be at your side.'

'I will make you proud of me, Lizzie,' she said. 'I will be a better person, I promise you.'

'I am proud of you already,' she answered. 'How could I not be?'

Dorothy sobbed thick tears full of pain and regret.

Christmas was a dismal affair. Sir William stalked the house, his face unshaven, reminding Dorothy of the last time their house had been in mourning. Lady Keyt remained with her daughter.

Thomas and Dorothy clung together, buoying each other in the uncertain waters.

Molly Johnson remained unseen.

'My relationship with Miss Johnson is over,' Sir William

swore to his family. 'I have sinned and now we are paying the price.'

'William, don't berate yourself; Elizabeth's illness has nothing to do with you. Pray for her, but don't sully her with your guilt,' Lady Keyt replied, and though Dorothy wanted to feel triumphant, somehow she did not.

Five days later, whilst Dorothy sat with her sister, Elizabeth squeezed her hand.

'Dotty, be nice to Molly when I'm gone. Promise me.'

Dorothy looked into the face of her dying sister, and could not deny her.

'Now, please, would you fetch Thomas?'

Running down the stairs, she found him in the library. 'Thomas, come quickly. Lizzie's asking for you.'

They entered the room, dark now, the curtains drawn against the light. Letitia lay on the bed, held close in Elizabeth's arms. 'Thomas, come here,' she whispered. 'I have little time left.'

'Don't say that. It's not true, is it?'

Dorothy turned away.

'This is not the moment for pretence, my dear brother,' she said gently. 'I'm going soon, and our parting must be honest and true. I'm not afraid, for soon I shall be with John.'

'But what will I do without you?' Thomas said, his voice quivering.

Elizabeth coughed, and then whispered urgently, 'Please call Mama and Papa. And I want to see Molly before I go. Thomas, will you get her?'

Dorothy ran from the room with a breaking heart. She found her father in his bedroom.

'You had better come quickly; Lizzie wants you.' They hurried back down the corridor. He sank to the floor beside the bed, the snake ring coiled around his finger. Dorothy stared at its ruby eye with suspicion – sometimes she believed it was evil.

'Lizzie, my darling girl, please do not leave me. I will do anything. Please don't die.'

'Hush, Papa,' she whispered. 'Have no fear, for I am not afraid. You have been the best father that I could have wished for. My only wish is that you will be strong and brave, and help me to the other side.'

She fell back onto to the pillow, lost for breath, and Dorothy left them, running down the stairs, running from the fear of losing her sister.

'Mama!' she screamed hysterically. 'What are you doing? Your daughter is dying!'

Her mother stood in the corridor. 'May God help me,' she replied, her face blanched, her hand fingering the cross at her neck. 'Please, God, give me the strength.'

Elizabeth's family gathered about her. Her passing, like her nature, was gentle. At just before three o'clock she last opened her eyes. 'The joy of parting is knowing that I will see you again,' she whispered as she sank against the pillows. She sighed, and the tension left her body.

Lady Keyt crossed herself and closed Elizabeth's eyelids for the last time. 'My beautiful child,' she moaned, rocking to and fro. Thomas fled the room, banging the door behind him, while Dorothy put her cheek against her sister's silent chest and wept.

When Sir William lifted his head, his eyes were dull and uncomprehending. 'Molly will make her better,' he said.

Appalled by her father, Dorothy ran from the room. As she opened the door to the gardens, the harsh wind knocked the breath from her, but she had to find her brother.

'Thomas!' she cried. 'Where are you?' She ran through the rose garden, under the archway, towards the wild garden. Then she heard his voice.

'Forgive me, Molly, but she's gone. Elizabeth died.'

She saw her then, Molly's arms beating upon her brother's chest.

'You didn't call me! I didn't get to say goodbye!'

'Forgive me, Molly. Please forgive me.' His lips were buried in her hair; his hands squeezed her shoulders. Dorothy stared, mesmerized at the tableau before her, and as Molly raised her face to Thomas's she turned up the stony path.

As she ran towards the gate, she tripped. She fell to the ground and let out a wail of rage and jealousy, her promise to her sister quite forgotten.

CHAPTER THIRTY-SIX

They buried Elizabeth during a blizzard, two days before Dorothy's twenty-second birthday.

White flakes settled on the coffin, obscuring her sister's name.

'Do something,' Lady Keyt said, frantically brushing the lid. 'It will cover the coffin.'

'Leave it, Mama.' Thomas took her hand. 'Lizzie won't mind; you know how she loved the snow.'

Lady Keyt sank against his chest and sobbed.

Dorothy hid her face in her shawl. She thought of her sister, flawless in death. At the service's end she placed a white Christmas rose upon the lid of the coffin. 'Goodbye, my darling. May you be free at last.'

The snow fell heavily, swirling around the gravestones until Dorothy could hardly see. She was aware of her family walking out of the church – her father, her brother, her poor mother who had lost three children – and yet she felt separate from their grief. She remembered only the circle of lilies and the white organza dress; she remembered only the coldness of her sister's hands.

Dorothy thought she glimpsed Molly Johnson at the lychgate, a dark figure swathed in a cloak, but when she looked again she saw only white.

After the funeral, while the rest of the family returned to the new mansion, Dorothy retreated to her old home. She found Letitia, cowering by her sister's chair. She looked up at her mournfully, and as Dorothy ran her hands through the dull coat, she felt the tiny bones protruding from her back.

'Poor little dog,' she whispered. 'You miss her as much as we do.' Miss Byrne's book lay upon the table. Picking it up, she remembered the last lines from her favourite sonnet: *So long as men can breathe or eyes can see, So long lives this and this gives life to thee*. Her sister would live on through this book.

She sat down in her chair and joined Elizabeth on her journey; she learnt of her pride in the new house, and of the love that had grown for her father. She learnt of her forgiveness of his mistress, and the friendship that had grown between them. She took Dorothy into the world of her imagination, the boy in the garden, his short hair and outlandish clothes. She recorded finally her desire for peace. 'God will take me soon, and I will be in his garden for ever.'

In front of Dorothy were her sister's fears and her triumphs, her suffering and her pleasures, and as dusk fell and the shadows lengthened, she felt her sister's life surround her.

When she could no longer see, Dorothy lit a candle and took up her pen. She resolved to continue Lizzie's work, and with a trembling hand she began to write.

Dorothy was putting on her bonnet, getting ready to go back to Stratford, when she heard a woman's sobs coming from Elizabeth's bedroom. She opened the door anxiously, expecting to see her mother, but Ruth stood there, a ragged sketchbook clasped against her chest.

The curtains had been thrown open, and sunlight shafted through the windows. A little vase of flowers was on the table by her bed, and the room smelt fresh and clean. Miss Johnson had found a way of showing her respects.

'What's happened, Ruth? Whatever it is, it is best to tell me. I won't be cross.'

'Nothing's happened, miss. She wanted me to burn it. But I just can't, it wouldn't be right.'

'Who wanted you to burn what?'

'Miss Elizabeth. Her sketchbook – I couldn't do it.' She passed the worn book to Dorothy. 'She gave it to me just before she died. She told me not to look at it and just to burn it, so I haven't, but I simply couldn't destroy it.'

'Thank you, Ruth. I'd like to be on my own for a moment, if you wouldn't mind.'

Ruth wiped her eyes and nodded. When she had shut the door behind her, Dorothy turned the book over in her hands. She recognized it; she had seen her sister working in it, even if she had not seen the results. She opened the cover and recoiled. Nothing could have prepared her: in the tattered pages, with the stark brutality of a nightmare, were her sister's private sketches.

Haunted faces with hollowed cheeks stared, begging her for something, she didn't know what. Stick figures in cages, cadavers in chains, birds with their wings clipped together. Text accompanied some of the drawings, but not in her sister's usual metered hand – the black charcoal scrawled across the page with restless urgency.

Dorothy felt dizzy. She dropped the sketchbook to her sister's bed and fell against the wall. As the room swirled around her, she moaned. Her sister had suffered in silence. Even in Miss Byrne's book she had hidden the truth. Her mother had told her of her sister's suffering, but her jealousy of Molly had blinded Dorothy to all else.

She staggered to the fireplace. She would burn it as her sister had wanted. No one should see this torment. Putting a taper to the fire she watched the flames grow. She had only to open her fingers, let the book fall from her hands, but she couldn't let go. Filled with panic, she ran from the room, carrying it in front of her.

She climbed the stairs to the attic, to Miss Byrne's room, now Molly's. Seeing it empty, she slipped inside. Blue and white china mugs lined the windowsill, and pictures hung on the wall. Some were Elizabeth's sketches of Norton's flowers and birds. Had Molly known the truth?

She sank to her knees and lifted the rug. Opening the boards she found the split in the joists beneath. It was just long enough and wide enough. Dropping the pad, she watched it slip down. No one would find it. No one would ever see it. It would be safe in its hiding place. Standing up, she replaced the rug.

She didn't hear the footsteps, or the door opening.

'Why are you in my room?'

Dorothy spun round. She couldn't think of anything to say.

'As long as I'm in this house, this is my bedroom, and I'd thank you to get out of it.'

'From what my father says, it sounds as if it won't be your bedroom for long,' Dorothy replied.

'That still doesn't answer my question. What were you doing poking around in my things?'

'Your things? Ha! Half of these clothes are my mother's or my sister's. You came here with nothing; everything you have has been cheated from us!'

Molly advanced until they stood eye to eye. 'You're a mean, spoilt girl. You spend your whole life thinking about yourself, and how someone or something is cheating you. My God, to think you are Elizabeth's sister – it doesn't seem possible. I warn you, years of hard work have made me strong, and if you don't get out this minute, I'll have no choice but to pick you up and throw you out.'

'You're a cheap and common whore, and I hate you, and all that you've done to this family!' Dorothy screamed, backing to the door. She slammed it behind her and ran downstairs to the carriage.

Her mother was waiting; Lorenzo was on the box. He got down and opened the door, but kept his face turned away from her. Throwing herself onto the velvet seats Dorothy bit her lip in an effort to control her emotions. As the coach drew under the archway a solitary tear escaped down her cheek.

CHAPTER THIRTY-SEVEN

January 1741

Three weeks after Elizabeth died, Molly and Ruth sat, doing the mending. Norton had already become a house of ghosts. The servants moved through the rooms silent and unseen, and Molly slipped in and out of the shadows, careful to avoid both William and his son.

Her conscience plagued her. The kiss should never have happened, but she relived every moment. She was miles away when Ruth brought her back to the present with an admiring glance at her work.

'Start a dressmaker's shop, love; you are gifted at stitching. I gave my mam the kerchief you made, and she won't blow her nose on it. Too precious, she says.'

Dear Ruth, with her simplistic ideas. A shop needed money. Molly needed money.

Ruth sighed. 'There's no reason you should stay. It's not like it used to be, is it, love? And with poor Letitia gone, God rest her soul, Master Thomas won't be here for long. Who can blame him – there's naught to hold him in this gloomy house.'

Molly dropped her work, barely managing to keep her composure before fleeing to the library.

Leaving the door ajar, she wandered aimlessly from shelf to shelf, running her finger along the leather spines. She read the titles hoping they would distract her; she could remember only too well the morning she had seen Thomas carrying Letitia's body in his arms. She had not meant to witness his private grief, but now the image of his despairing face haunted her.

'Molly! I was looking for you.' She looked up, startled. Thomas was in the doorway. 'I hope you don't mind; I saw you run down the hall. Don't look frightened, I just want to talk.'

'You mustn't, sir. What we did was wrong. You know that as well as I.'

'I understand. But don't go, please.' His face looked pale and his eyes strained. 'I want to show you something. I promise it has nothing to do with us, or what happened between us.'

He moved to the shelves and pulled down two heavy leather volumes, opening them on the large library table. 'I found these books after the funeral; they must have belonged to my grandfather. You may find them interesting. These are the Oxford colleges, Christ Church, Queen's.' He pointed to the black and white engravings. 'But this one,' he said proudly, 'is University College, my college, possibly the oldest and finest of them all.'

'You are lucky to be in a place like that. I always wanted an education. Lizzie taught me to read. Did she tell you?'

'She did,' he said. 'Perhaps now you have read the letters I sent you.'

'I never received any letters,' she replied.

'But I wrote to you several times.'

'The only thing I have is this poem.' She pulled the crumpled piece of paper from her pocket and held out her hand.

Thomas took it from her and opened it, his eyes widening in amazement. 'You kept it for all these years?'

'Of course I kept it. You gave it to me, and I don't know what happened to your letters – they must have been mislaid. But please, too much has happened. Too much hurt. Let's not create any more.'

'I know, Molly. But I must ask you this: how could you have gone with my father?'

'Because you were lost to me. I was at home in my father's house, emptying the slops and cleaning the fires, and Sir William wanted me back. He gave me a way out. What else could I do?'

'Oh, Molly,' he sighed. 'The fates are against us.' He moved towards her, and then he seemed to think better of it. He handed the poem back to her, and shaking his head, he left the library, closing the door quietly behind him.

Several hours later Molly was in the stillroom, her place of refuge. She took a bottle of rose oil from the shelf and opened the stopper. The sweet aroma reminded her of Elizabeth.

In the midst of her thoughts, the door opened and Thomas entered. 'I'm sorry, I am intruding again, but I always seem to be looking for you.'

'What are doing here, sir?'

'I have to see you before I leave tomorrow. Will you meet me in the temple at eleven o'clock? I beg of you, please be there.'

'What's wrong with here? We can talk now.'

'No. Not now. I want to be on my own with you, even if it's for five minutes.'

'You know that's impossible,' she said, but after he had gone, she leant against the wall, her mouth dry, her heart pounding.

That night, she took a shawl from the peg in the hall and made her way to the wild garden. In the cold evening air she could hear wildlife moving in the undergrowth. She sat down on the stone bench and shivered. A film of ice covered the pool. Staring at it, she tried to justify her longing, but she found no answer. Pulling her woollen shawl close around her shoulders, she stood up and walked towards the upper garden. Twice she turned back and twice she changed her mind.

She climbed the stairs and headed towards the temple; there the marble bust of Elizabeth, white and pure in the moonlight, seemed to glare in disappointment. She looked away and continued up the path. As she hurried through the door, the heat from the fire hit her. Thomas was standing by his sister's old easel. Molly noticed the half-finished watercolour. She turned the picture towards the wall.

Thomas touched her cheek. 'It's all right, my darling.' When she looked into his eyes and felt the warmth of his body, she believed him.

He kissed her gently, and then kissed her again, a deep ardent kiss, seeking to merge their souls. He cupped her thick chestnut hair, burying his face in her neck, breathing the heady sweet scent of her. He whispered her name, running his hand over her chest until Molly was lost to a desire such as she had never known in all of the nights with his father. She pulled at the buttons on his shirt and pushed her sleeves from her shoulders so that her naked breasts could press against his skin.

Her nipples crushed against him as a wave of need coursed through her. There was no time for caresses, for she wanted him to fill her. They ripped and tore until his clothes lay on the floor, her dress beside it, and as he entered her she cried out with relief. An urgent feeling possessed her; she thrust against him as he touched her more deeply. As he groaned her name and collapsed onto her she felt a great shuddering within her, the force so immense that she too fell back, satisfied as she had never been before.

As dawn broke they ran through the gardens, reckless after their night together.

'Molly Johnson belongs to me!' Thomas shouted to the sky. 'She is mine at last!'

Sir William woke from a drunken slumber and stumbled out of his study. 'Who's there?' he yelled. 'This is private property. I have a gun. Show yourself now!'

They stopped. Sophie ran towards them, barking, her tail wagging. 'Thomas, is that you? Oh my God, don't let it be Molly?'

As she shrank against Thomas, their terrible deception overwhelmed her. Staggering towards them, gun in hand, William reached the top of the steps. 'You whore. You disloyal ingrates! I'll kill you. I'll kill you both!'

'Father, for God's sake, don't.' Thomas held out his hand. 'Give me the gun.'

Molly stared at the barrel. 'Please,' she begged. 'This is all my fault.'

The gun discharged as Sir William stumbled on the top step and fell towards them. The shot rang through the air, shattering the bow on the statue of Diana the huntress; her arm lay in pieces on the ground. William lay beside it.

'We're all right, my love.' Thomas moved to embrace her, but in her terror she pushed him away.

'No, it's not all right. It's over. We'll pay for this.'

'Molly, don't say that. We will leave this place. I'll look after you.'

As she knelt beside Sir William and touched his unconscious brow, Molly's course was clear. 'Do you not see? I am a whore, just as your father said.'

'That is not true. I wanted you first. He took you from me.'

'I belong to no one. My past has destroyed any chance of our happiness.'

Thomas's eyes narrowed. 'Did last night mean so little to you?' he asked.

'It meant everything to me, but what would your family say? You would be cast out. We could never make a life together.'

'Never mind them. Is my love not enough for you?'

'We could never manage on love alone.' She avoided Thomas's eyes, knowing she would have to leave Norton once more.

CHAPTER THIRTY-EIGHT

Stumbling down the drive, Molly relived each moment of her night with Thomas. She thought of his breath upon her neck, his lips upon her brow. When he had touched her body, she had arched towards him, pleading that he take her, and afterwards, when they lay together, their bodies naked and spent, he had stroked her back, running his fingertips across her flushed skin.

'This is the beginning. There will be a thousand nights. You and I are meant to be together.' Now the memory of his hands would have to last a lifetime, his kiss upon her lips, for ever.

At the end of the drive Molly leant against a tree, her knees sagging with shock and despair as she considered her options. She had no money and only the clothes that she was wearing. The signpost pointed in two directions, Oxford to the right and Stratford to the left. After a moment's deliberation she chose the latter.

She had ridden this road in William's carriage. As she walked it now, every pothole seemed to claim her. Finally she heard a cart slowing. 'Can I take you somewhere, miss? I am going to market.'

She was in no position to turn down any offer of help. 'Thank you, sir. That would be kind.'

For the next two hours, she endured the man's foul smell and lewd conversation. When they arrived at Clopton Bridge, she stepped down with relief.

'Well, miss, if you ever fancy a jar of ale with an honest farmer, Pargetter from Mickleton, that's my name.'

'Thank you, I'll remember.' She headed off towards the centre of the market town, with the sole purpose of finding work and a roof for her head.

It was Friday, the busiest day; stalls of every description crammed against each other in the cobbled streets. Chickens in small cages clucked next to slaughtered carcasses and a rainbow of vegetables. Once she would have lingered amongst the ribbons and fabrics, but she couldn't spare the time. The coaching inns seemed her best option; they always needed serving girls. But when the White Swan and the Falcon turned her away, her confidence faltered. By the time she returned to the river she had been rebuffed from nearly every public house in Stratford.

She sat down outside the door of the Black Swan, but she couldn't muster the energy to face another rejection. Resting her head on her arms, she fell asleep.

'So! What have we here?'

Molly woke with a start, but she relaxed when she saw the amused face of the tallest man she had seen. 'Good afternoon, sir.'

'What are you doing outside my pub on a day like this?' he asked, wiping his huge hands on his leather apron. 'You could freeze to death, you could.'

'I'm looking for work, sir. I'll do anything.'

He raised a brow sceptically. 'Can you clean? Your hands don't look like a maid's hands.'

'Yes, sir, I can clean and serve. I've many years' experience, and I'm a hard worker.'

'Well, then. I'll give you ten shillings a month, and board and lodging. A word of warning: my wife, Mrs Quick, doesn't like lookers, so any trouble with the lads and you'll be out with the milk cans.'

Molly had never feared hard work. Soon she was serving the customers, swilling the floors, lifting the barrels and falling into bed, only to get up the next day and do the same. Such drudgery paid only in exhaustion. She was too tired to think, too tired to remember, and that brought her a kind of peace.

She accepted abuse from Mrs Quick because she believed that she deserved it.

'Where do you come from, landing on our step like a stray dog? I don't know what my husband was thinking. I don't trust stray dogs, you remember that.'

In the sixth week of her employment, while scrubbing the pantry shelves, the room began to spin. Putting out her hand to steady herself, she knocked the cream jug to the floor. She retched as the thick liquid spread over the stone slabs.

Mrs Quick was as good as her name. 'What's going on? I always knew you were trouble. Clear up this disgusting mess and get on with your work. Any slacking and you're out. And if there is a baby in your belly, you can pack your belongings and be off.'

Molly wiped her mouth on her soiled pinafore. It had never

occurred to her that she might be with child. In those precious hours with Thomas, she had taken no precautions.

Over the next few weeks she struggled to handle her workload. The nausea came regularly. It was difficult to escape the sharp eyes of her employer. In the twelfth week the sickness disappeared.

At night, lying on a straw mattress in the stuffy attic, she examined her options. When her belly became too noticeable she would have to leave. Though she longed for her mother, she could not return to the Charter House; her father would kill her before she reached the door. She faced a stark choice: either she could trust her child to the dubious care of the parish or she could enter the workhouse.

On a busy market day in late June when the public rooms were filled to capacity, Molly recognized one voice above all the others.

'Girl! Table, near the door – hurry! Can't you see I have baskets upon my arm?'

Molly turned, but it was too late.

'Good Lord,' said Mrs Wright, 'if it isn't Molly Johnson.' She stood in front of her, her incisive eyes sweeping Molly's body. 'Have we outlived our master's pleasure, or is there another reason? I think perhaps there is. Excuse me, miss, but I no longer need refreshment.'

She swept out triumphantly, and Molly felt her heart sink to the floor.

CHAPTER THIRTY-NINE

June 1741

Dorothy sat at her desk, gazing at the river. She imagined lying in one of the small boats, trailing her hand in the cool water, or strolling along the river bank amongst the parasols, picnics, and laughter. Instead she sat alone.

She was distracted from her self-pity by an insistent knock on the door. 'Come in,' she said, putting her untouched papers aside.

Mrs Wright entered. Sweat balled on her upper lip, and Dorothy could see that she was excited.

'Yes, Mrs Wright?'

'Forgive me, Miss Dorothy, but I have to impart news of extreme importance.'

'Go on,' she said impatiently, for she neither liked Mrs Wright and her affected speech, nor trusted her. 'What is it that you have to say?'

'Well, miss, I was doing the week's purchase in the market. It was that busy in the centre, so I went to the stalls down by the river – Mr Higgs, to be precise, very good meat, very tender—'

'Mrs Wright. Please get to the point.'

'Sorry, miss. I stopped at a hostelry on my way home to

obtain a glass of stout, not my usual route, you understand, and on entering the Black Swan, I ventured to a table. Before I had time to remove my bonnet, I recognized a certain person serving.'

'Yes?'

'It was none other than Molly Johnson. I was too distracted to stay, so I made my excuses and left.'

By the smirk on her face, Dorothy could see that Mrs Wright was saving the most salacious piece of information for last.

'What else, Mrs Wright?'

'She was pregnant, Miss Dorothy! Her belly was big with child.'

Dorothy's stomach dropped. 'Mrs Wright, you may go. You will keep this information to yourself. If I catch one member of this household gossiping, and it reaches my mother's ears, I will hold you responsible. Is that understood?'

'Of course, miss,' she replied. 'If that's what you wish.' From the frustration in her tone, it was obvious to Dorothy that she had denied Mrs Wright hours of pleasure.

She remained at her desk long after Mrs Wright had gone. The question hammered in her brain: who did the bastard child belong to, her father or her brother?

For two days Dorothy debated her course of action, and by the third morning she had decided. She dressed with care, putting on a lavender silk dress. Deciding it too frivolous, she took it off again, selecting a navy dress with a white lace collar and a small hat. These struck just the right note, for today she needed her clothes to reflect her authority. She hurried down the street, and because The College was only a short distance from the town centre, it took her just a few minutes to reach the Black Swan. She stopped outside, took a deep breath, walked up the steps and pushed open the door. It was ten o'clock and the parlour was still empty. A young girl polished the tables. 'Can I help you, miss?'

'Yes. Is Miss Johnson available?'

'She's in the kitchen, but I will fetch her for you.'

Minutes later Molly Johnson entered the room. She looked at Dorothy, and Dorothy had the pleasure of seeing her discomfort. The colour rose in Molly's cheeks. Neither of them spoke.

'So it is true,' she said, eyeing Molly's increased girth.

Molly's eyes darted around the room and she gestured to a table in the corner. 'Do you want to sit down, Miss Dorothy?' she asked.

Dorothy sat down and nodded for Molly to join her. 'Miss Johnson, I am not here to discuss particulars, but to offer you a solution to your predicament. Do you have private funds?'

'No, Miss Dorothy,' she replied, 'I have nothing.' Her eyes dropped sadly to her swollen waist, but Dorothy's loathing far exceeded any feeling of charity.

'Listen. I have a little money of my own and I am prepared to use it for the protection of my family. I will secure the safe delivery of this child in return for the assurance that you will never contact my brother or any of my family again.'

'What are you suggesting?'

Dorothy outlined a plan, simple in itself, but one supported by a web of deceit. 'A gentleman of my acquaintance, one Captain Thomas Coram, owes my mother a debt of gratitude. Some weeks ago, he opened his temporary foundling home in

London, for unwanted and abandoned children. He is prepared to take your baby.'

'I don't want my child to go to a home.'

'Do you have another option? If you do this, you will be giving your child a future. My mother, amongst others, campaigned tirelessly for Captain Coram. With their help his petition to the king was successful.' Dorothy smoothed the wrinkles from her gloves. 'At Captain Coram's hospital, your child will be trained – for the army or the navy, if you have a boy, and domestic service if it's a girl. Both are perfectly respectable professions.'

Molly shook her head. 'I have no wish to give up my child.'

'What will you do? With no money, you will go to the workhouse. Perhaps if you stay in Stratford, the parish will care for you. You and I both know what that means. Either way, your baby will have little or no chance of survival. What I am offering you is an opportunity for yourself and for your unborn child.' Dorothy did not relish her moment as much as she had expected.

'Does Lady Keyt know about this?'

Dorothy hesitated. 'Of course,' she replied. 'She considers it the only wise and sensible option.' It was only a small lie, but in her heart she knew her mother would not have condoned it. The child was, after all, a Keyt.

'I can't give up my baby.'

'Very well then, you must take your chances.'

'How can you ask this of me?'

'Because I want you out of our lives. You have caused injury to my family. With that child in your arms, we will never be free of your demands.' Molly opened her mouth to protest but Dorothy stopped her. 'Let me continue,' she said. 'In order to secure your promise, a settlement of seventy-five pounds will be given to you once the baby is handed over to the Foundling Hospital.'

'How will I know that my child will be safe?'

Dorothy thought back to John and the accident, and fought down a pang of sympathy for Molly. 'How can we know anything in life? I can only assure you the baby will have a home; Captain Coram has given me his word.'

Molly did not respond, so Dorothy continued, 'I will give you an allowance for your living expenses in London. I have five sovereigns in my purse, and a letter for the attention of my solicitor Mr Skarm. He will be your point of contact. He will pay you monthly, and after the infant is handed over, he will give you the final sum of money. I repeat, there will be no contact with my family.' She rose, taking the purse from her pocket. 'Will you take this opportunity or not, Miss Johnson?'

Molly nodded slowly. Dorothy's victory gave her little satisfaction.

'A final question: do you know the rightful parentage of this child?'

Molly looked at her defiantly. 'It is your brother's,' she said, and Dorothy hated her once more.

As Dorothy vanished into the throng, Molly sat, defeated. She watched the tilt of Dorothy's feathered hat and the assurance in her carriage. She had stood no chance.

Money, it seemed, could buy everything after all.

Despite her humiliation, Molly recognized that she had been thrown a lifeline. She would go to London. Her only contact with her previous life would be through an unknown solicitor. Wiping her eyes, she returned to her room to pack her meagre belongings.

'Miss Johnson, what are you doing upstairs? Come down this instant and get back to work.'

Molly grabbed her bag and met Mrs Quick on the stairs. 'Thank you for your generosity,' she said, determined to act with dignity. 'I am grateful; however, I have been offered a better position, and I am obliged to leave your service immediately.'

For a moment Mrs Quick was speechless, and Molly delighted in her small victory.

'Be gone then, you ungrateful bitch. Get out before I throw you out.'

CHAPTER FORTY

Late June 1741

Dorothy reached home, believing her objective accomplished, only to find two representatives had arrived from the bank to see her mother. When she joined them in the library, she realized regretfully that nothing was so simple.

'I'm sorry, milady.' The senior clerk cleared his throat as he addressed her mother. 'This is most difficult. It seems that your husband has mortgaged and remortgaged The College in order to raise money on his new mansion. The equity has gone. Unless you are able to find alternative funding, The College will have to be sold.'

'Sir, there must be some mistake?' she asked.

'I apologize, madam. There is no mistake.'

Lady Keyt's hands flew to her throat. Dorothy remembered her making the same gesture just before the carriage accident, all those years ago. 'How can this be?' said Lady Keyt. 'My son Thomas owns most of this property.'

'I believe your son has signed his inheritance away,' he replied.

Dorothy stepped in front of her mother. 'Please leave, sirs,' she demanded. 'I need some time to speak with my mother'. The men withdrew and she took her mother's hand.

'Oh, dear,' Lady Keyt said at last. 'My poor Dotty! What about your wedding?'

'It's not just my wedding. It's everything: our home, our future.' She paced the room. 'Have you no money of your own, Mother? What about your savings and the various properties you own in Stratford? What about the Tracy inheritance?'

Lady Keyt shook her head helplessly. 'I have never been very good with money; I suppose I never had to be. I'm not sure what I have.'

Over the next few days Thomas was called back from university. After assuring his mother that their downfall was not due to his actions, they then discovered the awful truth: Sir William had dishonestly squandered their fortune in order to pay for his folly. After meetings with financial advisors, Lady Keyt realized that her savings would not cover her husband's debts, and any property she might have once owned had gone the way of everything else.

With sickening clarity, Dorothy understood that their new life in Stratford-upon-Avon was already nearing its end.

Her mother would suffer most. In six months' time, Dorothy would be married and beginning a new life in Surrey. Her mother would be on her own, their home would be sold and her school would be closed. If Dorothy had any feelings of guilt over her treatment of Miss Johnson, the losses she suffered now far outweighed them.

Within days the house was put up for sale, and the agent made an appointment to see them. He told them of a distant relation, a certain James Kendall, a Member of Parliament and a gentleman of considerable wealth. He had apparently admired the property and was interested in buying it.

'I have never heard of Mr Kendall,' Lady Keyt replied. 'He is no relation of mine, but he may be of my husband's; however, if he must see our house, then so be it.'

For half an hour Mr Kendall walked through The College with strides of ownership and self-importance. Much against the wishes of Dorothy and her mother, he made and had his offer accepted. They were to move by the end of the following month

The thought of being near her father filled Dorothy with dismay, but it seemed Hidcote, a small manor on the Norton estate, was their only option. Again they packed up their lives.

Miss Byrne's book remained Dorothy's consolation. The imaginative stories still had the power to distract her, and she continued to lose herself in their magic. After she had read them, following the hand of her sister, she took up her pen.

CHAPTER FORTY-ONE

July 1741

Shortly before one o'clock, the coach left the Swan's Nest Inn in Stratford-upon-Avon.

Molly assessed the other occupants: a country parson and his plump wife, a governess in a black starched dress, and a young clerk.

'I've brought provisions,' the parson's wife offered kindly. 'Let me know if you're hungry.' Molly smiled and thanked them, but the governess avoided her eyes, staring resolutely out of the window.

After a few miles the clerk tried to engage her in conversation. 'Are you on a long journey?' he asked.

'Yes,' she replied. 'I'm to London to meet my husband.' She had no patience for young men and their flattery.

The horses were changed at Chipping Norton, and at just before midnight they arrived at the Angel on the High Street in Oxford. She retired immediately to bed. When she stepped outside the following morning, she was shocked by the traffic. Carriages, stagecoaches, men on horseback and pedestrians filled the streets. There were shops and street markets, stables and coaching inns, and not least the colleges.

Of course her thoughts were of Thomas. She remembered

him leaning over her in the library, the engravings open on the table in front of him.

At nine o'clock she climbed into the coach once more. They were crossing Magdalen Bridge when the sky opened into a violent summer storm. With thunder and lightning crashing around them, the startled horses refused to move.

'It's no use,' the coachman said, climbing down. 'If you're in a hurry, try the Mitre or the Greyhound in Longwall Street. The Flying Coach might leave, but my horses aren't going anywhere. You can walk back to the Angel or wait till it's done.' Climbing back onto the box he erected an oilcloth and huddled inside, leaving his passengers to decide for themselves.

Molly listened to the deluge subside, then tied on her bonnet and ventured out. She found University College easily. From the entrance lodge she could see into the quadrangle beyond. Now she could truly imagine Thomas going about his day.

On her return to the coach, the journey resumed immediately. She had just settled into the motion of the carriage when she saw Thomas from the window. In his beauty and casual elegance he stood out amongst his peers. He walked with a new confidence, and though her heart leapt, she felt the depth of the gulf between them. Still she put up her hand to wave.

He didn't see her at first, but when the coach passed him he stopped. For a second there was confusion in his eyes. Then he laughed in disbelief and jogged to catch up with his friends.

After what seemed an endless journey through unfamiliar countryside and impossible roads, the coach finally reached

London. It was early afternoon on the fourth day, and Molly had her first glimpse of the city. Oxford was a village by comparison.

A young attorney, Robin Hart, had joined the coach at its previous stop and proved a useful guide. He pulled down the window as they neared the city's centre and pointed to Tyburn, the infamous Triple Tree, where public hangings were held. 'The children are the biggest draw,' he said. 'And on those days the crowds are enormous. The rich book their seats in advance.'

'That's quite enough,' Molly said.

'Have mercy on their souls,' the vicar's wife whispered, clutching her husband's arm. Leaving Tyburn they saw the new tree-lined avenues, squares and gardens that were replacing the buildings destroyed in the Great Fire. He showed them Grosvenor Square, where most of the nobility of London owned houses. As Molly leant from the window, she felt the energy of the city. Builders and stonemasons swarmed over half-built houses, and gardens were laid out where once there had been fields. Flower girls, boot-black boys and milk girls all traded in the crowded streets.

'Watch the milk girls; they skim the milk, adding chalk and dirty water,' he told Molly.

'Thank you. I'll remember that,' she replied, concerned for the baby growing inside her.

Highly decorated sedan chairs wove through the traffic, and grand carriages bowled along the streets impervious to pedestrians. At Tottenham Court Road, they stopped. Molly had reached her destination.

It was easy to get lost in a city where the houses converged on the first floor and sewage swamped the gutters. It was easy to pity the children who ran through the waste in tattered rags. But Molly could not afford distraction. According to her instructions she headed east, and when she came to the bottom of Chancery Lane, she crossed Temple Bar to her final destination.

'Please, can you direct me to number nine Pump Court?' she asked the porter.

'Yes, miss. Follow me.'

In a matter of minutes, she was standing inside the private rooms of the solicitor engaged by Dorothy. Mr Skarm confirmed the details of the arrangements. She would receive money every month for the next three months. Once the baby had arrived and was safely installed in the Foundling Hospital, she would receive the final settlement.

'The living expenses provided are not large, Miss Johnson; I suggest you find a temporary position to supplement your income. For your confinement, a midwife will be arranged.'

As she listened to Mr Skarm, Molly reflected that this new life had been determined for her by Dorothy Keyt. Once again she was bought and sold.

Mr Skarm stood, signalling the meeting's end. 'Oh, one more thing, Miss Johnson. The temporary hospital has opened in Hatton Garden. You may consider it beneficial to present yourself to Captain Coram before the birth. My clerk will show you out.'

She took a room in the Old Cock Tavern on Fleet Street, a narrow, half-timbered Tudor building with leaded windows and crooked walls. She ate in the public rooms and listened to the conversations around her. Regional dialects mingled with strange accents, coming from seamen and tailors, silk weavers and patten makers, all with tales of hardship and fortitude. When she had finished her meal, she climbed the twisting stairs to her room. Standing at the window, she saw London spread out before her. The city enhanced her isolation; she had never felt so alone.

At that moment, even the thought of the child growing inside her could not sustain her. Taking her cloak she went back down the stairs and into the streets. The open air was a relief; even the vile-smelling streets were better than being cooped up inside. She was aware of the risk, but she no longer cared. Within minutes she was lost in a maze of alleys, surrounded by filth and degradation. Beggars accosted her, children followed her. She tried to turn back, but exhaustion blinded her, and one foul gutter ran into the next.

'Miss, spare a penny for a blind child?' She turned to find a small boy tugging at her sleeve. His tattered clothes hung from his body, and his face was covered with sores. Looking in her pocket, she took out her purse. 'Buy yourself some food,' she said, pressing a coin into his hand. Before she'd put the purse away she was surrounded. Boys of all ages charged towards her. Pushing her to the ground they grabbed her purse and ran off. Molly remained on her knees in the gutter. She could hear their laughter as they disappeared into the dark, polluted alleys. When she struggled to her feet, she smelt urine on her dress.

Molly ran, but she had nowhere to go; she had no money, she had nothing. Sinking down in a doorway she covered her head with her hands and wept. She slept there, and as dawn broke, with her filthy dress and dishevelled hair, she looked no different from any pauper begging on the streets. When a man tossed her a penny, she looked up dully. Then she thanked him and tucked it in her pocket.

She drank water from the spout, and when the hunger gnawed her belly, she used her penny to buy some bread. Her child turned inside her; she worried, would it be enough?

I must get back, she thought, heading down an alley that led into another that looked just the same. Ten minutes later she was back where she started. Crying with frustration, she asked a passer-by how she could get to the Old Cock. He looked her up and down and offered her a shilling for her services. Mortified, she hurried on.

She noticed three balls hanging above a doorway. She entered the pawn shop and waited while an old man came to the counter. 'Selling or buying?' he asked, his wrinkled face smiling.

'I've nothing to sell, sir,' she replied. 'I've lost my way, and I need to find the Strand.'

'You've ended up in the wrong place, but everyone gets lost here.'

Following his directions carefully, she left the last alley behind her. As she broke out of the darkness, she found herself in a wide street with shops and coffee houses. When she arrived at the Old Cock Tavern, her bag was in the store.

'So you're back,' the landlord said, eyeing her suspiciously. 'There's a pump outside. You can change in the privy, but you won't get the bag back until the bill is paid.'

Molly waited in the hall of the solicitor's offices. When Mr Skarm called her in, she explained her predicament and asked for his assistance. He listened with patience. 'I will give you an advance, but you will have to earn it. My wife mentioned her seamstress had lost an assistant. Can you sew?'

'I can, sir.'

'Well then, you may collect the money from my assistant, and come to my chambers later this morning, wearing, I suggest, a wedding ring. I'll have an address for you.' Over the next two hours, Molly went to a coffee house and ate hungrily. Revived and in clean clothes, she felt hopeful. She purchased a ring from a pawn shop in Hatton Garden, the cheapest she could find, and as she slipped it on her finger, for the briefest moment she thought of Thomas.

After collecting the address of the Misses Hogarth, two sisters living in Covent Garden, Molly resolved to find them. Avoiding the back streets, she took the long way around and found the house easily. Crossing Covent Garden, she reached James Street. Number five was a gracious house of good size. White stucco pillars adorned the front, and a neat iron staircase led to the basement. She walked down the steps, straightened her dress, and knocked on the door.

'Can I help you?' A young maid opened the door.

'Thank you, I have an appointment.' Molly waited in the small hallway amongst the silks, the muslins and the dressmaker's dummies, and the prospect of a future here excited her. She would make dresses for the wealthy, and she determined that in the years to come, she would save enough to reclaim her child.

The interview lasted an hour, but it passed with the natural ease of a social occasion in the company of good friends. In a surge of delightful chatter, the Misses Hogarth told her about their lives; instead of questioning her, they chose to reassure her. 'Well, dear, I am Miss Mary, and my sister here is Miss Anne. As you can see, we remain unmarried, much to the dismay of our brother.' The sisters laughed, the most infectious, kind laugh, and Molly almost wept with relief.

'Poor dear, such a long journey you've had!' Miss Mary said. 'You must be exhausted. My sister will make you some tea.'

'Of course, how rude of me. Your husband would think my manners atrocious.'

Whether they believed her or not, they chose to acknowledge her status as a married woman. It was not mentioned again.

When they told her their brother was William Hogarth, a distinguished artist and one of the founding governors of the Foundling Hospital, Molly's composure was shaken, but as they went on, unaware of her future connections with the Foundling Hospital, she regained her self-control.

'He lives by his conscience, and much of his work depicts the vice and cruelty within our very streets. He wishes to expose the darker side of humanity; I believe he would change the world if he could. Oh, would you like a muffin, dear? And one of my sister's special tarts? Am I boring you, Mrs Johnson?'

'Of course not,' she replied, honestly, for Miss Mary and Miss Anne Hogarth were willing to give her a chance. 'And I would love a tart, please.'

Gradually, as her confidence grew, she asked them questions, and with great enthusiasm they told her about the position available in their small but reputable business. They explained about London, the pitfalls and the benefits, and when with considerable tact she led them on to the Foundling Hospital, they were able to enlighten her. She learnt about the uniforms designed by their brother: dresses with stiffened bodices for the girls, and jackets and breeches for boys. She tried to imagine what her own child might look like, wearing them.

When she left the Hogarths, she had a job and a future.

CHAPTER FORTY-TWO

The summer of 1741 was one of the hottest on record. London sweltered in the fetid heat, ravaged by sickness and disease. Molly struggled to work each morning.

When she arrived at James Street, she entered an oasis of tranquillity. She worked hard, and her employers rewarded her accordingly. They taught her with generosity, imparting their knowledge and their secrets until she became accomplished in the dressmaker's art.

'Such beautiful stitching,' Miss Anne admired. 'I can no longer sew those tiny pearls; it's my eyes, I'm afraid.'

That week Molly was assigned her first appointment.

Mrs Carmichael was pregnant like herself, and as Molly pinned her loose-fitting gown, she forgot her own circumstances while she gossiped and laughed with a woman of a similar age. Only later, as she stitched the silk of the peacock-blue mantua, would she reflect on the differences between them.

With the gown successfully completed, and a satisfied customer singing her praises, Molly was offered an important commission. It was a wedding gown for a valued and long-standing client.

'My sister and I feel that you are quite capable of making the dress,' Miss Anne Hogarth said, taking her hand, and smiling happily. 'We have watched you carefully, and the standard of your work is exceptional.'

'Thank you, miss. I will not let you down,' she said.

When they told her the name of the client, Molly felt the force of the past catching up with her.

'The Keyts are marked with tragedy. They had been on the way to London when the accident happened. We had a fitting booked for Miss Elizabeth's presentation dress. To this day it hurts my heart to think of it, and now poor Miss Elizabeth is dead, God rest her soul.' She paused, unaware of Molly's distress. 'I used to make dresses that showed her figure. Mary, do you remember the blue dress with the gold thread? There was another for Lady Keyt, so pretty, mint green with Brussels lace.'

At the mention of the mint-green dress Molly sat down heavily.

'Mrs Johnson, are you unwell?'

'I am known to Miss Dorothy Keyt and her mother,' she said at last. 'They would not appreciate my involvement.' With the sisters' usual discretion no further questions were asked, and it was agreed that while they fitted the dress and cut the patterns, Molly would do the more delicate work.

When the fitting date arrived, Miss Mary Hogarth tended to Dorothy. Against the familiar voices drifting through the door, Molly fought to maintain composure.

'My daughter wishes for organza. Would you consider organza fashionable, Miss Hogarth?'

She caught Dorothy's voice, confident and unchanged. 'My brother will give me away. He has just come down from Oxford with a first-class degree. We are very proud.'

'What a clever young man,' Miss Hogarth said.

'Absolutely,' Dorothy replied, 'and we are keeping our fingers crossed that he too will be married before the year is out.'

That evening Molly left work early, absorbed in her misery. Thomas to marry. It was another punishment. She took her usual route past the Shakespeare's Head, hurrying past the pimps and the prostitutes, past the church of St Paul's, where they gathered at night. While she waited to cross the Strand, a little boy darted into the road in front of her.

'Stop! There's a child!' she screamed at the driver, but the carriage rolled on, crushing the boy beneath the relentless wheels. When she called for help, no one came, and as she held the limp body in her arms, no one faltered in their stride.

CHAPTER FORTY-THREE

September 1741

Though Dorothy and her mother saw few outsiders, it was impossible to escape the rumours within the village of Hidcote.

'He's mad,' Thomas said, banging his fist upon the table. 'Is it not enough to empty the family coffers? Now he will ruin our reputation. I refuse to join him for dinner tomorrow.'

'Of course you must,' Lady Keyt said gently. 'He is still your father. The women, the gaming – I believe it is caused by his melancholy. Poor William has never recovered from the deaths of John and Elizabeth.'

'Mother, how can you be so forgiving?' Dorothy cried. 'He has destroyed your life; he has destroyed everything he has touched.'

'It's not just about forgiveness, it's about understanding. Circumstances beyond our control caused our downfall.'

Dorothy could see there was no use arguing. Her mother refused to accept the truth.

Her brother took her hand. 'Poor Dotty. You will have your wedding, and your beautiful dress. Fortunately Gilbert gives not a fig for money or dowry. Don't worry, I'll go to Father and try to reason with him. He will stop this excess, I assure you.'

The next evening Thomas rode to Norton. A few hours later Dorothy heard him return. She put down her book and ran outside to meet him.

'He was most odd,' Thomas reported, passing the reins to the waiting groom. 'He'd forgotten that he'd sent for me. He asked me if I had come for the "Last Supper". He even apologized for his conduct, for The College, for everything. It seemed quite out of character. I think I should ride back, don't you?'

'Don't be alarmed. It will just be one of his drunken fantasies.'

'Dotty, that's the problem: he was sober. Maudlin, but certainly not drunk. I've a bad feeling.'

'Go to bed, Thomas. I'm going to see him tomorrow. And I'm quite prepared to stand up to him.'

Thomas smiled. 'Always my fiery sister. But please be careful, he seems a little disturbed.'

When Thomas had gone to bed, Dorothy tried to read but found it impossible to concentrate. She was fearful of the dark, of the shadows from the past, and of her imagination.

In the morning she fetched Fidelia and rode towards Norton. It was a fine day, and she decided to take the long route through the woods. She turned Fidelia's head and cantered towards the larch fence, and as the horse jumped cleanly through the air, Dorothy felt a surge of elation.

Her skill as a horsewoman had come from her father. He had taught her to ride, and he had given her Peter, Ophelia and Fidelia. All desire for confrontation disappeared. By the time she arrived at the house, she had decided to treat him with understanding and forgiveness, just as Elizabeth would have wanted. She would encourage reconciliation with him, perhaps not immediately, but in time.

Lorenzo walked across the courtyard to meet her, his face betraying only professional intent. 'Hello, Miss Dorothy. Do you wish to see your father?' he asked.

The study curtains twitched behind him. Without warning, all her previous goodwill disappeared.

'No, thank you, Lorenzo,' she said, for suddenly she wanted to run, away from the indifference in Lorenzo's eyes, away from her desperate father. 'Will you tell him that I called, and tell him that I'll come tomorrow?' Turning Fidelia's head, she cantered back through the archway, shame spreading through her chest.

CHAPTER FORTY-FOUR

Only five members of the indoor staff remained at Norton: George Heron, who felt an instinctive loyalty towards his self-destructive master; three housemaids, all daughters of a tenant farmer; and a cook.

Outside, Lorenzo carried out his duties with a sick heart. It was a thankless job, for with only five horses, one carriage, and a master who never ventured out, there was little to do. Even Lorenzo couldn't explain why he stayed; perhaps it was his affection for Apollo, or his grateful devotion to Sir William, or perhaps it was because he held onto a dream.

Sir William lived in private misery, emerging only to host the occasional dinner or an evening of gambling. His guests were usually women of dubious reputation and any dissolute members of the gentry who wished to take advantage of his generous cellar – or, indeed, of Sir William himself.

After these debauched evenings, he would wake to a few hours of sobriety before the reality of his situation hit him with painful clarity. Memories of life before the accident haunted him: recollections of Ann, laughing with his four children; of Elizabeth resting in the garden, her features tranquil in the dappled light, and John running towards him with his arms outstretched.

Everyone he loved had either left him or died. He raged at Molly, but in rational moments he realized the fault was his own. His words had sent her away. He tormented himself, imagining her beautiful body entwined with his son's.

Only when entertaining on a lavish scale did he take to the new mansion. At other times, he would wander through the vast, empty rooms, marvelling at his foolishness.

William was sitting in his study when Dorothy entered the courtyard. He heard Fidelia's hooves before he saw his daughter. Inching back the curtains he looked outside. She was standing next to Lorenzo. The body language between them was unmistakable.

He smiled for a moment. 'So that's how it is,' he said. 'How alike we are. Have courage, Dorothy. Take life with both hands.'

He let the curtains fall back into place. 'Come to me and I'll tell you so. Come to me and I'll beg your forgiveness.'

He waited, willing her to enter his study. 'If she comes,' he whispered, 'I can start again. Please God, let her come.'

He heard the hooves ring on the cobbles once more. 'Well then,' he said, 'it's done.'

Taking a sheet of paper from the top drawer he refreshed his pen and started to write.

When he came to the end he thought for a moment and signed it.

Be happy, my child, and forgive me.
Your loving father, always.

He smiled, a wry smile. Dorothy would rummage through his drawers, as she always had. She would find the letter; she

238

would find the ring. He looked at its ruby eye for a moment before gently removing it and putting it in a small box which he perched on top of the telescope. It seemed the fitting place. 'Oh Dorothy, how well I know you,' he sighed.

He looked carefully around his study, patted Sophie and went upstairs.

CHAPTER FORTY-FIVE

Her brother's voice woke Dorothy.

'Mama, I'm going to Norton. Something is wrong, I can sense it.'

Dorothy ran downstairs. Her mother and Thomas were in the hallway. She was trying her best to pacify him.

'Nothing is wrong, my love.' She pulled back the curtains. A pink tinge lit the sky. 'It's a beautiful night and all is well. I will pour you a brandy, and we will return to bed.'

Lady Keyt had just picked up the decanter when hooves rang on the cobbles – galloping hooves, clattering into the courtyard. Dorothy's heart hammered against the walls of her chest. Shouting followed as someone banged on the door. It was a stable lad.

'Mister Thomas, come quickly!' he yelled. 'Norton is on fire! We need help.'

Her mother dropped the decanter. It shattered, spreading its amber contents across the floor.

'Mama, be brave. Everything will be fine, I promise you. Get Pike to harness the cart and bring the water butts. I will ride on first, but you must stay with Dorothy.'

'I will not stay here!' Dorothy cried, images of her father and Lorenzo vivid in her mind. 'I'm coming. You can't stop me.'

'And William? What of William?'

Thomas put his hands on his mother's shoulders. 'I will do my best, but you must promise not to come.'

Thomas and Dorothy galloped along the track towards Norton. At the end of the drive, they jumped down.

'Go home,' Dorothy yelled, smacking Fidelia's rump. With little encouragement the horses galloped back towards Hidcote.

Taking Dorothy's hand, Thomas led her through the yard, past the hay cart and the feed store, past the stable lads trying to soothe the terrified horses. They were barely through the garden door before a suffocating heat hit them like a wall, burning their throats and stinging their eyes.

Estate workers, servants, men and women formed a chain of black silhouettes against the red sky, passing buckets of water from hand to hand, but it was too late. The magnificent new mansion had blossomed into an inferno. Flames leapt through the roof, and one by one the windows shattered and the columns crashed to the ground. Thomas ran towards the front door.

'Come back!' Dorothy screamed, but he ignored her, pushing his shoulder against the smoking wood.

The door burst open, and the flames exploded, forcing him out.

George Heron ran from the house into Thomas's arms. 'I tried to stop him! I did, sir, but he bolted the door from the inside! We managed to remove a few of the pictures and some small pieces of furniture, but that is all. Come, we must get away, there is nothing we can do.'

Dorothy looked beyond the pictures and the items of furniture discarded on the lawn towards her father's window. There he stood, dark against the fire, his arms raised in supplication as the flames licked around him. She would never forget his face, that mask of agony; she would never blot out his screams as they carried on the smoky air.

Her brother ran forward once more, but Heron blocked his way. 'Sir, I told you, it's too late.'

They stopped at the sound of Sir William's final cry: 'Forgive me, Father, for I have sinned.'

For minutes Dorothy remained immobile, transfixed by the unspeakable horror in front of her. She wanted to turn away, but she couldn't move. She could only stare at the window above her.

When at last her father had vanished into the flames, Dorothy fled back across the lawn, past the villagers, gawping in shock and amazement, and the estate workers, standing bowed and defeated, until she reached the garden door. She pushed against it and fell into the stable yard beyond. The horses, wide-eyed and restless, snorted and stamped as Dorothy entered. She went to each one, soothing and comforting them as she tried to quell her own rising hysteria. Her father, who had loved her and spoilt her, and who had caused her so much anger and confusion, was dead. Now, when it was too late, she was filled with unbearable sadness.

Finally she entered Apollo's stall. He turned his head and looked at her, bewilderment in his clouded eyes. Did he know? she wondered, wrapping her arms around the horse's neck, her sobs growing as the full horror of her father's death overwhelmed her.

She hadn't realized that Lorenzo had entered the stable until he touched her shoulder. She spun round.

'Lorenzo! You are safe,' she cried. 'Thank God, you are safe.'

'I will take you home, Miss Dorothy; there is nothing you can do here.'

'But I can't leave my brother – I must find Thomas.'

'He is looking for the dog. He'll be fine, I promise you.' She let him lead her away, and as he guided her into the cart she turned to look back; behind her a pall of smoke hung in the night air.

They travelled to Hidcote, the wheels bumping along the rutted track. When they arrived, he helped her down and she leant against his scorched coat.

'Why did he do it, Lorenzo?'

'He died because he wanted to. There was no peace for him in this world; perhaps he hoped to find it in the next. I am so sorry.' He took her by the shoulders. 'You'll be all right?'

She would have fallen into his embrace but her mother ran out of the front door. 'He's dead, isn't he?' she cried. Dorothy nodded silently, her head bowed.

'What will I do without him, Dotty? I love him. I never stopped loving him. If only I had known the depth of his despair, I would have gone to him. Now it's too late.'

Dorothy slept an hour in her mother's bed, and as the early morning sun rose in the sky they drove to Norton together. She held her mother's hand as they entered the courtyard. The new mansion had been reduced to a jagged, smouldering ruin: the elegant windows, the fine stonework, the statues. It was a scene from hell. The passage between the two houses had also been destroyed, but apart from some charring on the external walls, the original house remained unscathed.

'I must look for Thomas,' her mother said at last. 'Where is the poor boy?' They found him beneath the cedar tree with Sophie at his feet.

'She was hiding in the bushes,' he said. 'Thank God she's alive. You know he torched it, Mama? He used the candelabra from the hall table. He piled the curtains into the centre of the room. Heron tried to stop him, but he broke away and locked the bedroom door. I should have gone back with Dorothy. I could have prevented this. He tried to tell me when I went to dinner, but I didn't listen.'

They stood on the bank, staring at the nightmare in front of them. Occasionally small pockets of smoke burst through the rubble, and though most of the internal walls had gone, one fireplace remained intact. Dorothy looked at the blackened skull buried amongst the foliage She called to the workmen. 'Pull that chimney piece down – take it away, every part of it.'

Two days after the inferno, when the ashes had cooled, George Heron put on his best white gloves as a mark of deference and searched amongst the rubble for any remains of his master. Dorothy held her mother back, while Thomas joined him in the search.

'I'm sorry, my lady,' Heron said sadly, his gloves soiled, his breeches covered in the powdery residue, 'but I have found only his hip bone, his gold pocket watch and his keys. Perhaps more will be found as we continue. It's a bad do when all is said and done.' He placed the meagre remains into a small clay casket and they followed him across the courtyard to

Sir William's study. Standing in a circle around the fire, her mother led a few short prayers.

'Dear God, take my husband to your side,' she said gently. 'May you give him peace at last.'

George Heron spoke. 'Sir Thomas, my lady, I expect you will no longer need my services.' Dorothy saw uncertainty in his face.

'Mr Heron,' her brother replied, 'your services and your loyalty have been invaluable to this family. As long as I am able, I will continue to keep you in my employment.'

Dorothy was instantly aware of the change in position. Her brother was now head of the house, the new baronet.

'If you will forgive me, Mama,' he continued, 'I must talk to the household. I have asked them to assemble in the hall in ten minutes.'

'Of course, you go, and Dorothy, if you don't mind, I will sit in the library.' Dorothy took her mother's arm and settled her in a chair.

'I'll be back in a minute, Mama. I won't be long; there is something I must do.'

'I'll be fine, don't worry. I'll be fine.'

Dorothy left her mother and returned to the study. She looked at the urn on the mantelpiece, all that remained of her father. If she had gone to him, would things have been different? If she had seen him, could she have prevented this?

'Tell me, Papa,' she whispered, 'was this my fault?' She remembered his diary. She knew the answer would be there. She opened the drawer, but the diary had gone. She was about to search in the bookcase when she saw the letter.

The envelope had her name upon it.

My dearest Dorothy,

By the time you read this letter, I will have committed my soul to God.

You will look for my diary as you have before, but this time you will not find it. I have taken it with me, my companion to the grave.

You would ask me how I know. On the day you left Norton with your mother my suspicions were confirmed. I found the comb I had given you on your ninth birthday on the floor of my study. Look in the drawer below and you will find it.

She put the letter down, and opened the drawer; it was empty, save for a small jewelled comb. She turned it over in her fingers, and suddenly it was her ninth birthday once more and her father was handing her the tiny wrapped package. Clutching it tightly she continued reading:

I kept it, Dorothy, I couldn't let it go, but there is something else. There is a velvet box. Find it and open it. You always were inquisitive. You love riddles; this shall be your last from me.

She pulled open the other drawers, but they held only papers. She looked around the small panelled room. There was nothing beneath the wing chair in the corner – John's chair. She remembered her brother sitting there, his chubby legs tucked beneath him. Behind the velvet curtains she found nothing. At last she saw the box; it was resting on the telescope. She opened it, and her father's ring fell to the

246

floor. She knelt to pick it up, when a smaller note dropped from the box.

Dorothy, you must have it. You have always loved it. I probably wouldn't have given it to you yesterday, even if you had come in. Of course I wanted to see you, but I quite understand. You hate me, and quite rightly so.

'I don't hate you, Papa, I don't hate you,' she cried, her tears blotting the paper.

You may now have the perfect wedding, and when you are Lady Paxton-Hooper, I will not be around to embarrass you. But make your choices well, and go where your heart lies, for position is not everything.

Wear the ring, my child, wear it with pride. One day, if Thomas has a son, give it to him; if not, give it to your own. Know that I have loved you especially, for we are quite alike, you and I. We desire things we should not desire, and we both know jealousy.

Tell my beloved wife that I have loved her always. I have never stopped loving her.

Be happy, my child, and forgive me.

Your loving father, always.

PS Please ask Thomas to discharge all outstanding debt. There is a sum of money hidden beneath the floorboards in this room.

Dorothy put the letter down. As she slipped the ring upon her finger, she sank to the floor once more.

'I should have gone to him,' she moaned. 'I should have forgiven him.' Cowardice and pride had prevented her. She buried her face in her hands and sobbed.

CHAPTER FORTY-SIX

At the end of September, Molly received a letter from her brother.

My Dear Molly,

Our mam has asked me to write to you. What I have to say will shock and distress you, for it is news of the gravest nature.

On the ninth of this month, Sir William burnt himself and his new mansion to the ground. The butler tried to save him, but he locked the bedroom door and set fire to the bedclothes. They thankfully managed to save the old house, but that is of little consolation.

They say he was mad when you left, as mad as a raging bull.

Forgive me, my dear sister, for imparting such wretchedness, but I would rather you heard from people who love you, rather than from those who do not. Our father, as you can imagine, is not of good heart. He had great hopes for his daughter, and they are now buried along with Sir William.

Loving you always,
Will

Night and day Molly tortured herself, haunted by images of William's charred and frightened face. She wallowed in guilt, but guilt does not stop an unborn child from growing. In October she made an appointment to visit Captain Coram at the temporary Foundling Hospital in Hatton Garden.

'Your baby will be safe within our care,' Captain Coram assured her, his long silver wig moving with his jaw as he spoke. Although he was of dishevelled appearance, his round belly bursting through his crumpled red coat, his black stockings sagging, she was struck by the compassion and understanding in his eyes.

'Did you know that seventy-four per cent of children born in London die before they are five? In the workhouses the death rate is over ninety per cent. We offer a far safer alternative; we have every intention of giving our foundlings the best start in life.'

She trusted Captain Coram and began to believe wholeheartedly in her decision. The Foundling Hospital would provide for her child's good.

'Come, my dear,' he said. 'I will show you around. Forgive me if I'm a little proud, I have faced many years of struggle. It's only a start. One day every child will have a future, but at least for now, a few children will have a home.'

He ushered her through the long tiled corridors, into the simple accommodation for girls and boys. She was struck both by the cleanliness of the spotless beds and the scrubbed faces, and the longing in the children's eyes.

Do any of them know love? she wondered sadly, then shook the thought from her mind, knowing it was better than the alternative.

They were near the front door when Captain Coram pointed to an architectural plan. 'This,' he said, tapping the wall with his stick, 'is the design for our wonderful new hospital in Bloomsbury Fields. The foundation stone will be laid next year, and it will house up to four hundred children. It will be built almost entirely from private donations, proving that the people of England are finally developing a social conscience. There will be a large garden, giving our children freedom to run and play in safety, and in the glorious chapel they will learn that despite everything, God still watches over us. We shall have choirs chosen from amongst the children. They will learn music, as well as scripture and Bible reading, and the girls will learn needlework and the domestic duties necessary for their future lives. Is it not incredible?'

Molly said goodbye to Captain Coram, certain that within the austere walls of the Foundling Hospital her child had a chance. She walked past the railings, past the desperate women who held out their babies for the weekly selection. That torment, at least, she would not have to endure.

The following week she looked for temporary lodgings near Hatton Garden.

'Don't forget me,' she said, hugging the Misses Hogarth on her final day. 'I can never thank you enough.' She walked up the iron stairs for the last time, and entered her own small room to await the birth of her child. As the baby turned within her body, she worked upon two mementos: a handkerchief for herself, her initials embroidered within the centre of a heart, and a matching tiny stitched heart as a trinket for her child. Even at the Foundling Hospital, her child would know a mother's love.

When the contractions began she sent an errand boy to fetch the midwife. 'For Christ's sake, be quick!' she yelled. As the pain ripped through her body she cried out, and screamed at the poor woman who knelt between her legs, until several hours later, she gave birth to a fine and healthy son.

She spent one week of perfect contentment with her child. She examined every inch of his tiny body. She counted the fingers, the delicate pink nails, and stroked the soft down upon his head. 'Charles,' she whispered, looking deep into his blue eyes, 'you shall have your father's middle name.'

On the eighth day she opened her eyes, with a crushing pain in her heart. She dressed her son in a delicate gown she had made; she put a shawl, knitted from the finest yarn, around his shoulders, and a tiny woollen hat upon his head. She carried him the short distance to the Foundling Hospital. As the fog came down on the cobbled street, she hurried on.

Reaching the tradesman's entrance she pulled the bell. It echoed down the corridor. The seconds ticked by: she pulled again, a flicker of hope expanding in her chest.

'They can't be expecting me,' she whispered, daring to hope. 'We can go, love. We'll manage.' She kissed her son's head and was about to leave when the door opened. A scrubbed, unsmiling face appeared.

'I heard you the first time, Miss Johnson. You're late.'

'I'm sorry,' she muttered. 'I had to feed him, he was hungry.'

'Late is late, miss,' the matron replied. 'You are lucky to have a place. Half of them will have to take the bairns away.' She gestured to the women who lined the railings. 'You got lucky, just listen to them wailing. They know their babes will die of disease or starvation, so I have no truck with the likes of you, someone who knows someone. There is no preference in here. They are all treated the same. Now give him to me, I have fifty babies to attend to.'

When Molly could not let go, the matron's voice became harsh. 'Are you able to provide for this child? I think not, or you wouldn't be here. Looking at you, you probably earn it on your back at night, and drink it during the day. If you know what is good for your child, you will unhand him. If you stand there blubbering in the cold he will die, and that will be one less child to trouble with.'

'I don't want to give him up!' she moaned. 'You don't know anything about me! I will collect him soon and take him home.'

'That's what they all say,' she replied callously, pulling Molly's son from her arms. 'We'll give him a medal engraved with his number, and a new name, and when the documentation is done, he'll be sent out to a wet nurse, so it's no use you coming for him.'

She was about to close the door when Molly grabbed her sleeve. 'His name is Charles, please call him Charles, and give him this when he is old enough to understand,' she pleaded. 'Tell him his mother loves him. I beg of you, if you have any mercy, tell him his mother never stopped loving him.' She put the embroidered heart in the woman's hand, and the matron's harsh face softened.

'I'll do it. I'll tell him one day,' she said. 'Now be away with you before I change me mind.'

As the door closed behind her, Molly dropped to her knees, keening with despair.

For three days she drank little and ate nothing. Only the sound of the landlady's key in her lock forced her out of her soiled bed. She dropped the coins into the landlady's fingers. 'Here is your rent. Now get out,' she screamed, shutting the door to the woman's prying.

She hardly recognized the wretch in the washstand mirror – the greasy hair, the pallid skin. She hardly knew the demented eyes that stared back at her from the dirty glass.

When the fever took her she prayed for death. As she tossed and turned, she lost consciousness, and William laughed at her from the flames.

When the fever abated she lay exhausted, her sheets wet with sweat, her breasts tender and full of milk. Crawling to the cupboard, she found some bread and forced herself to eat. Binding her breasts until she cried out with pain, she resolved to return to the country and build a new life with one aim: to reclaim her child.

Before leaving London, she returned to James Street. If the Misses Hogarth were surprised by her appearance they did not show it; instead, they took her hands and led her to the fire.

'Sit down, my dear. Perhaps you would like to talk,' Miss Mary said.

The sisters listened quietly to her story. They neither judged nor condemned, but nodded their heads in sympathy and concern.

'God has given you a hard path to follow,' Miss Anne said solemnly, 'but we know that you are strong and worthy of his love.'

'Please, will you ask your brother to watch over my child?' she asked as she rose to leave. 'And will you tell me how he is? I will send an address when I have one.'

They nodded. 'We give you our word,' said Miss Anne.

Her last call was to Mr Skarm. She entered his room and sat before the great desk.

'Good luck, Miss Johnson. I hope that fate will be kind to you,' he said, handing her a promissory note. 'Take this into a bank, and they will exchange it for you. Travelling with money is dangerous; it will be much safer this way.'

'Thank you,' she said. 'I will try to make good use of it.'

CHAPTER FORTY-SEVEN

The remains of Sir William Keyt were interred under the chancel steps of the church of St Eadburgha in Ebrington.

The following week Norton was closed and dustsheets shrouded the furniture. The indoor staff left, with one exception. Sir Thomas found George Heron in the strong room.

'The silver is being removed to Hidcote for safety, sir,' the butler said, as he shut the last of the green baize bags.

'You are a wise man, and I believe it would be in all of our interests if you would stay at Norton until we have made our plans. Will you do this?' When it was agreed, Thomas went to find Lorenzo.

'I am told you are going back to Italy. We shall miss you, Lorenzo,' Thomas said, clasping his hand. 'You have been a true friend to our family.'

'There is no longer anything for me here,' he replied sadly. 'Now . . . you promise you will never sell Apollo?'

On the day Lorenzo was due to leave Dorothy took the small cart and drove to Norton. The wind had picked up, and as she set the pony at a brisk pace, falling branches and twigs caught beneath the wheels. She finally arrived, her bonnet removed and pushed beneath the seat for safe keeping, her hair falling in a tangle around her shoulders. In the empty yard, buckets rolled across the cobbles, and the stalls stood empty.

There was no sign of Lorenzo. She was back in the cart and about to leave when she saw Apollo and Lorenzo, horse and rider in perfect harmony, flying up the hill towards her. The enormity of her loss hit her as she ran down the track, not stopping until she reached them at the gate.

'Look after Apollo, Miss Dorothy,' he said, his face flushed from exertion. 'He is old now, and although I must, I can't bear to leave him.' She nodded, unable to speak. She couldn't help but put out her hand to him. He leant forward over Apollo's neck and accepted it, pressing it to his lips.

She shut her eyes, lifted her face. Her body longed for him. She moved towards him involuntarily, before remembering that she was betrothed to someone else. She pulled away.

'Keep safe, for I'll miss you,' she said. 'I'll always remember you, Lorenzo. Always.' She ran from him, up the path, past the dovecote and the ice house, and only when she reached the courtyard did she turn to look back. They were still there, horse and rider, motionless, frozen in her memory for all time.

In years to come she would remember him as he was then, and she would wonder what would have been had she heeded her father's advice.

CHAPTER FORTY-EIGHT

The next September, Dorothy married the Honourable Gilbert Paxton-Hooper. Her wedding was a simple affair, as seemed appropriate.

On the eve of her marriage she went to bed with a heavy heart. She tried to think of her dress – the organza sewn with a thousand pearls, the wide hooped skirt, the scalloped hem. She tried to imagine the silk slippers, her mother's diamonds, but she could summon little enthusiasm.

During the night she awoke. The sheets were wrapped and knotted around her thighs; her body was clammy with sweat. She climbed out of bed, threw open the window and stared up at the sky. Inhaling the crisp autumn air, she watched the clouds sail across the moon, and she remembered a story Miss Byrne had told her on a similar night many years before.

'It's a galleon,' Miss Byrne had said, her arm around her shoulders. 'Don't you see, it's collecting treasure from the moon?' She could picture herself as she was then, a young girl gazing in wonder at the night sky. If Miss Byrne were here now, she would be giving Dorothy sound advice. 'If you love him truly, 'tis the most natural thing in the world,' she would say. But did she love him? Did she feel passion for the man she would marry? By virtue of having to ask, she knew her answer.

A pier glass stood in the corner; she stood before it, a shadowy figure, watching her reflection. Her dark hair fell to her shoulders, and her blue eyes looked black in the gloom. She lifted her nightdress above her ankles, assessing her white skin, her delicate bones. She wondered what it would be like. Her experience was limited to animals mating in the field and stolen moments in her novels. Hesitating for a moment she raised her arms, pulled the nightdress over her head and stared at herself: the triangle of hair between her legs, the dark nipples on rounded breasts, the slim waist. Letting the breeze cool her skin, she lay back on the bed. A sigh escaped her lips, and her fingers became Lorenzo's. As they touched her skin every sense in her body awakened. His hands stroked her breasts until the nipples were standing erect and waves of sensation pulsed down her body. One hand strayed across her stomach and down. The other came up to her mouth and traced the outline of her lips. At the same time she felt his fingers between her legs, touching her with lingering strokes that tantalized and teased, until her body arched towards them. Now it was Lorenzo's mouth pushing her lips apart, Lorenzo's body rising above her. There was no turning back as her legs parted and she started to move faster and faster against his fingers, no hesitation on this strange voyage of discovery. It was all-consuming, taking her until she exploded into the light. When she had finished, she lay breathless in her bed, confused and alone.

At noon the following day, Dorothy's hair was dressed and her stays tightened, but it was hard to return to reality and her mind still wandered. As the tiny buttons were secured along her back she faltered, and as the gloves slipped over her scented wrists and along her arms, her hands quivered. She had slipped away from the present, from the inevitable, towards a man who smelt of meadow hay and saddle soap, and whose smile would haunt her for ever.

Entering the church of the Holy Trinity in Stratford-upon-Avon, kneeling within feet of Shakespeare's tomb, she said her vows to the man at her side, and hoped that she would be worthy of his love.

Afterwards she bade farewell to her small family.

'Goodbye, Dotty,' her mother said softly, holding her at arm's length, staring into her face. 'I hope you will love him truly.'

Thomas hugged her tightly and shook his friend's hand. 'Goodbye, Dotty. Look after my darling sister, Gilbert. I'll write to you both. I'll miss you.'

As the carriage drew away, she remembered Elizabeth's words: 'Follow your heart, but follow it honestly.'

Not for the first time, she doubted her integrity.

They stayed in lodgings on the way to Surrey. As she looked at her new husband, she hoped he would inspire passion within her. Standing in front of the fire, in her new negligee of lawn and lace, she waited for him.

'Stop, my love,' he said, taking her hand. 'It is not necessary to undress. Do up your buttons, for I would not embarrass you.' She redid the buttons, rebraided her hair, and when he snuffed the candle, which she had pleaded for, he laughed.

'That is for whores,' he said. 'Not for my virgin bride.'

Gilbert fumbled with his britches, then released himself into her with no joy. When it was over, her body was sore and unsatisfied, and she turned her face to the pillow to weep.

The years passed. Dorothy's children were born and christened, and though she didn't achieve the fulfilment she longed for, she discovered the joys of motherhood. As she held a sleeping baby, she reflected on her mother's pain – on the loss of her children, her husband, the unnatural order of her life. Each year she returned to Hidcote, and each year she was saddened by her mother's suffering. On these occasions she saw her brother, unmarried, his energy and beauty fading. When she returned to her own family once more, to the children who demanded her time, she tried not to think of Thomas or of the hand she had played in his destiny. She tried not to think of Lorenzo.

In the spring of 1749, she received a letter from Thomas.

Dearest Dotty,

I hope life is treating you well, and that you and Gilbert are happy.

Firstly I must tell you that we have found a purchaser for Norton. As you know, my agent has been looking for some time, and at last Sir Dudley Ryder has made up his mind. He will complete the purchase over the next few years. I know this news will make you sad, but if I am honest, I'll be glad to be relieved of the financial burden. Mother is of the same opinion; it is time to move on, to put the past behind us.

We are both in good heart, having stayed with Cousin Jack in London for the last two weeks. We went to the opera, the theatre, and even a few social gatherings, but then something unexpected happened.

Six days ago, we attended a benefit concert at the Foundling Hospital. George Frideric Handel conducted the first performance of his Foundling Hospital Anthem. It was a wonderful affair: the Prince of Wales and many public figures were raising money to fund the new chapel. Before the concert started, we were invited to view the paintings on display. The hospital is unique, for on the one hand it rescues poor foundlings, but on the other it promotes British art. I wish you could have seen the paintings; perhaps I can persuade you to leave the country for a few days.

The evening was a glorious occasion, but that's not all of it. We were shown to our seats by the choristers, fine young lads in black robes and white cassocks. Our guide was a boy of about seven or eight years old.

Dotty, though the child was well fed and clean, and cheerful enough, my heart was moved by the longing in his eyes. He made me want to put something back into a society where children are ill-treated and abandoned by their mothers, where infants are left on the streets to die.

I asked the boy his name, and he told me that he was Charles Coram, and that he loved to sing. He asked me to hear him perform, and when the choir sang, I was moved once more. I now feel I have a purpose.

I have no children of my own, no obligations; I want to do something for that young man and others like *him. Before we sell it, I have decided to have one last party and hold my own concert at Norton, and I will ask Handel to perform his work, Messiah. I believe we could alert people to the plight of these poor children, and raise money at the same time. We can call it the farewell concert. Will you assist me, Dorothy?*

Your loving brother,

Thomas,

In anticipation of your reply.

Tightness closed around Dorothy's chest. For years she had tried to justify her behaviour to herself. If she had been a better person, she would have owned up to her actions, would have lifted the veil from her brother's eyes. Instead the lies continued.

Of course I'll help you, she wrote. *It will be a pleasure.*

CHAPTER FORTY-NINE

Molly survived these years of hardship and toil. She kept going, for there was a child in London without a mother's love. One day she would claim him and make up for all the lost years.

She did get her shop, a small property outside London. As she had envisioned since she was a child, a blue sign with gold lettering hung above the door, but as the roads improved, her customers drifted to the city. Before long someone else's sign hung above the door, and Molly returned to Gloucestershire, with Dorothy's money all but spent.

For two years she worked as a seamstress in a small hilltop village. 'Stow-on-the-Wold, where the winds blow cold,' they said, and it was true, and the cold seeped into her bones at night. Every morning she read the trade cards in the village shop, until her opportunity came.

Premises for sale, Chipping Campden.

It was perfectly located on the High Street near the centre. She lacked the money, but Will, who had found marriage and success, gave her a loan. Molly worked hard, and her reputation for excellence spread. Soon she would go to London. She dreamt of collecting her son.

Next year, perhaps, she would be rich enough.

She was turning the hem on a client's gown when Ruth surprised her with a visit.

'Well well, Molly Johnson,' Ruth said, looking her up and down. 'Still pretty, still slim – how do you do it after all these years? Look at me. I've gone to the dogs: too much food and no fine men. That's my problem, no reason to take care of myself.'

Molly hugged her and laughed, then hugged her again.

'Ruth, dear Ruth, I am sorry I didn't contact you, but I have had to keep my head down around here.'

'Well, you were a hard one to track down. "Miss Jones", for heaven's sake! Whatever next? It was your lovely brother Will who told me where you were, and indeed who you bloody were. Lord, if you do it again I'll give up on you.'

For the next hour they caught up on old times.

'I work for Lady Keyt at Hidcote. I'm her housekeeper now; I suppose that's why I'm still with her after all these years. I haven't been to the old house since it was closed; it still scares me to death when I think about the fire. They say a gent from the city wants to buy it – the Attorney General, whatever that is. Word has it, his sights are set on a peerage and he needs a country seat.'

They slipped back easily into their old friendship. Ruth was on the point of leaving when Molly asked her to accompany her on a trip to Norton. 'I have not yet seen the ruin, Ruth, and I would like to pay my last respects.'

'Tomorrow is my day off. I'll be here at three.'

The following day, as their cart bumped along the rutted track, Molly remembered her arrival at Norton.

I can't imagine why Papa employed you; you're hardly old enough to be a lady's maid.

She remembered Elizabeth: *Dorothy, be polite to poor Miss Johnson. We must make her welcome in our home.*

As they entered the ruins, voices and memories reverberated around her.

Molly, what do think? Do you like bronze silk for the curtains, or red damask?

We have to do the menus. I wish it to be the most memorable evening ever.

My radiant girl, would you dance with me?

'Ruth,' Molly cried at last, 'everything that I have touched has broken. I gave my son away, sold him for money. He's growing up without his mother, without even knowing his real name, and I pay for it every day.' They sat on the wall, the tangle of ivy softening the crumbling masonry, and Ruth heard her story. She heard about Mrs Quick, and about Molly's agreement with Dorothy; she heard about the Hogarth sisters, who sent occasional reports of her son, and of her dreams of reclaiming him.

'Lawd,' she said at last, 'it's not that bad. We all make mistakes and you've made yours. You can make it up to your lad; you gave him away with the best intentions. Now you can get him back.'

CHAPTER FIFTY

On 1 May 1750, Handel's sacred oratorio *Messiah* was performed at the Foundling Hospital. It was a great success, raising a large sum of money, and after donating an organ to the new chapel, Handel was elected a governor of the hospital. Thomas attended the presentation and had the opportunity to approach the famous composer with his request.

> *Darling Dotty,*
>   *In haste,*
>   *Handel has agreed. He will come to Norton next summer with his choristers. I am elated beyond words. Please, will you ask Gilbert if he can spare his wife for a few weeks? He's probably busy on the estate, but I hope that he will join us eventually too. I will of course expect my nieces and nephew.*
>   *Always*
>   *Your devoted brother,*
>   *Thomas*

Shortly after receiving this, Dorothy wrote a letter to the Foundling Hospital.

Dear Sir,

The Foundling Hospital choristers are performing the Messiah *at Norton, my brother's house in Gloucester-shire, next summer. I have an interest in a particular child, the son of a Miss Molly Johnson. I would be most grateful for the following information. Will this boy be amongst the choristers, and what is his name? Any information will be treated in confidence.*

Please could you send your reply to my solicitor in London? I enclose the details.

Two weeks later, Dorothy received the answers to her questions. The child would be performing, and his name was Charles Coram.

When Dorothy left Surrey with her children, Gilbert wished them well and waved goodbye as the carriage swept them away. She smiled, for he was a good man. He knew nothing of the anxiety she felt, heading back to Norton for her brother's concert. How could he? He knew nothing of her.

Dorothy persuaded her mother to spare Annie from Hidcote to supervise the cleaning and to look after the house when the choristers arrived. Under her direction, Norton awoke from its long sleep. The house was scrubbed, the rooms were aired, and the furniture was polished until it shone. Dorothy hired local men to cut back the neglected gardens, and the ruined mansion rang once more with the sounds of life.

In late July, Handel arrived with his musicians and thirteen foundlings. The coaches entered under the archway, and as the foundlings piled out, George Heron and his staff formed a welcoming party. Thomas escorted the blind Mr Handel as Dorothy watched uneasily from the steps.

Children of various shapes and sizes filed towards her. She wondered if she would recognize her nephew.

One young boy lingered behind the rest. When he looked up he saw a woman standing at the front door. Though her hair was dark, she had the same blue eyes and the same bearing as Sir Thomas. He met her glance and approached her. 'Hello. You must be Sir Thomas's sister?' he asked.

Something struck a chord: the delicate face, the curly hair. 'I am,' Dorothy replied. She took a deep breath before asking the question to which she already knew the answer: 'And what is your name, young man?'

'Charles Coram,' he said proudly.

As the concert approached Dorothy struggled with her conscience. The time had come to tell her brother, but she could not.

On the night before the performance, everyone gathered informally in the drawing room. They had finished supper and the choristers, tired but happy, were sprawled on the floor playing cards and chequers. The adults sat on chairs grouped around the large room, sampling the last of Sir William's port. Everyone stopped talking when Thomas stood up and cleared his throat.

'Mr Handel, friends,' he said, his voice filling with emotion. 'Thank you for coming. This is a very special occasion; it marks the end of an era, and I can think of no better way to say goodbye to my family home. The last few days can be counted amongst my happiest. Norton needs life, and nothing brings more life than these delightful children. It has been a joy to have you all here. You have rejuvenated this old house with your singing, and for that I thank you. I also wish to welcome Sir Dudley Ryder to his future home. You have been most generous, sir, in your contribution to our festival, and I hope that you will be as happy here as we have been.'

All eyes turned towards Sir Dudley, who rose and bowed, to warm applause.

CHAPTER FIFTY-ONE

July 1751

Molly and Ruth wore cloaks to disguise themselves as they took the wooded path through to Norton. 'I feel like a child,' Ruth laughed. Molly looked anxiously at her. 'Thank you for agreeing to come with me. I wouldn't have been brave enough to sneak in on my own.'

They slipped through the gate, and running through the yew trees they reached the temple. Molly stopped at the entrance. Elizabeth's statue remained, but the stone had aged and was covered with lichen. 'Hello, Elizabeth,' she whispered.

She touched the stone columns, remembering her night with Thomas. In the shade of these trees, unseen by the one hundred and fifty guests who stood on the lawn drinking champagne, they could see the theatre. Chairs were arranged in a semicircle, and a stage had been constructed behind the round pool. The lime trees planted by Sir William had grown to form a proscenium arch.

'Though I admit to financial folly, I believe future generations will thank me for this theatre,' he had said, and at last Molly saw wisdom in his words.

The orchestra arrived. They filed into their places, followed by the audience and family members. Dorothy led

Mr Handel, and Thomas led a small band of choristers onto the stage.

Seeing him, Molly shrank back against the pillar. Thomas had changed; his jawline was the same, and his hair still curled over his collar, but he looked significantly older and worn. She glanced at the choristers, sweet boys with black cassocks and white ruffs, but her eyes returned to the man she still loved. Watching him now, she realized the intervening years had done nothing to lessen her feelings.

When he went to the podium and lifted his hand, the crowd fell silent.

'Mr Handel, I thank you,' Thomas said, 'for coming to give us this performance. I am honoured to be your host, for it has a purpose beyond the music – it is also to honour the children who will sing to you tonight. May I ask you to raise your glasses to Mr George Frideric Handel, to the orchestra and to the choir of the Foundling Hospital? I also raise my glass to Captain Thomas Coram, whose benevolence and perseverance helped each and every one of these young people. Though he is recently dead, his legacy lives on.'

Molly would have fallen, but Ruth caught her. 'It's the foundlings!' she gasped. 'My son must be amongst them. You didn't tell me they would be here.'

Ruth held onto her friend's arm. 'I didn't know, but we ought to go, Molly. No good can come of this.'

'Ruth, I must see him.'

Scanning the faces in the choir, she grabbed Ruth's sleeve. 'I think that's him,' she hissed. 'It is him, I'm sure of it.' She leant forwards against a tree, her eyes now fixed on the small boy in the black cassock. The music that filled the theatre made only a distant hum in her ears. Her focus was on one child, a boy with unruly curls and restless hands so like her own. She could see both Thomas and Elizabeth in the fragile face. Molly knew Elizabeth would have loved her nephew and would have forgiven her friend.

When the boy stepped forward, and all eyes were upon him, he stood alone, his sweet voice soaring through the trees. Molly moved towards him automatically. Ruth pulled her back.

When the glorification of Christ was over and the voices were stilled, Thomas stood on the podium once more. When he toasted the choristers, each child came forward. As he named them, Molly held her breath. Her instinct had been correct; the child was Charles Coram. He was her son.

'Come away now, Molly,' Ruth said anxiously.

'You go, I must stay.'

'Don't you embarrass yourself, and don't do anything hasty. You have plenty of time to put things right.'

'I promise you,' she replied.

When Ruth left, Molly remained in the shadows. She wanted to go to Thomas, to reveal the identity of their son, but Ruth was right, she should wait. For the moment she was happy enough to watch Thomas unobserved, and to gaze adoringly at her son. Next week she would go to London and claim Charles. Then she would tell Thomas, be damned the consequences.

Thomas moved amongst the crowd. He talked to Mr Handel; he helped his mother from her chair. Molly noticed his solicitude towards the elderly, and his easy manner with the guests, but then he stopped at their child. He patted Charles's small thin shoulder, knelt beside him and took his hand. He pulled something from his pocket. It was a small wrapped gift. Molly watched the child tear the paper and saw the adulation on the boy's face.

'Thomas knows!' she gasped. 'He has known all along.'

Drawing the hood of her cloak over her face she ran towards them. She was halfway across the lawn when she stopped. If she confronted Thomas now, her son would be present. It was no way to meet his mother. The poor child had suffered enough. No, she would go home tonight, but by God Thomas would hear from her tomorrow.

How could he deceive me? she thought, running back through the woods, her skirt catching on the trees, her hair escaping its pins. 'How could he make me give up my child?'

Had Molly waited, she would have realized that the present was in fact given to Charles in recognition of his solo, and that every soloist received the same gift. But flushed in renewed passions she did not wait. Arriving at her cottage she grabbed pen and paper, and she began to write. They were harsh, angry words.

Dear Thomas,

I may have sinned, but yours is the greater. Was it a game, your sister's plan to betray me, or was it your idea? You are a vile coward; you have ruined my life and your son's, for every child should have a mother. The years spent preparing to collect him from the Foundling Hospital have now been in vain. You are a hypocrite and a liar, and I despise you both.

Molly

Her mother had always told Molly to sleep on her stronger impulses. 'Sleep on it, my love, for in the morning you will sing from a different sheet.'

But Molly didn't sleep, for she didn't go to bed; she sat up with her letter, waiting for the day to break, and when the milk carts rattled down the street, she gave the letter to the farmer's boy. 'Please deliver this letter to the big house; there's a penny in it for you.'

Molly Johnson had cast her die.

CHAPTER FIFTY-TWO

'There were shepherds, abiding in the field, keeping watch over their flock by night, and lo the angel of the Lord came upon them.' The child's voice was pure in the still evening air. The audience leant forward, listening intently, but Dorothy felt only shame. Despite every challenge of his birth, the boy before her, in voice and appearance, was a Keyt.

Slipping away amidst the clapping and the cheering, she fetched her horse and galloped along the drive towards Hidcote. Throwing the reins at the groom, she jumped down and ran into the house. She pulled off her gloves, threw them on the settle, and ran upstairs to the long gallery. Her boots clattered on the wooden boards. She looked up at the portraits of generations of the Keyt family and burnt with shame. She had dishonoured the family, and now she felt her ancestors look down upon her with surprise and disapproval.

She quickly left the room, swearing that she would tell Thomas tomorrow.

The following morning, Dorothy returned to Burnt Norton.

'Good day, my lady,' Annie said. 'You're up early. Can I get you anything?'

'No, Annie, thank you. I'll wait until breakfast.' She noted an envelope in Annie's hand and thought it must be from Gilbert. 'Is that letter for me?'

'No, my lady, the letter is for Sir Thomas.'

'Give it to me, Annie, and I'll make sure that he gets it. Are my children still asleep?'

'They are. They were up half the night with the foundlings. They seem to like that young Coram lad.'

'Thank you, Annie,' she replied tersely.

When the housemaid had gone, she put the letter on the breakfast table beside her brother's place. She picked up a book and tried to read, but then looked at the letter again. Apprehensively she broke the seal and read Molly's letter.

Panic gripped her. Running to the study she sat at her father's desk, and with his pen, she wrote to the Foundling Hospital.

Dear Sir,

I am aware that Charles Coram will be enlisted as an ordinary seaman in Her Majesty's Navy in two years' time. My brother and I, as a gesture of goodwill, would like to give a financial incentive so that he may be enrolled immediately as captain's servant, thus giving him the best possible chance to rise within the ranks.

Enclosed is a sum that I hope will more than suffice.
Sincerely,
Lady Dorothy Paxton-Hooper

The courier took the letter from her outstretched hand, and as he cantered down the track, Dorothy tried to run after him, but he had gone too far, the horse disappearing into the distance.

She cried and wrung her hands in despair. 'Dear God, what have I done?'

That afternoon, the foundlings piled into the coaches for their return journey to London. Charles Coram was the last to say goodbye. 'Thank you, mistress. I wish it hadn't gone so quick. May I come again one day?'

'I am sure you can, I would like that, Charles.' Another lie. Dorothy knew she had ordained this child's fate.

When Mr Handel took her hand, he held it for a second. 'Thank you. Your kindness will have its reward,' he said, as the coach door shut behind him.

After the last coach had left, Thomas and Dorothy returned to the house. Her children played in the ruins.

'How dismal and empty it seems.' Thomas sat down heavily in an armchair. 'If circumstances were different, and I had plenty of money, I would do so much for those children.'

Dorothy couldn't look in her dear brother's face.

Within the day, the house was closed once more. 'I hope Sir Dudley will make good use of our possessions,' Thomas said. 'All I wish for is a simple life. Take the harpsichord, Dotty, and when you play, think of our childhood.'

'Thank you,' she replied, wishing she could go back to those earlier times and untangle the lies.

With the harpsichord safely secured on the cart, and the children stowed inside, Dorothy's long journey to Surrey began. 'Goodbye,' she called, as her brother faded into the distance. 'Goodbye and forgive me,' she whispered.

CHAPTER FIFTY-THREE

July 1751

Charles Coram didn't want to leave Burnt Norton. During the week he had spent there, he had experienced a totally different world: he had known freedom. He climbed trees and slid across the polished floors; he jumped ditches and snagged his clothes. At night he climbed from his bed and leant from the window. Across the lawn, silver in the moonlight, lay the crumbling ruin of the mansion. While the other boys saw it and laughed fearfully, Charles wondered about the poor man who had burnt inside.

But one emotion outshone all others: a sense of belonging. Sir Thomas had touched his heart; he had given him more attention than any adult so far in his young life. Of course, Mr Handel had been kind, as had his choirmaster, and from a very young age, Thomas Coram had shown him affection. Certain teachers had inspired him, but nothing compared to this new friendship. He didn't try to understand it; he just knew Sir Thomas was special. When their eyes met, and the older man's face broke into a smile, Charles felt his whole being light up with happiness.

He felt nothing of the sort for Lady Dorothy. There was something in her face he didn't trust, a look about her that scared him. She skulked around at the oddest times, and he suspected that she had been watching him, a nagging doubt that disturbed him long after the coach had left Norton behind. Her last words to him had been dishonest. She didn't want him to return, he was sure of it.

Back in London, life at the Foundling Home returned to normal, and the trip to Burnt Norton took on the proportions of a distant dream. When the choristers went to St George's Chapel in Windsor to sing to the King, Eton College Chapel was pointed out to the boys. Charles saw it rising far above the school and thought of Sir Thomas. *He had sung there.* Whenever Charles leant against the solitary yew tree in the Foundling Hospital garden, he imagined the whole coppice of yew trees at Norton. Amongst them he had played hide and seek, concealed himself in their dark boughs, held his breath in excitement. How he longed to be back.

Charles applied himself to his lessons and his singing, believing that hard work would help him to shape his own future and avoid recruitment into the navy. Some of the boys looked forward to such a future, with its possibility of travel and adventure. Not Charles. To his gentle, artistic nature, the sea, with its weather, tides and harsh conditions, was anathema.

Late in the summer of 1751 a messenger came to the hospital. It caused a stir amongst the staff. 'An anonymous benefactor – who could it be?'

When Charles was singled out and told of his imminent departure, he was not surprised. He also believed that he would never return to London.

'It's an honour, young man,' the kindly Mr Handel said,

trying to console him. 'Not many of our boys are captain's boys. You could rise through the ranks.'

'I don't want to go, sir. I could stay here with you. I want to sing.'

'But your voice will break soon; you can't rely on it for ever.'

His best friend, Moses, whose skin was black and whose mam left him by the river without the basket, tried to reassure him. 'Like as not, I was born on one of them slave ships. I'm used to the sea, Charlie boy. I'll be there for you.'

'Thank you, Moses,' he said, 'but I won't be coming back.'

'Hush now. You have a good friend to look after you. You'll do that, won't you, Moses?' Mr Handel said.

'I'll try to, sir, if a powder monkey is allowed to care for his friend.'

Along with thirteen other boys from the Foundling Hospital, Moses and Charles boarded HMS *Lancaster* under the command of Admiral John Byng. As Mr Handel and the staff waved them goodbye, there were many amongst them who wondered if they would ever see the boys again.

On 19 May 1756, five hard and desolate years after boarding his first ship, Charles Coram wrote a letter to Sir Thomas Keyt. It was the night before engagement with the French off the coast of Minorca.

Dear Sir Thomas,

Before battle, most of the crew send messages to their loved ones, but I don't know my family, and I'm hoping you won't mind if I turn to you instead.

My apologies, sir, but tomorrow will be my first

battle, and you've been kind to me. I want to tell you what is in my heart. If I'm done for, my best friend will make sure you get this letter. He's called Moses and he's given me his word.

Thank you, sir, for ensuring my position as captain's servant. I know it was you and it has made things easier. I'm no powder monkey, but if I'm honest, I didn't want to go to sea. Not that I'm ungrateful, but it's nothing but rats, sickness, floggings and exhaustion. Sometimes at night I hear my mates' tears. We all pretend to be brave, but it's not easy. We just want to come home. The hospital was strict and there were rules and more rules, but at least you got to lie in a bed at night, not in a hammock in the gun deck of a ship. Most of all you weren't cold and scared, more scared than you can imagine.

At first light we will fight the Frenchies. I don't want to. I've got nothing against them. I hope you will forgive me for seeming ungrateful, but Mr Handel said it's no crime to be scared. If you get this letter, I will have gone to the maker. Would you be kind enough to find my mother? I feel sure she would like to know.

Goodbye and thank you,
Charles Coram

He sealed the letter with borrowed wax and went below to find his friend.

When the battle came, Moses, as apprentice seaman and powder monkey, ran the gunpowder from the ship's magazine to the gun deck. Charles was in the rigging as lookout, high above the ship. He didn't see it coming, but he heard the earth-shattering splintering of wood as the mast crashed towards the sea.

CHAPTER FIFTY-FOUR

In July Dorothy made her annual journey to Gloucestershire. She was shocked to learn of her mother's growing blindness.

'Why didn't you tell me, Mama?'

'Darling, it's of little importance. I am most sad about losing access to my precious books. There is still so much to learn,' she sighed, 'but then, what use is knowledge to an old woman like me?'

'You are such a good woman. You never burden others with your pain, and you never judge anyone.'

Lady Keyt laughed. 'I do, my love, and if you ask my poor servants, I'm sure they'd tell you that I complain all the time.'

'Mother, have you ever done anything that you're ashamed of?'

'Of course I have, but I'm hoping that God will forgive me quite soon, for I'm ready to make his acquaintance.'

That night they dined alone. Afterwards, Dorothy helped her mother into the drawing room.

'Dorothy, I believe we have letters today. Would you read them to me? They're on the salver in the hall.'

Taking a candle, she walked through the panelled hallway. She lifted the letter from the silver dish, and at once her hand started shaking. Though the letter was addressed to her mother, the Foundling Hospital seal was unmistakable.

'Are you coming?' She heard her mother's frail voice.

'In a moment, Mother.'

Breaking the seal she opened the envelope. Inside were two letters.

The Foundling Hospital
Bloomsbury
London

Dear Lady Keyt,

I have had the pleasure of meeting you in the company of your esteemed son on at least three occasions, though principally at Norton House, when I performed Messiah for your guests. Unfortunately, I am unable to contact Sir Thomas directly, for I believe he has since moved.

Moses, a young gentleman and former foundling who serves in His Majesty's Navy, recently delivered a letter into my hand. He was insistent that I should help locate Sir Thomas. I am greatly distressed, for I have now learnt that my principal soloist was lost at sea. I am told that during a conflict with the French, off the coast of Minorca, Charles Coram was thrown from the rigging. He is presumed to be dead.

I can only tell you that he was an inspiration to all of those around him and he shall be sadly missed.

In accordance with his wishes, I am determined that the enclosed letter should reach your son.

Your servant,
George Frideric Handel
Written by the hand of my assistant, John Christopher
Smith.

Dorothy put the letter down and buried her head in her hands. She had caused the death of an innocent child, her own nephew. Tucked inside the smaller envelope was a letter from the boy himself. As her tears fell, smudging the ink, she read the letter and her shame increased. Charles Coram had trusted her brother, and she had betrayed them both. Returning to the drawing room, she looked into her mother's sweet face as she slept.

The following evening, Thomas joined them for dinner.

'Hello, Thomas, are you well?'

'Yes, Dotty, I'm fine,' he answered. But Dorothy could see the pain in his gaunt face. His eyes, once a startling blue, had dulled with worry.

He trusted me, Dorothy thought miserably, and I have stolen his every chance at happiness.

They ate in silence, each lost in memories.

'Do you like your new house?' Dorothy asked finally.

'It's small, but well enough, for I have only myself to care for. I would have loved a wife and children, but life is not always as we wish it to be.'

He looked at her, but Dorothy could not meet his eye.

'You can still get married, have children – you are young yet.'

'No, I can't. There has been too much pain in this family, too much loss.' He paused. 'There was a child that I was fond of, a foundling. Do you remember at the concert, the boy they called Charles Coram? I could have given him a home, but they sent him to sea. Now of course we are at war, and I may well never see him again.'

Dorothy put her hand into the pocket of her dress and felt the letter. The words trembled on her lips but she looked at her plate and said nothing.

Afterwards, when they stood in the porch to say goodbye, Thomas took her hands. 'Dotty,' he said earnestly, the lamplight illuminating his haggard face, 'you take care now, for you are very precious. And watch those children of yours, for they are precious, too.'

In her dreams that night, hell came for her. The devil dragged her from her bed. He threw her into the inferno and laughed as the flames consumed her. It was nothing less than she deserved.

CHAPTER FIFTY-FIVE

August 1756

Despite her best intentions, the five years since the concert had not been kind to Molly. Through no fault of her own, her hard work had reaped less than she had hoped. However, a recent increase in clients had changed her position, and at her own insistence she had paid the final instalment of her debt to her brother, and any outstanding bills were cleared. It was only now that she felt able to claim her son. She still had not heard from his father.

She was making the final adjustments to a client's gown when she heard a knock. She opened the front door to find the two Hogarth sisters standing outside.

'Miss Anne, Miss Mary, what a wonderful surprise!'

'Our apologies, we came at such short notice, my dear,' Miss Mary said. 'We didn't have the time to let you know.'

'How lovely to see you. Are you visiting friends near by?'

'No, Molly,' Miss Anne said, coming towards her at last, holding out her hands. 'We are not visiting friends; we came to see you. I'm afraid we have some very bad news.'

'What's wrong? It's not my son? Please don't let it be my son.'

Miss Mary took her hand.

'Molly, your son is dead. We don't know the details, but he was lost at sea. I am so very sorry.'

They approached her with their arms outstretched. Avoiding their embrace, Molly staggered to her desk, her head spinning with grief.

'But it's not possible; I've seen him. He sang like an angel.' She sank to the floor. 'I have made my arrangements, I'm going to get him, despite his family's plans to keep us apart. He can't be dead.'

'We had to tell you ourselves. A letter wouldn't do.'

'No, it's not true – please don't let it be true!'

For days the Hogarth sisters remained at her side.

'Take this my dear, it will help a little.' The bitter concoction did nothing to lessen her agony, but it did dull her senses, and despite herself she slept.

Each time she awoke the awful truth overwhelmed her again. Her son was dead. The child she had strived for was gone.

A week later, the sisters departed for London.

'Will you be all right, dear? We must return to our customers and clients.'

'You are so good to have come. Thank you. I wouldn't have survived without you. '

'Molly, we treasure your friendship. How could we let you hear any other way? Besides, we gave you our word.'

When they had departed, Molly shut the door behind them. Her cat jumped through the kitchen window, pushing aside the checked curtains, rubbing his back against the wall. She had created a home for her son, and he would never see it.

He would never know his mother; he would never know her struggle to win security for them both. Ruth came to see her, her arms filled with flowers. 'I know you love roses so I brought you some. Poor love, you look a wreck. Have you eaten?'

'I don't want to eat, I want to die. What is there left?'

'There's always something, love.'

'No, not now. There is nothing, no one.'

'Someone as pretty as you will find love again.' She stroked her hair.

'I've lost my son, Ruth. Don't you see I can never be happy again?'

Ruth looked into her lap. 'I have other news. Sir Thomas wants to see you; he calls your name through the fever.'

'So he's ill, is he?' Molly looked at her furiously. 'Well, I'll tell you what I think: he deserves to die. He sent our son to his death. He's ruined my life. I hate the Keyts. May God curse each and every one of them.'

'I understand your feelings, but he is dying, Molly – you can't deny a dying man.'

'Trust me, I can.'

'I'll take you on the cart. Please come. Her ladyship asked me to find you. Please come; I fear there's not much time left.'

Molly went, not for Thomas or his mother, but for Ruth, who had proven herself a most loyal friend.

They arrived late in the afternoon. Molly climbed from the cart. The farmhouse had turned a salmon pink in the setting sun, and smoke curled from the chimneys.

'This way, madam,' the housekeeper said, wiping her floury hands. 'Come in. Please forgive me, but I've just been baking. We are trying to encourage Sir Thomas to eat.'

She followed her down a short passageway to the foot of the stairs.

'Up there, madam,' she said, indicating a room off the landing above. 'I won't come up, if you don't mind. Her ladyship is waiting for you.' Molly climbed the stairs, smoothed her hair, and knocked on the bedroom door.

'Is that you, Molly?'

'Yes, my lady, I'm here.' Molly entered the room; in the corner a small elderly woman sat in a Windsor chair. Molly was shocked, but when the woman spoke it was the same refined voice.

'Will you take me downstairs, for I can't see. I have been waiting for you; Thomas has, too.'

Molly took her by the arm and settled her in a chair by the fire.

'Thank you. You have always been so patient.' Lady Keyt sighed. 'Have we wronged you, Miss Johnson?' she asked.

A thousand replies clamoured in Molly's head. 'No, my lady,' she replied. 'You have never wronged me.' She longed to ask if Lady Keyt had known the truth, but thought the better of it. What good would come of it now?

She returned upstairs, pausing on the threshold. Books lined the shelves, and in the corner a desk overflowed with papers. It was a simple room, but somehow it was appropriate. Elizabeth's paintings covered the walls. One stood apart from the rest; she remembered the afternoon it was painted.

'Molly, be still. You are hopeless. How can I make a likeness when you fidget thus?'

'Why would you wish to, when I am such a poor sitter?'

She could hear their laughter echoing through the years; she could see Elizabeth's sweet face, and now to her amazement, she could see her portrait hanging on Thomas's wall.

Walking over to the bed, she stood over the dying man.

'Is that you, Molly? It cannot be.'

'It's me, Thomas,' she replied, appalled by the change in his appearance: the sunken cheeks, the yellow complexion. The arm that protruded from the covers was no more than bones with a papery covering of skin. It was as if his life had already gone, leaving only a phantom behind.

He grasped her hand and looked at her with dull eyes. 'Why did you run away? I loved you so much, and you deserted me.'

'Too many reasons,' she said, after a moment. 'Guilt, fear, and I thought you deserved more. We were from different worlds; I believed you would never survive the disgrace.'

'Was that not for me to decide? Have I married, had children, happiness? There was only ever one woman in my life. Look around you. I live in a simple farmhouse. Do you see extravagance, excess? This is me, Molly. This is who I am.'

Molly's anger returned. 'Then why did you betray me? Why did you force me to give up our son? You took him away from me, when I could have looked after him. I worked for years to be able to look after him.'

'What on earth do you mean?'

'If it were not for your family, he would be alive today.'

He dragged himself up in the bed. 'What are you saying? I have no child. Please don't torment me.'

'Don't lie to me, Thomas. I'm not a fool. When I saw you together at the concert, I knew immediately. How could you let your own son go to sea, to fight a wretched war? How could you abandon him?'

292

'Oh my God,' he gasped. 'Charles Coram was our son?'

'Of course he was our son. You knew he was our son. He was the image of you. Now unburden your conscience before you meet your maker.' Molly stood above him in a frenzy. 'You are pathetic, Thomas. I would have given my life for you and our son, but you! You deserve this.' She let out her breath, as if she could rid herself of her grief. 'You Keyts are all the same!' She turned to go, but he caught her arm with surprising strength.

'Molly, I didn't know! You have to believe me. I didn't know!' She saw the disbelief and horror on his face, and realized in a flash that he was speaking the truth. She sank down to the floor, keening with despair. She saw it now; Dorothy alone had orchestrated this. If Dorothy had entered the room at that moment, Molly would have killed her.

She looked at Thomas and picked up his hand, knowing her words would destroy him.

'Listen. Your sister paid me to give him to the Foundling Hospital.' Her grip tightened on his hand. 'Then I saw you with him, Thomas. On the night of the concert you gave him a gift. What was I to think?' She paused to control herself. 'Now I have paid for my sins. Our son was killed in a fruitless war on a distant sea; I will have to live with that for the rest of my life.'

He cried then and she took him in her arms.

'It's all right, my love, it's all right.'

'But it's not all right,' he replied, sobbing into her chest. 'I am a coward, it's true. I was afraid to find you, to come after you. Look where it has brought me: I am dying with no love and no life, when I could have had it all.'

'We can have it now, Thomas. Get well and we can still have it all.'

He fell back to bed, exhausted. 'Yes, my love, we can start again.'

Molly bent to kiss him. 'I'll come again tomorrow,' she said, brushing his dry lips with her own.

They enjoyed one week together.

'It will always be like this when you are well, Thomas. I'll look after you; I'll never leave you again.'

'Molly, I won't be well. It has gone too far,' he answered sadly. 'But there is something you can do for me. I wish to leave my papers in order. Perhaps your brother can help us?'

She sent for Will, and as Molly watched them, she indulged in imagining the life they could have had together. Pride and preconceptions had kept her from Thomas. She had assumed he would want a different life, refusing him the chance to prove otherwise.

'So, I've finally met the author of the poem,' Will said as he sat beside the bed.

'I have always loved your sister,' Thomas replied sadly. 'Please will you ensure that she receives this farm and the living that goes with it? All my possessions, my books, my writing, I bequeath to her. I wish my sister to retain only my prayer book, for she has wronged me, wronged us both. Perhaps she will find forgiveness within its pages, for I cannot find it within my heart.'

When he had finished, he lay back against the pillow, his face grey. Molly took his hand and sat beside him. He smiled and shut his eyes and she could see he was at peace.

'I can go now, knowing that you will never struggle again. I came to this house in the knowledge that you loved it. I remember your words when I asked your opinion of Norton: "Master Thomas, I like it enough, but the house in the dip with the chickens outside reminds me of home. That one I like a lot." When I moved here, I felt close to you. Now it is yours. Perhaps, when I have gone, you will feel close to me.'

Molly put her head upon his chest and wept, for how could she let him go when she had only just found him again?

'Molly, look at me,' he said. 'I can't bear to see you cry. Please be brave for me.'

'Your sister said the same thing: "Be brave for me, my dear friend, and let me go." But how can I?'

'You can let me go now because I have found happiness. You can help me through the door, and I'll wait for you, and then we'll be together for eternity.'

She did let him go. She held him while he slipped away, and though their time together was brief, it gave her the strength to go forward.

CHAPTER FIFTY-SIX

August 1756

On Dorothy's arrival in Surrey, the children hurled themselves at their mother's skirts.

'Mama, I've missed you!'

'Mama, thank goodness you are home!'

'Dorothy, I may not be the most demonstrative man,' her husband said as he welcomed her. 'Sometimes I believe I am not all that you had hoped for, but may I say that the house has been quiet and wretched without you.'

When the children were in bed, they ate together in the small dining room. 'You are a remarkable woman,' he said, putting down his fork. 'You make the journey to Gloucestershire each and every year, unselfishly and with devotion. I am proud of you, even if I would like more of your time, and possibly more of your heart.' Dorothy was ashamed. She was sorely tempted to tell her husband that the woman he loved had lied, cheated and deceived, but she couldn't bear to shatter his belief in her.

'Thank you, my dear,' she said, 'I only wish I could live up to your expectations.'

'Nonsense,' he said, 'you are too modest.' Dorothy watched his slim fingers play nervously with the stem of his glass, the brown eyes cautious and diffident.

She was married to a good man, a truly kind man, and she had hurt him, too. His belief in her decency gave her the courage she needed. She would return to Gloucestershire. She would tell Thomas. When the truth was out, she would tell her husband, too. Afterwards, if he still wanted her, she would give him all of her love.

'Gilbert, I'm sorry, but I am going back. There is something I must do.'

'But my dear, you have only just arrived.'

'Please, Gilbert, trust me. I will not be able to rest until I have met with my brother.'

'Of course I trust you. Go if you must. Just come home soon.'

On the long journey back to Gloucestershire, Dorothy rehearsed her lines.

'Thomas, I have betrayed your love and trust. I know you will never forgive me, but if I can give you a chance of happiness, your contempt will be a small price to pay. I can never make up for the past, but perhaps you will now have a future.'

Refusing to contemplate the consequences, she took the red leather volume from her bag. As Miss Byrne's writing swam before her eyes, she remembered the day she had left. *Take care of that brother of yours ... I have all the faith in you, all the faith in the world.*

The coach arrived at Hidcote as the sun sank behind the gabled house. Stepping down she waited for George Heron, who had entered her mother's service.

'May I take your bags, my lady?'

'Thank you, I would be most grateful.' She was climbing the steps to the front door when she froze. Hanging above the entrance, a black canvas hatchment stirred in the evening breeze.

'Heron, what does this mean?' she asked, pointing to the hatchment. 'It carries only a single coat of arms. What is going on?'

'Forgive me, my lady. I'm truly sorry.'

'What do you mean you are sorry? Tell me quickly, man!'

When his eyes shifted away, avoiding her own, she knew the worst.

'Sir Thomas is dead, my lady, struck down with the fever. The good Lord saw fit to take him. We sent word by messenger, but you had already left.'

'Why wasn't I told that he was sick?'

'I don't know, my lady.' He looked away in embarrassment. 'We had our orders.'

Throwing herself to the ground, she hammered her fists upon the cobbles. 'Thomas!' she cried. 'Thomas, forgive me!' Through her tears she could see the bleak years ahead. There would be no deliverance, no absolution.

They buried the last of Dorothy's siblings in the family vault, and, as the bearers lifted the coffin upon their shoulders, Dorothy held her mother's fragile form in her arms.

'It's an unnatural order,' she cried. 'Three children, my husband – what in heaven's name have I done, that I should be punished thus?'

'You are blameless, Mama. Let us go inside.'

They were sitting in the pew when she saw her. She had

chosen a place in the south transept, and as Dorothy looked at the handsome woman who sat beneath the Keyt coat of arms, she was bombarded with emotions. With appalling clarity she realized that her hatred and envy had blinded her to the truth. If in the eyes of the Church Molly Johnson was an adulteress, she knew at that moment that her sin was still greater.

When the tomb was sealed, she turned to her mother. 'This is the end, Mama; God has done his worst.'

'I wish to be amongst them,' Lady Keyt replied. 'I am too tired to fight any more. You have your own family. May you know peace and a measure of happiness. It is my only remaining desire.'

She kissed her mother's cheek, and as she looked up, she saw Molly waiting.

'If you will forgive me for a moment, there is someone I must see.'

Shivering, she pulled on her gloves and walked outside. Skirting the gravestones, Molly Johnson approached her; there was a new assurance in her bearing.

'So is it finished? Have you ruined enough lives?'

'Miss Johnson,' she replied, for there was nothing she could say.

'Are you satisfied? You are a wicked, manipulative woman, with your misguided principles and self-righteousness. Your father may have been weak, but you, Dorothy, are evil.'

If she had struck her, Dorothy would have welcomed it.

'You shall live and die with your conscience,' Molly declared. 'And I hope you rot in hell.' She turned to leave, then she turned back. 'And you think we didn't know about the Italian?' she said. 'You broke his heart and discarded him, but there's an irony, for I believe you loved him. But it wouldn't do, would it? It just wouldn't do.'

The stark accusations threw Dorothy, even as she accepted that every one of them was true. Though she would not see her again, Molly Johnson would haunt Dorothy's conscience for the rest of her days.

That evening she took up her pen and wrote the final chapter of their family history. She wrote quickly, and she wrote honestly, sparing no detail. When it was done and the light was fading, she closed the cover.

Looking through the window towards the Vale of Evesham, over the stark fields, she remembered galloping through the lanes; she remembered the acrid smell of burning, and riding with Thomas to the fire.

Thomas, the flames! I'm frightened.

It's all right, Dotty, I'm at your side.

She had returned his loyalty with deceit.

The next morning she took the cart and drove to Norton. She visited the pools, the woods, the gardens of her childhood. In the grounds she could see her handsome father astride Apollo, her brothers and sisters running through the long grass, and Lorenzo, her dear Lorenzo.

She found the caretaker in the room above the archway, the room that had been his.

'Excuse me. I lived here once. May I see inside?'

'There's naught inside the big house, save for a few sticks of furniture and plenty of dust. They don't come here, the Ryders – too busy in the City. Sir Dudley is dead, poor sod, passed away on his way to receive his peerage. His son Nathaniel will have to earn it for himself.' He took his coat off the peg, the same peg that Lorenzo had used, and walked into the courtyard. Dorothy followed him. He spat superstitiously into the ground.

'I'll not be going upstairs. 'Tis dark and full of spirits.'

Had he seen her family? Did they remain in the shadows?

She went first to the shared nursery, later her bedroom, two beds side by side.

Thomas? Would you read to me?

Go to sleep, I'm tired.

She retrieved Hastings from the bed, where he had remained untouched for years, and held him to her breast. 'We are going on a journey,' she murmured, 'and this time, old friend, you will come with me.' She walked through the house, up the stairs to the very top. She lifted the iron latch, opened the small oak door, and entered Miss Byrne's room. Leaning back on the old iron bed she could hear her parting words: *Now always remember, my child, how exceptional you are.*

She lifted the boards, placed the book inside, and her sister's shawl. She could just see the side of her sister's sketchbook. When it was done and the boards were closed, she stood beneath the crucifix. She prayed for forgiveness, not in this world but the next. She prayed for Charles Coram, for Lorenzo, for Miss Byrne and her family.

The following week her luggage was packed once more.

'Come with me, Mama, I can't bear to be without you,' she begged Lady Keyt, knowing it would be the last time she saw her.

'How can I leave?' she replied. 'What is left of my life is here. Your life is with your own family. Hold onto them, for they are everything. Teach the children what is right, but don't judge them harshly. We can't play God, my child.'

The carriage moved onwards, and Dorothy watched her mother's fragile form become fainter until it finally disappeared.

They reached the farmhouse; she walked along the flagged pathway, knocked upon the door. 'I would like to see my brother's room. Would that be convenient?'

'Miss Johnson hasn't moved in yet, madam, but under the circumstances I am sure she wouldn't mind. Do come in.'

'Miss Johnson?' she queried, her hand trembling.

'Sorry, madam, didn't you know?' the housekeeper said gently. 'He left her everything. Poor lass, she is inconsolable.'

Dorothy climbed the twisting stairs and opened the bedroom door. The room, though small, was light and cheerful. Elizabeth's drawings decorated the whitewashed walls. There were sketches of flowers and trees, of Letitia and of John, but she was drawn to one sketch in particular: a drawing of Molly, with laughing eyes and soft face. Her mother's words echoed in her ears. *We can't play God, my child*.

She was about to leave when she saw the letter. It had her name on the envelope.

Dorothy,
*   I have little to say to you, for throughout my life you have had my love and my trust, and yet you have deceived me in every conceivable way.*
*   Did you think I was your puppet? Was I not capable of living my own life in my own way? Your actions have*

proved fatal in the case of a young man, your nephew. They have proved fatal in the case of your brother. I am dying because you stole my reasons for living.

I hope that you will live and die knowing that I never forgave you.

Thomas

PS I bequeath you my prayer book. Let it enlighten you, and let it heal your troubled spirit.

As she picked it up, opening the delicate pages, the brittle remains of the violets she had given him so many years before turned to dust in her hand.

CHAPTER FIFTY-SEVEN

'Seventeen fifty-six,' Molly would later say, 'was the year the ponds froze over, and icicles like sharpened swords hung from the lintels.'

They were challenging times. Food was limited and wood was hard to come by, but Molly welcomed the hardship. Work remained her only distraction. Through Thomas's legacy, she no longer relied on work for money; rather, the hours bent over her stitching numbed her pain. At her lowest ebb she thought of ending her life. William had taken his destiny into his hands; it was tempting, but Thomas's final words prevented her.

'I love you, I've always loved you. You will go on for me and for the memory of our son. Everything you strive for will be a memorial to us both. Marry someone, Molly. Be happy. We have taken so much from you; if I have one last wish it is that you shall have a new life, a good life. Please do this, if not for me then for him.'

And so she had struggled on, day after endless day. At some point in those bleak, desperate months she started to look for her son. She could not stop herself. Any child was subject to her scrutiny, regardless of their age – a boy with curly hair, a boy in the village choir. Any mother would do the same, she told herself, but later she would chide herself for her stupidity.

Had he lived, her son would have now been fifteen, no longer a child. But the search continued, and until she had proof of his death she would go on looking. In March of the next year she made arrangements to travel to the Foundling Hospital. They had been responsible for his welfare – surely they would know the details of his death. The journey was long and arduous, how well she remembered it, but on the fourth day the coach arrived in London. As she walked through the streets and avenues, avoiding the alleys, she remembered walking through these same streets heavy with child.

The Foundling Hospital had moved; the temporary home in Hatton Garden had long since closed. The new buildings were large and spacious, the result of Thomas Coram's dreams. She could see him showing her the architectural plans as if it were yesterday, and now his vision was before her, the new chapel, where her son would have sung, and the refectory, where he would have eaten. She smiled softly, remembering the kind old gentleman. If only she could turn back the clock, how different it would be. She steeled herself once more. She would not give up on her son. Reaching the end of the carriage way, she climbed the steps to the front door. No longer would she use the tradesman's entrance. Her courage faltered when she was ushered inside. 'I wish to learn the details of my son's death,' she requested.

'Come this way.'

The hospital secretary was solicitous. 'Forgive me, madam, only his death is recorded, but let me reassure you, mistakes in His Majesty's Navy are most unusual.'

Defeated, she had one last request. 'I wish to enter the chapel.' Inside the lofty chapel she imagined her son amongst the choristers who even now were rehearsing evensong, and she thought her heart would break for all the emotion crowding it. She dabbed at her eyes with her embroidered handkerchief, the same handkerchief she carried always, and paid her last respects to Thomas Coram, buried beneath the altar. As she stood and turned to go, a young man passed her in the aisle. He wore a naval uniform, the white ruffles on his shirt glowing against his black skin. He touched his hat in deference. She smiled at him, and he returned her goodwill with a broad smile that lit up his face. I wonder if he knew my son, she thought as she walked away, lacing the handkerchief between her fingers. She turned and looked back at the boy, but his broad smile had gone, and he stared at her with a puzzled expression. He made as if to speak, then thought better of it and returned to his prayers. Molly sighed and closed the heavy door behind her.

She returned to Gloucestershire immediately, and though the secretary's words should have reassured her, they did not.

Late March

She was pinning a dress on the dummy when she heard the noise. She smoothed the folds of the unfinished skirt until the damask hung softly and, rubbing her raw fingers, blew out the workroom lamp. It was only a short distance to the parlour. She stopped and listened; there it was again, a tapping, rhythmic and constant in the street outside. Hurrying to the door, she opened it and peered into the dark. There was no one there. Returning to the fire, she threw her last remaining log onto the embers and lay down on the sofa. She pulled the blanket up to her chin and tried to sleep.

That night, lying on the cramped sofa, once again she dreamt of her son; she could hear his voice, see his eyes, blue as Thomas's, but as the day broke she woke to the reality of a cold, empty room and tears of despair.

Weeks later, when the town was shrouded in fog, she heard the tapping again. She was delivering a dress to a client, and as she hurried along with purposeful steps, the haunting sound stopped her in her stride. Her eyes darted around the gloom but could see nothing. She waited, her heart beating fast. Finally, the shape of two men emerged from an alley, one with a stick, which tapped against the cobbles, the other with a dark face. It was like seeing ghosts, the wraithlike creatures bundled in their coats, coming in and out of the vapour. She made to follow the men, find out who they were, but before she could the fog enfolded them, leaving Molly on the cobbles with a bemused expression and the new gown limp across her arm.

As the nights lengthened she made plans to move into the farmhouse. She visited the property occasionally and was surprised to see the vegetables sown and the garden tidy.

'A young lad tends to it,' the housekeeper told her. 'He says little, and won't take payment. He says he's a friend of the master and it's his way of thanking him.'

Molly smiled sadly; Thomas's kindness had touched many hearts.

When July came, Molly decided to take up residence in her new home. She wrapped a shawl around her shoulders, and putting her cat in the basket, set off down the high street towards the Norton woods. She remembered the last time she had taken this route on the night of the concert, and her more recent visit to the ruins with Ruth. 'You can make it up to your lad; you gave him away with the best intentions. Now you can get him back.' Even after the fire there had been room for optimism and hope. Now all that was left was a legacy from the man she had loved.

Molly walked on. She was luckier than most; she had a good house, Thomas's house. She skirted the gardens, refusing to look back at Norton, and continued down the track. Standing in the park she could see it below her, resting in the hollow, just as she had seen it on her first journey all those years before. The farmhouse was her future, and with the trees in leaf and life bursting through the ground she felt a glimmer of hope. Thomas had wanted her to be happy in his house, and as much as she could, she would be. Opening the small garden gate she walked up the path.

'Welcome, Miss Johnson,' the housekeeper said, coming to greet her. 'The young lad's working in the vegetable garden. I told him you'd be arriving today, and he's very eager to meet you.'

'Thank you, Mrs Parker,' Molly replied.

She walked around the house to the plot at the back, interested to see the young man who had valued Thomas so highly. He didn't see her at first, and as he dug the spade into the ground she watched him. His white linen shirt was open and there was something vaguely familiar about the line of the young man's neck as he leant over, tending the seedlings that pushed through the toiled ground. Something stirred in her memory – the way his shoulders sloped a little, and his hair, visible beneath his cap, curled at the ends. What was it about this stranger that seemed so intimate?

Her chest tightened. An extraordinary thought started to grow in her mind, but no, it was impossible. It was then that she recognized the walking stick propped against the wall. She stopped, unable to move.

The young man looked up and straightened. He stared at her and neither of them spoke. Around his neck hung a small medal, on it the number 171 was just discernable.

'Who are you?' she said, her eyes moved from the medal to his face. He took off his cap and held it in his hands.

'My name is Charles, miss.'

She gasped. 'Charles? Charles who?'

'Charles Coram,' he replied.

Molly was silent, the breath knocked from her body. She leant against the wall to steady herself.

'That can't be. My son is dead.' Every fibre of her being wanted to believe him, but her rational mind said it was impossible.

'But it's true, you have to believe me. Don't you recognize anything about me?' The young man was frantic. Doubt made him panic. Was the woman in front of him his mother; the woman he had searched for? If it was, would she accept him? His good leg felt weak and he worried he would fall. He was frightened, more frightened than he had ever been before. Moses had told him to come here, his dear friend who had seen the lady carrying the exact same embroidered heart that Charles Coram kept with him always. Perhaps he'd been wrong and the address he had found at the hospital was out of date. This was Sir Thomas's house – how could his mother live here?

'If you are my mother, I believe you made this for me,' he said, his hands clumsy as he pulled something from his pocket. He edged nearer to her. In his palm lay the small embroidered heart, grubby with years of handling, the edges worn and tattered. Molly stared at it, remembering again the moment she had handed over her child.

'It can't be true,' she whispered as the young man stared at her with steady eyes, blue eyes like Thomas's.

'But it is. It's me.'

They remained silent while she studied him. Was this some cruel trick?

'How?' she said at last. 'How are you here, when they told me you were dead?'

'I didn't die. My will to live was stronger – my need to find you.' The young man found his voice, and as he spoke she listened. She heard how the mast that had nearly killed him had ultimately saved him, keeping him afloat in the turbulent water; she learnt of the fisherman who had rescued him and taken him home to his family, splinting his shattered leg, nursing him back to health.

'And so,' he said at last, 'I worked my way home on a merchant ship. The thought of finding you saved me. It's what kept me going, but then I was scared you wouldn't want me and so I worked in the inn for my board, and I worked here in memory of Sir Thomas, the man who was most kind to me.'

They kept the truth to themselves; Dorothy must never know. Only one person was invited to share in their reunion and joy.

'If Lady Keyt ever hears, it won't be from my lips,' Ruth

swore, her eyes dancing. 'Now where is he?' As Charles entered the sitting room, she was at a loss for words.

'Well,' she pronounced at last, 'you're a fine bonny lad if ever there was one, and as God is my witness, you're more like your father than he was.'

'This is Charles,' Molly said, her eyes shining, 'my son.'

EPILOGUE

Time past and time future
What might have been and what has been
Point to one end, which is always present.

The train sped on. Edward leant against the window, lulled by the comforting repetition of steel against steel. Through heavy lids he watched the landscape flash by, until at last his eyes closed. He was going home, returning to the house that had captured his imagination and his heart.

He remembered his first visit, that hot day at the end of summer, a boy propelled from childhood into a strange new world. His journey had taken him into the past, into a family torn by tragedy; he and his stepfather had pieced the story together until the jigsaw was complete. They had discovered the theatre, hidden for centuries in the undergrowth. They had found the name Thomas Charles Edward Keyt carved into a desk at Eton, and on a night he would never forget, he had crossed the line between the present and the past.

It was the night of the leavers' concert, his last performance at school, and as the windscreen wipers battled ineffectively against the driving rain, the school gates closed behind them for the last time. Conroy, Edward and his mother were silent, each lost in their own thoughts. When they arrived at the house, Edward climbed from the car. Pulling his jacket over his head, he ran across the courtyard, into the house and upstairs to his bedroom. With the wind rattling against the window panes he lay down and shut his eyes, the music from the concert still ringing in his ears. Some time later he opened them. The wind and the rain had gone, the air was balmy and warm, and he found himself in the upper garden. He felt no surprise to discover that the theatre was prepared for a concert, an audience in place. A hush descended, and the conductor tapped his baton on the music stand. The choir began. And Edward knew the music; it was the solo from Handel's *Messiah*, the solo from the leavers' concert. He stepped forward to sing.

When he awoke the following morning, Edward noticed a loose floorboard by his bed. He lifted it easily, finding a space below. There, hidden between the joists, he found a large, leather-bound book. Sitting down, the book cradled in his arms, he touched the crumbling spine, brushed the dust from the brittle cover. As he opened the first page, Miss Byrne's fairytales, hidden for so many years, came to light once more. If the stories were initially unfamiliar, he recognized the ending to each and every one.

When a delicate ribbon bookmark indicated a change of hand, he whispered the name to the silent, empty room. He knew with a certainty he couldn't explain that this was the girl he had glimpsed in the window: Elizabeth who had filled his dreams, the girl with the sea-mist eyes. In this book, through her selfless voice, the Keyt family were revealed. He was shocked, too, to read about himself: *I believe I saw the* strange young man again. Is he is a figment of my imagination? It doesn't really matter any more, because in my mind he is real.

And he came to her closing words:

Dear loved ones,
Do not weep for me. Open this book and I am with you. Look upwards in the sky and you will see me liberated from my chains. Look upwards, for like the kite, I will be free.

Edward gazed at the window uncertainly. He had seen her in this house. What did that mean? Had she found her freedom?

Then the writing changed again into a hand laden with suffering.

Death is everywhere: my brother, Ophelia, and now my sister, too. Is there any justice?

And Dorothy revealed her jealousy and anguish:

I have to keep her out of our lives, for Miss Johnson would destroy us.
I did not give my brother the only letter from his son, for I am a coward,
I have seen her sketches. They are visions of hell, but like Ruth I couldn't burn them.
Forgive me, Elizabeth.

There were letters tucked inside – letters from Eton, from Elizabeth, from Sir William on the eve of his death. These fragile testimonies of love and life remained. Edward read them all. One stood apart from the rest: the letter from Charles Coram, a foundling boy on the eve of battle. Edward read it slowly. Dorothy had manipulated the life of a young boy. By revealing her sins, had she hoped for absolution? He sank to the bed, his legs giving way beneath him. He felt sure that she was there in the shadows, begging forgiveness.

I have done my worst. Let those who find this, judge me as I should be judged. May God forgive me, for I am a sinner and I have betrayed them all.

He shut the book, then opened it once more, drawn to a single line: *I have seen her sketches.* He looked to the void beneath the floorboards, pulled towards an unseen yet certain goal. He knelt down, and with his torch, swept the empty space. The beam shone on a narrow opening. Just as he suspected, something was wedged there. Getting a screwdriver, he levered the board until it broke with a crack, releasing the contents. The pad was large and brittle; he lifted it out with care. For a moment he stood motionless. Dorothy had hidden it; perhaps it was best left alone. Then, holding his breath, he opened the cover.

Elizabeth Keyt. The name was scrawled across the page, black charcoal scored onto white paper, as if the very act of writing was a declaration of misery. He lifted another page and gasped. The gentle face he'd seen in the window masked a tormented soul. Sketch after sketch of desperation devoured the pages. Elizabeth had not accepted her plight; privately, she railed.

Taking the sketchbook, he went downstairs. Checking to see if he was alone, he walked quickly towards the old kitchen garden. Pushing open the door he could smell the remains of yesterday's bonfire. Hens pecked behind the high brick wall, and in the distance a car clattered over the cattle grid. He stood beside the dying embers, hesitant, holding the pad in front of him like a sacrifice. Before he could change his mind, he hurled the pad into the middle of the bonfire. There it rested amongst the rotting vegetation until, with new kindling, the flames took hold. Edward felt a heavy burden drop from his chest as the paper blackened, flared up and finally reduced to a pile of ashes. Walking back to the rose garden, he felt certain it was over. 'It's finished, Elizabeth,' he whispered to the sun-filled silence. 'I've finally set you free.' In the window above him, only light moved across the irregular glass.

At Conroy's suggestion, they visited Coram Fields. Only a playground remained, a green oasis amongst the traffic. Leaning against the solitary yew tree, Edward closed his eyes. Children filed through the gardens before him, wearing brown uniforms with red trim. When he opened his eyes, the cars hooted once more, and the children had vanished. In the Hospital Museum, amongst the inventories, the billet books, the petitions by mothers, the accounts, the rules and more rules, he saw the keepsakes, the tokens of love and of desperation, of hope and of hopelessness. They found an entry in the register, Charles Coram no. 171, admission date 10th November, 1741.

Edward woke as the train pulled into Moreton-in-Marsh station. He had reached his destination. He picked up the worn copy of the *Four Quartets* from the seat beside him, a present from Conroy on his twenty-first birthday, put it carefully in the breast pocket of his jacket and rummaged in the other pocket for the car keys. After stepping down onto the quiet country platform, he went to find the car. He passed through Chipping Campden, his eyes seeking the corbels and elaborate capitals that dressed the simple village houses. Some of the stonework was charred, some was a little broken, for it had been plundered from the ruins of two much grander houses: Campden House, the seat of the Gainsborough family, burnt by its Royalist owner Lord Noel in the civil war; and Over Norton House, burnt by Sir William Keyt. Two men, both involved in the destruction of their houses, and in the death of their dreams. As he drove on past the almshouses, the gatehouse, and through the Norton entrance pillars, he reflected that in some way the dreams of these two men did live on, though not as they may have imagined. These relics were testimony to their lives.

His mother opened the door. 'You have some letters in the hall,' she said, hugging him. He collected them and, taking a jumper from the peg, retreated to the wild garden. Sitting on the bench beside the dry, empty pools, he looked at the large brown envelope:

Edward Coram James
Burnt Norton
Chipping Campden

He opened it, drawing out a letter and a piece of copy paper. He put the envelope on the bench beside him and read the first.

Dear Edward,

I live locally and I've heard you are searching for information on the Keyt family. I am enclosing the copy of an entry from a diary that has been passed down through my family for generations. My grandmother gave it to me before she died. Apparently it was found amongst the possessions of Dorothy Paxton-Hooper and now eight generations after my ancestor's death, I believe it may be of particular interest to you. I am reluctant to send the diary itself, so will call by in the next few days. I believe for the obvious reasons you will wish to see it.

Regards,
Helen Keyt

Edward shivered and his heart lurched uncomfortably. What would this hold?

In the distance a motorbike roared through the country lanes. He waited until it had passed, then unfolded the second page.

Many years have passed, but still our story continues.

Now in my sixth decade I have made my last pilgrimage to Norton. My dear husband has passed away after a long illness, and my children gone. How strange to return in the twilight of my life, and though my memory is dulled with age, remorse endures. The caretaker's son lives there now. From him I learnt that Sir Dudley Ryder is dead. His son, the first Baron Harrowby, rarely visits Norton. The house remains empty.

Ruth met me by arrangement; she is old now and fat. She lives comfortably on the stipend from my mother – how well she served our family. She told me that ten months after his presumed death, Charles Coram found his way to England, and in July of that same year he was reunited with his mother. I don't know where his life has taken him, and the question is not mine to ask, but Molly is happy with her adored son and has at last shown me mercy. I thank God her heart is bigger than my own. I never gave him the ring, the one that was worn by his grandfather. Instead, I returned it to the Roman. I climbed the hill and buried it with my bare hands. I hope that the curse on my blighted family will now be buried too.

May you, the future generations, attest to this.
Dorothy Paxton-Hooper, 1779

Edward stared at the entry for a long moment, and then, holding it tightly, he ran from the pools. Panting, he reached the house and went inside. He leant against the wall, breathing deeply, trying to gather his emotions. He could no longer see the children, and he would no longer see the girl in the window. Despite his relief, he felt bitterly disappointed. Amongst the secrets and the ghosts, the past had finally taken its place.

The bell rang, interrupting his thoughts. Mentally exhausted, he moved his limbs sluggishly towards the door.

Putting his hand on the latch, he looked up. The girl in the window stood before him, her grey-green eyes staring incisively through the plate of glass. Slowly he opened the door.

'You must be Edward,' she said. 'I am Helen Keyt. I've been looking forward to meeting you. Tell me, have you received my letter?'

'Elizabeth,' he answered faintly. 'I have.'

Dry the pool, dry concrete, brown edged,
And the pool was filled with water out of sunlight,
And the lotos rose, quietly, quietly,
The surface glittered out of heart of light,
And they were behind us, reflected in the pool.
Then a cloud passed and the pool was empty.
Go, said the bird, for the leaves were full of children,
Hidden excitedly, containing laughter.
Go, go, go, said the bird: human kind
Cannot bear very much reality.
Time past and time future
What might have been and what has been
Point to one end, which is always present.

T. S. Eliot

AUTHOR'S NOTE

I am privileged to live at Burnt Norton, the Gloucestershire estate which inspired T. S. Eliot to write the first of his *Four Quartets*. I hope my story may bring Burnt Norton to life once more.

It is a story based on real events, although I have embellished the facts and where necessary added or changed things in the interests of narrative colour and coherence. It tells of the Keyt family (pronounced 'Kite') who lived at Norton from 1716 when they bought the estate from the Saye and Seale family to increase their already large local holdings. Sir William Keyt was christened at Blockley on 6 July 1689. He married Ann Tracy on 23 November 1710 at Toddington. Sir William died in the fire that engulfed his new mansion on 9 September 1741.

In 1753, twelve years after the fire, my husband's ancestor Sir Dudley Ryder, Lord Chief Justice and father of the first Baron Harrowby, bought the estate from Sir Thomas Keyt, and it has since remained in his family's ownership for over two hundred and fifty years. Over the years, Norton House, though itself untouched by the fire, became known as Burnt Norton.

For the purposes of this book I have used the original names where possible but in the interests of my story I have used only four of the original eight children. I have omitted Jane who was born in 1713 and was christened at the church of Holy Trinity, Stratford-upon-Avon; Agnes, who was christened in 1715, Anne christened in 1717 but who died in infancy; and lastly Robert who was christened at Holy Trinity, Stratford, on 18 December, 1724. Robert succeeded to the title of the fourth Baronet upon the death of his brother Thomas, but he remained childless. The baronetcy became extinct upon his death. I do hope that descendants of the Keyt family will forgive my omissions and indeed my impudence in altering some of the dates and facts for the benefit of my story. Elizabeth was in reality born in 1721 and she died in 1741; she is buried at St Eadburgha's church in Ebrington. Dorothy was christened in Ebrington in 1727; there is no record of her death. John Keyt died in early childhood. Thomas was in reality born in 1712 and died on 24 July 1755. Gilbert Paxton-Hooper is a fictional character.

If we are to believe local legend, both Sir William Keyt and his son Thomas were infatuated with Molly Johnson, and her famous words 'What is a Kite without wings?' were genuine. Sir William's affair resulted in the end of his marriage to Ann Tracy, and led to his eventual downfall. The unusual circumstances surrounding the attempted murder of his butler Thomas Whitstone are also recorded.

It is quite possible that Molly Johnson did have an illegitimate child but her association with the Foundling Hospital is imaginary. Facts relating to Captain Coram and the hospital are genuine.

George Heron served Sir William faithfully until the end. A poem written upon his gravestone in Weston-sub-Edge was removed in the nineteenth century; only a small portion of the stone now survives.

To my knowledge Handel never visited Norton.

I have gleaned facts from the Sandon archives, from the eighteenth-century diaries of Sir Dudley Ryder, the Gloucestershire County Council archives, and from the research of Roger Keight, Margaret Causer, Dr Christine Hodgetts, Jo Xvereh-Brenner, Guy and Lucile Wareing and Margaret Fisher.

My research has been considerably aided by the diaries of Samuel Pepys, *Dr Johnson's London* by Liza Picard, and the Foundling Museum in Brunswick Square. I am indebted to my husband Conroy Harrowby for his patience and fortitude, and to Marge Cloutts, James and Viathou Parker, Kate Sloane, Medina Marks, Nicola Finlay and Ellis Rogers for their invaluable advice, and to Pink Harrison for her beautiful artwork. The biggest debt of all goes to five people without whom this book would not be possible: Lorenzo Soprani Volpini for making me write it; Sheila Crowley, my wonderful agent, who believes in my book; Lara McDonnell, my initial outstanding editor; and Charlotte and Nick Evans, who have encouraged and helped me along the way, and without whom none of this would have happened. Last, but by very means not least, my publisher Anthony Cheetham and his wonderful editor-in-chief Laura Palmer, both of whom have made this happen.

My thanks go to them all.
Caroline Sandon

(Sandon is a courtesy title given to the eldest son of the earl. My husband, Dudley Ryder, is now the eighth Earl of Harrowby.)